Beneath the Burning Sun

Anna Healey

Cover art by Serpents and Doves Publishing.

Map created by author using rollforfantasy.com and kmalexander.com resources.

Published in Australia in 2025.

Paperback ISBN: 978-0-6458074-3-1

E-book ISBN: 978-0-6458074-9-3

A catalogue record for this book is available from the National Library of Australia

This book is for everyone who dreams of a secure and joyful world, and especially for those who fulfil their role in achieving one.

I dedicate this book to Abby and Ellie. Don't settle for just surviving.

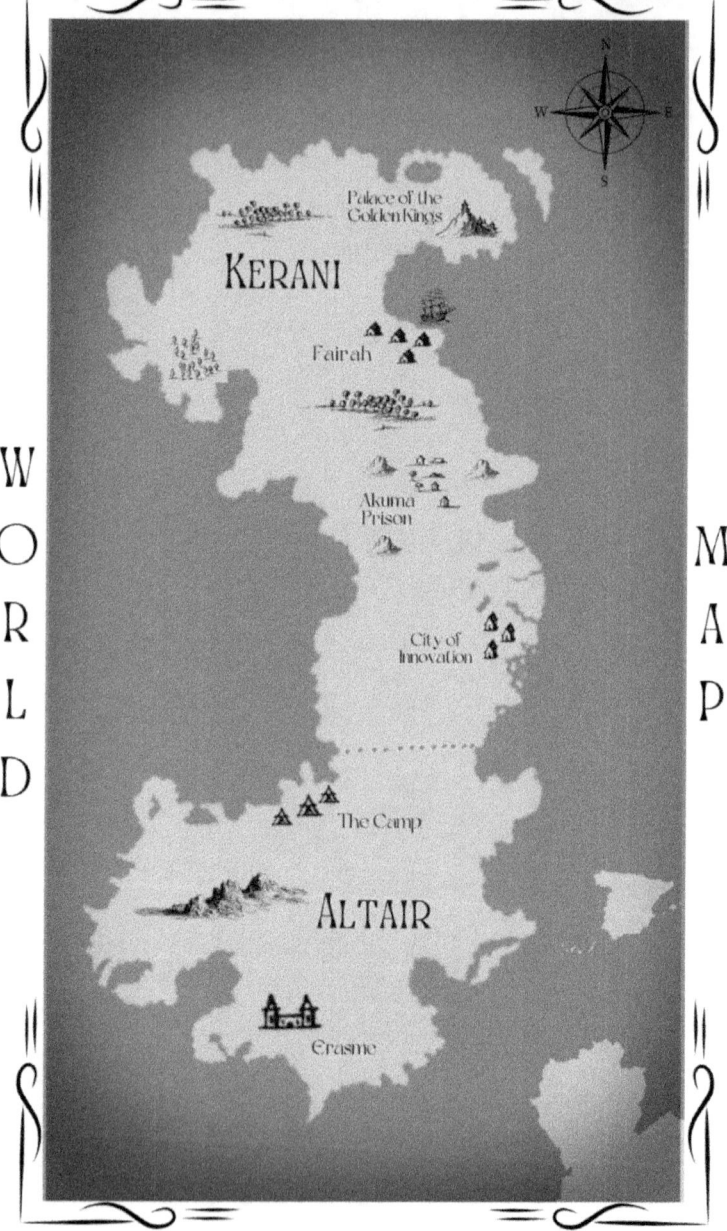

CHAPTER ONE

The humid wind blows the dusty yellow sand into the eyes and mouths of anybody within its reach, no matter how hard the people try to keep it out. Sometimes, nature dominates like that.

Kaira lets out a cough, feeling the grit sticking between her teeth as she's battered by the relentless force of the desert gales. She should be used to it by now. It's been years of living here with nothing but the thin cloth erected as tents to keep them protected from the elements.

The loose pants Kaira wears are whipped against her legs as she treks up the only road in the camp that sees the army vehicles. The rest of the so-called 'roads' are dirt tracks organising the tents into small blocks.

Kaira glances at the people making their way to and from the toilet blocks that sit isolated on one side of the road. Their faces are as weathered as her own.

As soon as she's close enough to be recognised by the other prisoners, the calls of her name begin.

The children break into a run towards her, almost sending Kaira tumbling to the ground as they crash into her. Their dry, dirty hands grip her as their smiling faces bring Kaira to laughter, even as she feels that familiar saddening weight in her chest. It won't be long before some come of the age where the smiles are wiped from their youthful faces.

1

"Hey, look at all of you!" Kaira exclaims. "If I didn't know better, I would've guessed you were waiting to ambush me!"

The children let out innocent giggles, pushing each other in attempt to be the closest to Kaira.

"Come on. Are you all ready?" Kaira asks as she begins moving again, the children following at her heels as she diverts from the main path and weaves through the tent houses.

"Miss Kaira, will we be able to run around the track again today?" one of the children asks, tugging on Kaira's hand to make sure they have her attention.

"We'll see how quickly you complete your work," Kaira responds, opening the flap door to their destination tent, distinguishable from the others by the thicker canvas. She'd fought tooth and nail to use this building, not only for its sturdier build but also for its centrality that means they're further away from the main roads skirting the prisoner-of-war camp where the army vehicles pass.

Inside, more children await, having come from the other side of camp. All up, there's about thirty of them, their ages ranging from around two to ten.

As the children let go of her to settle into their spots on the rug covering the dirt ground, Kaira smiles at Nora, another girl around her age—seventeen—who helps care for the children.

Nora has a selection of arts and crafts—scraps from the worksites—set out already. Kaira smiles upon seeing the activity. It's one of her favourites to do with the kids as it spurs their imaginations beyond the walls of the camp.

She keeps watch as the children are given free reign over their projects, some working together and others individually.

"What are you making?" Kaira asks, squatting next to one of the little girls as she brushes the girl's knotted hair back from her face.

She glances over the girl's shoulder to look at the scene she's creating with thin twigs. There's a figure lying horizontally, whilst three more crowd over them, holding guns.

Kaira winces. She wishes she can leave the scenes untouched, as if not making the children speak about them will erase their existence, but it's important to use every opportunity for the children to develop language that'll otherwise go unlearned within the cage they're kept in.

"It's Papa," the girl, Eloise, responds. The lack of emotion in her voice is a stark reminder of their position.

These aren't regular children; they're children of war, living under the harsh regime of their conquerors. Some mightn't have been old enough to witness the fighting, to witness as they were shoved from their homes and forced into the camp four years ago, but they've seen enough even here, in what should be their refuge. The things they create are almost enough to make Kaira stop it, but ignorance doesn't bring healing; it just seeks to hide the problem as the children are left to battle those thoughts alone.

Whilst the guards and the restrictions have eased since 'The Fall', as the conquest of their country has been dubbed, it hasn't all been good. Every day the resources dwindle and they already struggle enough from that.

There's a loud scuffle behind Kaira and she gives Eloise a comforting squeeze on her shoulder before making her way to the source of commotion.

"Come on, boys. Stop that," Kaira calls out, pulling the makeshift stick weapons from the hands of the three fighting boys. Kaira tilts her head to the side as she waits for them to respond to being stopped.

"Sorry, Miss Kaira," the boys mumble, looking down at their shoes as they dig their feet into the rug.

Kaira sighs heavily, gesturing for the boys to get back to their creations. She can't blame them for their actions that come from boredom, having tired of the crafts already. Faster and faster each day this has been happening, as though the children can feel the nervous energy that lies in every conversation.

She's not the only one noticing the dwindling resources. Everyone recognises that some change must come soon. They can't survive like this much longer, yet nobody seems willing to be the one bring it—especially their Elders.

Kaira clears her throat, adjusting the jewellery adorning her body. She's long wished there was a way to give it value, to use it to buy food for the children, but it's worthless when all that matter are the ration cards they're given.

"Well, haven't we worked brilliantly? Who thinks you're deserving of a reward?" Kaira asks, smiling at the children as she attempts to leave thoughts of their situation behind.

The children call out in agreement and Kaira nods to the door, giving permission for them to head out. They lead the way through the houses until they draw to a stop at the cliff that forms one edge of the camp's border.

"Let's race for the end!" Kaira urges the kids along the path that follows down into the cliff, enclosing them in a cave. The only light comes from the one open edge that's on the cliff's face.

"I'll go ahead," Nora says, cocking her head in the direction of the path where the fastest kids have taken off to.

Kaira nods, agreeing to bring up the rear.

As the kids around her take their time absorbing the moment, Kaira draws in deep breaths. She soaks up the salty air as the barrier the cliff's cave provides offers them a reprieve from the weather, wind and sand. Many have tried to erect their tents down here to take advantage of the escape from their harsh desert climate, but with how often it's patrolled and the warnings from the guards, it's a death sentence to do so. You can't be seen lingering in the shadows.

"Benji, be careful near the edge!" Kaira calls out as she sees him peering over it to catch a glimpse at the water crashing against the rocks below. The force with which the waves collide causes sea foam to float in the air around them.

Benji heeds the warning and carefully steps back, though the slight glare he throws in Kaira's direction says he wants to ignore her. His glare softens into a smile as an idea takes form in his mind. "I bet you can't catch me, slowpoke!"

"Oh, you picked the wrong person to challenge, mister."

Kaira takes off after him as he sprints along the edge of the wall, his screams echoing as it's just the two of them remaining.

Kaira catches up to him, pulling him into her body. He squirms in her grip as he calls out for her to stop her tickling amidst his squeals of laughter.

Abruptly, Benji's giggles are cut off as he's torn from Kaira's grip. Panic courses through Kaira's body before she's slammed into the ground in the next second. Arms go around her, trying to subdue her as she thrashes in the grip of her assailant.

The ground beneath Kaira's shoulder gives way and another dose of fear makes its way through her body. The cliff's edge is just centimetres from her, her struggle bringing her and the guard holding her closer and closer to it.

Kaira freezes, giving up her fight. She can't risk falling, especially not when Benji might see. With the reminder of the boy, Kaira's eyes move from the cliff's edge back to the main path.

There, Benji is in the arms of another guard. Where had they come from, though? All there is ahead of them is a long, straight path before the final bend that lets them out into the lower portion of the camp.

Kaira's eyes search the path. A resigned sigh passes by her lips as her eyes land on a hole just deep enough to conceal the two guards carved into the inner wall of the ledge.

"Let go of the boy!" Kaira shouts, throwing her anger at the guard that holds Benji. The little boy has frozen in fear, his eyes wide and staring at Kaira.

The assailant that has Kaira on the ground elbows her harshly in the ribs and, in her moment of shock as her breath is taken from her, pins her arms to her sides. The guard looks behind him to the other one. "Take the boy back to the camp," he orders in Keranian, his native language.

The other guard obliges and Kaira lets them go without more of a fight. It's better than she could have hoped for; they're letting Benji go.

"Yeah, don't want to cause a scene, do you?" the guard huffs, switching to her language—Altairian, the language of the camp—as he shoves her further into the ground.

Kaira realises her mistake in that he's misread her silence. She shouldn't have known that they're going to return Benji to the camp. The blood drains from her face as she sees the scene the way they have—like a kidnapping.

The guard rolls her over before he pulls her hands behind her back to force her to her feet.

"Let go of me!" Kaira demands, pulling on her arms in attempt to slip from his grasp. "I didn't do anything wrong."

The guard lets out a disbelieving laugh as he turns her around to face him, moving them a few steps away from the edge of the cliff. Her back hits the inside wall of the cave as he presses against her to hold her still. Weapons hidden in sheaths poke awkwardly into Kaira's ribs.

Kaira throws him a sharp look that dissolves in seconds as her eyes go wide, landing on the details of his uniform: the golden buttons, the golden trims and seams. Kaira swallows, looking away.

"Is it that easy to take your fight away, little birdie?" the guard taunts.

"Knowing when to pick your battles isn't equivalent to having your fight taken away," Kaira spits back, the Keranian language falling unnaturally from her tongue. Her stomach rolls at her foolishness. What has gotten into her today? In what world did she ever think it was a good idea to speak their language? "What? Is it that easy to render you speechless?" Kaira pushes.

The guard stays silent, his eyes running over her in scrutiny. After a minute, he asks carefully, "How do you know our language?"

"How do you know mine?" Kaira responds, her eyes watching him to get a read on his feelings.

The guard's eyes flicker in annoyance and his grip tightens, making Kaira flinch from the pain. Before he can say anything in response, loud footsteps echo from the end of the path, bearing down on them.

The guard pushes Kaira away and she barely catches herself in time as she's suddenly released. Her hand reaches for the wall to steady herself.

"Go," the guard orders.

Kaira blinks at him, the words not registering.

"I said go," he repeats before rolling his eyes. "You don't speak our language, now? Need me to say it in your language: go!"

Kaira still doesn't move, feeling the same paralysing fear as Benji earlier. The guard moves back towards her, pushing her roughly. This time, instead of meeting the wall, she slots perfectly into the crevice the two guards had been hiding in.

The other guard returns, brushing their blond hair from their face as they look at Kaira's assailant, who subtly adjusts his ferronnière and golden eye mask, accessories typical of Kerani's army.

"Where'd the girl go?" the returning guard asks.

"It was a misunderstanding. I let her go," her guard responds.

"What? You saw it with your own two eyes! How could that be—"

"I said it was a misunderstanding," her guard interjects. "Do you want to question my authority?"

The other guard's gaze follows over the first guard's golden details before they shake their head. Kaira eyes their own uniform colour—blue—which shows they're a level below her guard, if her memory's right.

Without further argument, the guards begin to move off. Kaira peers around the wall to make sure they're leaving and catches her assailant looking back at her, his eyes marking every detail of her.

Shivers race down her spine and she turns back into the crevice, allowing her body to collapse to the ground as she buries her head in her hands. What has she done?

CHAPTER TWO

"You're going to get in further trouble if you're caught staring out there," Nora says, leaning on the half-wall made of rocks beside Kaira.

Kaira sighs heavily but doesn't move nor divert her gaze from the dry plains beyond the wall that have been cleared of trees. It used to be the border between their country, Altair, and Kerani, before the conquest, when Kerani's side had been lush forests.

"What happened yesterday, Kaira?" Nora asks, her eyes taking in Kaira's appearance, lingering on Kaira's hand that plays with the necklace around her neck.

"They know," Kaira answers simply. "One of the guards knows I speak their language."

Nora's silent for a while as wind sweeps at the dusty earth. "Well, if they haven't come for you yet... Maybe they're one of us."

"Gold," Kaira says. "They wore gold."

Nora bites her lip. She doesn't need more than that to know why Kaira is so stressed. Some Altairians may have been able to integrate themselves into the ranks of the Keranian armies, but no-one would be able to ascend that high. The gold order represented only the best of the best.

"Still, it must mean something that they haven't yet come for you," Nora offers.

"You're right. I wonder if it means they're just checking Akuma Prison has space or they're figuring out how to dispose of me—"

The end of Kaira's sentence is overtaken by the roar of a truck coming up the main road. Kaira's head whips up to spy it before she spins back to Nora. "Go, now. Whatever happens, keep the school going. Go!"

Nora hesitates, her hands digging into the crumbling stone wall before she offers one last look at Kaira and turns. She runs across the road in front of the green-painted vehicle as it trundles to a stop in the middle of the road.

Kaira crosses her arms over her chest as she faces the figures clambering from the truck, feeling the gazes of other prisoners burning into her. She stays silent as one guard waits at the front of the truck, barely coming up to the height of the bonnet, whilst another crosses the sand towards her.

"Well, fancy seeing you here," the guard remarks as he leans on the wall next to Kaira.

Kaira swallows her annoyance at the fact she recognises him not from his uniform or voice but from the design on his ferronnière. It's a gold metal that hangs down across his brow to meet in a design that reminds Kaira of the dream catcher that used to hang above her bed before The Fall. There are three dangling chains connecting to light blue gems that settle perfectly between a cutout in the golden mask he wears. The colour brings out the green in his eyes.

"What do you want?" Kaira asks, her voice harsher than it should be if she wishes not to anger him. *Forren*, she's come to call him in her mind, meaning foreigner in her language.

"Have somewhere to talk?" Forren responds, gesturing his head towards the camp.

"No."

Forren tilts his head sideways. "Shall I show myself to your tent?"

Kaira rolls her eyes. Of course he'll have found out which tent is hers. "We're doing just fine holding our conversation here."

"So, you don't mind if all the camp witnesses this? Do you think they'll want to have you instructing their children when you're in trouble with the guards?"

Kaira swallows. They've certainly found out a lot about her—more than she expected.

"Look, Miss Aziz, I'm done with this. Either show us to your tent or we take you back to the capital."

"You're deceived if you think a tent is going to make this conversation any more private."

Forren huffs out a frustrated breath before spinning on his heel and heading back to the truck. "Come on."

Kaira wants to refuse, but the judgement on the faces of the people watching and the look on the face of the guard by the truck has her following. It's best not to cause any more of a scene.

She reaches the truck and Forren opens the door before offering a hand to help her up.

"What? Not going to put me in the back like one of your prisoners?" Kaira questions.

"Should I?" Forren responds, quirking a brow.

She huffs before ignoring his hand and pulling herself into the vehicle, having to step onto the tyre rim to get to the first step. Behind her, she senses Forren rolling his eyes before climbing in as the other guard walks around to the driver's side.

Kaira drags sand into the vehicle as it falls out of her sandals. Once she's seated, she fixes her clothes, as if it'll make her feel any less inferior to the guards' pressed uniforms, and drops back her headscarf.

"Getting comfortable so quickly?" Forren taunts.

Kaira shoots him a glare as he leans back in the seat, draping an arm over the headrest. Anything she goes to retort dies on her tongue as the driver's side door opens and the other guard gets in. It's the same one from yesterday who had taken Benji.

The other guard looks at them both before shaking their head and returning their gaze to the road, easing the grumbling truck into a roll.

"I'm Tuomas," the second guard offers. "He's Mikko."

"I'm Kaira," Kaira responds before tilting her head in Forren's direction. "How'd you know I didn't know his name?"

"Don't tell her that stuff, Tuomas! We can't trust her. She knows our language; who knows what else she knows about our country," Forren—well, Mikko, but Kaira's keeping the name—says.

Tuomas looks at him before rolling their eyes and answering Kaira's question. "I've spent my whole life partnered with him. I know he isn't the type to offer it freely."

Forren huffs on Kaira's other side. "If for some unlikely reason you require to speak our names, you can call us by High Guard Arias and Guard Koski." He points to himself before pointing at Tuomas.

"No, thanks. I'll stick with Forren for you," Kaira disputes.

Forren huffs, muttering what sounds like 'ridiculous' under his breath.

Tuomas laughs, looking over at Kaira. "I like you. It's about time that Mikko has someone put him in his place."

Kaira gives them an appraising look before returning her attention to the road, trying to ignore how comfortable she feels in their presence. If they weren't wearing the uniforms they were, she might've been able to trick herself into believing that they were like her. They seem to be around her age, maybe a bit older. She should be able to trust that they weren't directly involved in The Fall, but given how early on Kerani trained their soldiers, they were probably on the battlefield long before it.

They continue past the rows of hole-speckled tents, but instead of turning at the barrier of the camp to continue around the border, the truck continues past the guards at the opening in the low brick wall.

Kaira's heart constricts in her chest as she passes over the threshold for the first time since being in the camp. Her hand goes to her necklace, fiddling with the small bird pendant, but she stays silent, not wanting to show her fear.

Not long later, they're pulling into an establishment that consists of three mud-brick buildings. Despite the small collection of structures, the number of Kerani guards around worries Kaira. She doesn't move as Forren jumps down from the vehicle and offers a hand to help her out.

Tuomas sighs as they open their door. "Look, if he hasn't put a bullet through you yet, I doubt he's going to. At least, until you do something to anger him, that is."

Kaira, despite her mind screaming at her not to, decides to trust them. She gives them a slow nod before turning and climbing from the truck. Her feet meet the ground and she looks down at the hard dirt.

"So, you're more intelligent than you seem," Forren taunts, crossing his arms over his chest.

"That's still to be seen," Kaira mutters. "This might turn into the stupidest decision of my life."

The guards in the complex turn to look at them as they catch sight of Kaira, her brown clothing standing out stark against the black of their uniforms. All of them wear masks, like the kind you'd find at a masquerade. The pieces hide all facial features apart from their scowls. As Forren turns his glare on them, it's made clear the authority he has as the soldiers clear the way.

Kaira pulls her headscarf back on as she silently follows Forren and Tuomas into the smallest building. The door opens to a single room that's sparsely furnished with a table and four chairs.

As Forren slips into one of the chairs, Tuomas beside him, it's like a mask—a figurative one, his literal one hasn't moved—comes down over his face. Kaira can no longer deceive herself into thinking he might be like her. He's nothing but a cold, hard soldier, a gold-decorated guard for the Kerani army.

"Miss Aziz. Sit." He gestures to the chair opposite him, his expression staring Kaira down as if daring her to disobey.

Kaira swallows and does as he says. There are two metal pieces on her side of the table, places to hook handcuffs to. She shifts on the spot as the silence continues, Forren waiting for her to say something as she waits for him to do the same.

Eventually, Forren looks to the door as if he can see outside before sighing loudly and leaning back in his seat, folding a leg to cross over the other. "Miss Aziz, you know what this room is, don't you?"

"I thought I did," Kaira comments, "but you don't seem to be doing a good job at interrogating me, so maybe I was mistaken."

Tuomas shifts in their spot, moving their gaze from Kaira to the far wall as they attempt to hide the twitch of their lips.

"Miss Aziz," Forren pushes on. "Yesterday, you revealed to me that you speak our language. How do you know our language?"

Kaira pushes her lips together, shaking her head.

"I must warn you of the consequences of not acquiescing to our inquisition. According to our law—"

"You don't need to spell it out," Kaira cuts in.

"Well, I'll ask you again. How do you know our language?"

"I learned it growing up. My father taught me."

"Your father taught you? And how did he learn it? Was he a Kerani citizen? A defected soldier, perhaps?"

"Is that something your country struggles with? Soldiers defecting?"

Forren glares harder at her in response.

"No. He wasn't," Kaira answers. "He's a scholar—was a scholar."

"A scholar? And how much about our country did he teach you?"

Kaira shrugs. "As much as one can learn with how private you are."

"So, you understand the significance of the colours we wear?"

Kaira looks at the golden details that adorn his uniform. Though she looks away, it doesn't hide the fear that flashes past her eyes. "Yes."

"It's protocol for us to...eliminate...any threat to our country. Do you think you're a threat?"

Kaira snorts. "Does it look like I've done anything threatening yet?"

"You're running a daycare in the camp. Instructing the children. Who's to say you haven't taught them all you know?"

There's something in the way Forren speaks that purposefully gets on Kaira's nerves, pushing her to respond before she can consider her answers. "That 'daycare' is to help the children process the trauma you put them through, not to teach them anything about your country. You don't deserve to take up any more of their mind than you already do."

"I have a proposal for you," Forren states suddenly.

"Is it really a proposal or is it an ultimatum?"

Forren chuckles dryly. "Yes, it's a proposal, though one with less than appealing choices for you."

"What is it?"

"I want to form a partnership with you, where you report conditions inside the camp to me."

Kaira looks over to Tuomas who has so far kept silent. "And the other option?" she asks, turning back to Forren. There's no way she's agreeing to work with him. She'd take death over that. Torture. Anything.

"You come work at the capital. We have a lot of...detainees...needing interrogating. Sometimes they act like they can't understand us but if they're talking to one of their own? We also have a need for more teachers of your language; things get lost in translation if they don't come directly from the source. You have experience teaching, don't you?"

"Get lost if you think I'm going to 'interrogate' your wrongly accused prisoners or teach more of you our language so you can continue to control us."

"So, you agree to work with me within the camp, then?"

Kaira swallows. "Why are you doing this?"

"Because the alternative is executing you," Forren says bluntly. "I know how rare it is for an Altairian to know our language and I'd hate to see that go to waste." He stands, pushing his chair back. "You have two days to decide. Take her back, Guard Koski."

Forren exits the room, leaving Tuomas and her sitting in silence. After a while, Tuomas taps their fingers on the table before standing. "I should take you back before Mikko changes his mind."

Kaira nods, scrambling to her feet to follow. They load into the truck, ignoring the looks following them from the other guards.

"I suppose you don't really bring people back," Kaira says as they head back to the camp.

"You're the first," Tuomas says, their eyes steady on the road ahead.

Kaira leans back in her seat, letting her head fall against the headrest. "What have I gotten myself into?"

17

CHAPTER THREE

The daycare's tent flaps open, causing a stream of sunlight to fall across the room. Kaira lets out a loud sigh as she stands to see who's at the door, only having to catch sight of their black uniform and the golden buttons to know who it is.

"Nora, watch everyone," Kaira orders.

She steps past the children to make it to the door before Forren can enter. The children watch her movements intently, though nobody moves as they identify the uniform.

"Not here." Kaira grabs Forren's sleeve and directs him out of the tent.

Outside isn't any better for avoiding the stares, whispers starting as she leads the guard past rows of tents.

"Wow, I'm getting an invite to your house?" Forren quips sarcastically as he follows her.

"Only because there's nowhere else to go." Kaira huffs as she finally reaches her tent.

Other tents have a small collection of objects outside: tables, chairs, any areas for conversation. Hers is empty. It's shared with her mother—whom she barely sees with the hours she works—and two other women she didn't know before The Fall.

She pushes open the flap and gestures Forren in, ignoring the looks they're getting. She's already received enough this week after *returning* in the truck and being set free. No doubt some people are already questioning if she's colluding with them.

"Where's your trusty sidekick?" Kaira questions as she gestures for Forren to settle onto a set of blanket-covered crates they use as beds. She speaks in Keranian, hoping he gets the hint that it's the only way their conversation can be somewhat private.

"Didn't think I needed them today. You don't seem like any sort of threat, do you, now?" Forren kicks his legs up onto a nearby drum, casting his gaze around the room as his lips curl up in distaste.

"Stop judging. You're the one putting us in these conditions."

Forren huffs. "Yeah, as if you guys had no part in this outcome. It was your country's stupid visions of the future and 'we're all one big happy family' ideas that led to this." Rolling his eyes, he offers out a handful of pages Kaira hasn't realised he's been carrying. "But because you hold those ideas, I know you're going to choose the first option."

"I don't want to be spying on my people," Kaira argues, her voice low as she speaks through her teeth.

"It's my people you'll be 'spying' on."

"What?" Kaira stutters over the word.

Forren taps the buttons on his uniform, pointing out the golden colour as if Kaira hasn't noticed it before. "As you may have put together, I'm the highest-ranking guard that oversees the camp. That means not only am I responsible for your people but for mine, too. I've been noticing that our performance has been less than subpar."

"What does that look like to you? Less of us are being murdered every day?"

Forren shrugs carelessly. "If that's what you think. What I know, however, is that if I don't get this under control, the King will send people much worse than me to draw the lines in the sand. Do you want to know what that'd look like?"

"Humour me."

"I'm assuming you'll have heard of the King's Hounds, right? Imagine them roaming between the tents. Imagine the number of guards here doubled. Imagine the required hours of physical labour tripled to make you too tired to revolt. And, if all that fails, why not just eliminate you from the equation completely?"

"All that's about controlling us still. What about controlling you?" Kaira asks.

"I have a question for you: how many people have been killed in the last week here?"

Kaira stares at him as if it's a trick question before answering, "Thirteen."

"And how many more have gone missing?"

"Six."

"Do you want to know how many of those I ordered to be arrested? Three."

Kaira tilts her head as she looks at him, trying to figure out his motive as he stares back at her with those green eyes through his emotionless mask.

"That leaves three unaccounted for. Three that have escaped the borders and haven't been caught. Three times that my guards have failed at their jobs."

There's a small commotion outside the tents and Forren jumps at the sound of metal scraping against metal. He stands from the makeshift bed and approaches the door, but Kaira holds out a hand, blocking his way. Forren looks at her questioningly.

Kaira drops her hand quickly, red creeping up her neck. "Sorry. I suppose they won't kill you on sight. You can leave." She's too used to stopping others leaving their tents at such commotions.

Forren tilts his head, displacing the ferronnière on his brow. "Why are you afraid to find the source of danger? Wouldn't you rather know if something's coming? If you need to run or prepare to fight?"

"Maybe I would if you stopped your men from killing anyone on sight that dares leave their tent when a fight arises. Once you stop them from immediately assuming that we're trying to hinder them from delivering your twisted sense of justice."

"Walk out there."

"What?" Kaira cries in dismay.

"Walk out there," Forren demands again. "Walk out there and show me that they do that. If they make a move on you, I'll step in."

Kaira can hear the double-meaning behind 'step in'; not only will he step in now and make sure she isn't harmed, but he'll also step in and make sure his men don't act like that in the future.

Kaira takes a deep breath and before she can second guess herself or the guard opposite her, she pulls open the fabric of the tent. She hardly takes a step out before the eyes of the guards two tents down fall on her. Their swords are raised, pointing towards a man cowering before them.

"Someone deal with that," one of the mask-clad guards mutters, gesturing carelessly towards Kaira.

Kaira spins on her heel, feeling that familiar dread settling over her. She's too slow, as with almost impossible speed, one of the guards separates from the circle, cuts through the row towards her and grabs her by the arm. Twisting her arms behind her back, the guard kicks out her legs, sending her to the ground. Kaira clenches her teeth against the pain that shoots through her body. The cold press of a knife marks her neck.

"Lay another hand on her. I dare you," a voice speaks up from beside them.

Kaira manages to turn her head enough with the surprise of the guard above her to see Forren leaning—well, as much as one can when they're only supported by fabric—casually against the flap door of her tent.

"I...I'm sorry...I didn't..." the guard splutters, fear lacing their voice as they identify who's speaking.

The other guards have stopped their tormenting of the man, but they don't move, as if afraid doing so will bring attention to them.

Kaira spins her head back around as movement in her periphery catches her attention. Her breath catches with an audible gasp as she sees Forren has moved and is now holding the knife that was seconds ago at her neck against the guard's.

"Can you explain to me, Guard Julius, why you were holding a knife to this woman's throat?" Forren asks, though his tone shows he knows there's going to be no valid answer.

"She was threatening us, sir," the guard—Guard Julius— stammers.

"Threatening? Since when have Keranians become so weak we find a woman exiting her house a threat?" Forren scoffs.

"But, sir—"

"That's High Guard Arias to you," Forren cuts in. "And you know what? Who even gave you the order to harass that man." He points towards the collection of other guards who fidget under his attention.

"We believe he was attempting to steal rations, sir—I mean, High Guard Arias."

"'Believe', huh? Well, from now on, no one makes a move unless they have evidence for a claim that goes before me and waits for my approval. Got it?"

"But, sir—"

"No," Forren cuts in, "you know what? All you come with me. You can explain yourselves back at the station." He turns roughly to face Kaira, who's still lying sprawled on the ground. "And as for you" —he opens and shuts his mouth a few times as if debating what to say— "behave yourself."

Kaira lowers her head in acquiesce.

Forren nods before turning his attention back to Guard Julius. He moves his hand that's holding the guard's throat to the shoulder of his uniform, leading him like an animal to slaughter. Forren tips his head, motioning for the other guards to follow as he pushes past Kaira's tent and aims for the truck idling on the main road.

"The man—" one of the guards begins to protest.

"Leave him," Forren barks.

As the guards are led away by the gold-decorated soldier, heads start peeking from the tents nearby. Kaira lifts herself from the ground slowly, waiting for the guards to reach the truck, before she slips between the tents to meet up with the man the guards had been pestering.

She offers out an arm, helping to pull him from the ground. She ignores the hesitant look that passes by his eyes, like he's judging whether to trust her.

No-one else moves to help, their eyes still watching the truck as it trundles away. Kaira watches it go, her mind turning over as fast as each wheel on the vehicle.

Maybe this is all an act to make Kaira think Forren's truthful about wanting to discipline his soldiers, where he'll get to the boundary and let the guards go scot-free or maybe he really is being honest and he'll punish those guards and do something to stop the poor treatment of her people.

Kaira supposes that there's no other way to find out other than to keep playing his game and watching him closer than she's required to watch his men.

CHAPTER FOUR

Over the weekend, Kaira's even more aware of everything that goes on within the camp. She hides behind her headscarf as she watches the guards dragging the 'unfit' workers away from the vehicles that'll take them to the forests for logging, as she watches the citizens be denied their rations for cards being slightly damaged, as she watches for the guards that slip extra food to the children.

"I was wondering when I'd see your face around here again," Kaira mutters, otherwise ignoring the presence at her side as she focuses on lugging the bucket of water she has.

"I trust you've been performing your role, then," Forren says, keeping stride with her.

There are eyes on them, but Kaira ignores them as she makes her way into the shower blocks. She dumps some of the water over the ground before brushing her long hair out of her face and grabbing the hand-made mop.

Forren watches her silently as she moves about the showers, pushing the dirt to the dug-out draining hole that lines one wall of the concrete-floored building. He moves around, looking at the open-stall showers that are rigged up using gravity-fed hose pipes with holes punched through them.

Kaira keeps her gaze diverted, attempting not to laugh at Forren as he steps around the dirty spots of the ground. He kicks his boots with every step, shaking off whatever has gotten on them.

"How often do you shower?" Forren asks, turning to watch her.

"Is that your way of telling me I stink or are you going to use it as reason to cut back our allowance as we use too much water?" Kaira returns.

Forren tilts his head in her direction. Kaira wishes he wasn't wearing the mask so she could more easily discern the emotion on his face; his green eyes aren't enough to go by.

"Once a week," Kaira mutters.

"Huh, yet you still manage to keep your hair so nice?" Forren gestures at her dark brown hair before brushing a hand through his own. "I wash my hair every second day and it still turns into this mess."

Kaira looks up from her mopping to glance at his hair. It's a medium brown colour, staticky as it curls around his ears. "Maybe you wash it too much."

Forren chuckles, putting his hands in his pockets as he leans on the closest wall. "So, what observations have you made?"

"You said in our last meeting all you expected was for me to spy on your guards. I did. That's my job complete."

Forren hides a smile. "Ah, yes. I did. But, if I remember correctly, I did word it in our meeting prior as having to report back to me."

Kaira puffs out a breath of air before looking around the shower block, checking the shadows for eavesdroppers. "What do you want to know?"

Forren follows her gaze. "Why don't we go somewhere more private?"

"Get lost if you think I'm going anywhere 'private' with you."

Forren takes an intimidating step towards her as he lifts one finger to point at his chest whilst his other hand goes to the weapon at his side. "Do you really want to challenge me, little birdie?"

Kaira drops her gaze. "I must finish my mandatory work hours. After, we can meet wherever suits you."

"I'll have you exempt from your chores for today. We can go now—"

"No," Kaira cuts in. "I didn't say that to appease the guards. I said it because we're a community here. 'One big happy family' as you said. It shows...camaraderie. It earns my place. If everyone else must, then I will, too."

Forren huffs. "I tell you I'll take you from your work which is wearing you down to the bone with exhaustion and fatigue and you refuse?"

"I'm not going to grace that with a response." As if it isn't the work hours he sets that has such an impact on her body, as if it isn't the food rations he dictates.

"Fine. Finish your chores. I'll be waiting outside."

Forren leaves in an annoyed huff of breath, tugging at his uniform as if uncomfortable. Kaira lets out a sigh, relieved to not have his shaded eyes boring into her, watching and judging.

She finishes mopping the bathing rooms sooner than she wishes—for once. It just so happens to be the last thing on her list for the day as well. Besides, it isn't like she could've slipped out of the building without Forren coming after her, not when he's standing outside the only door or so Kaira assumes from the shadow that's been lingering there.

Kaira pulls her headscarf over her hair as she exits the building, in part for protection from the sun and sand but also to hide the scowl that she aims at Forren. She's drawn to a stop abruptly as she sees another figure with him.

"Oh, hello," she says to Tuomas, offering them a forced smile.

"Hey," they respond, tilting their head in her direction. "So, I hear you're the cause of Mikko's interrogation of those guards earlier this week."

"If his men had acted in line, there would've been no need for my involvement," Kaira responds.

"If this is the disrespect you show to your superiors' faces, I can only imagine what you say behind their backs." Forren chuckles dryly.

Tuomas looks between them before turning away with a smile. "Come on. We haven't got time for this imbecile bickering."

"*Imbecile?*" Forren and Kaira screech at the same time before turning with scathing looks to each other. Agreeing on something seems to be the simple answer to their arguments as both turn to fuming in silence, following Tuomas as they lead them towards the camp's perimeter wall.

The trio hop over the wall before sitting on it. Kaira and Forren perch on either side of Tuomas, who sighs dramatically at their behaviour. "I thought you guys had some sort of partnership going on."

"We do," Forren says.

"More like coercion," Kaira contributes.

"Besides the point, guys," Tuomas sighs. "One of you needs to keep the discussion on track because I don't even understand why you're working together."

Forren sighs dramatically, looking over his shoulder at the collection of tents that starts a bit back from where they are. As soon as he looks, the peeking eyes are quick to dart back to protection, hiding from his view as if he hasn't already seen them.

He turns back to look past Tuomas to meet Kaira's eye. "I'm assuming you want this to be over with before your people can grow too big of ideas about you colluding with us."

"As if they aren't already." Kaira rolls her eyes.

Kaira can imagine the twitching of Forren's eye behind his mask before he hurriedly swings his leg back over the wall and hops down. In a few steps, he passes Tuomas to stand behind Kaira.

"You can hop down off that wall by yourself, or I'll drag you off it," he warns.

Kaira can see the burning fire behind his eyes as his hands clench at his side, one unconsciously going to hover above where one of his weapons sits. Still, she remains on the wall, crossing her arms over her chest.

Tuomas removes themselves from the wall, standing between Forren and her. "Let's talk about this calmly, okay? You don't need to get worked up for no reason."

"No reason?" Forren repeats. "You think the disrespect she's continued to show me is no reason for my anger? I shouldn't be compromising my position by working with her and trying to improve the treatment of her people. Not when she acts like this." He turns on his heel and storms off.

Kaira slips down from the wall, feeling her own anger growing. She catches up to Forren just as he's reaching the truck Tuomas must've arrived in.

"Are you really that cowardly that you're going to blame me not reporting back to you for the treatment of us prisoners?" she growls.

Forren scoffs. "I fail to see how that shows I'm cowardly. All it does is show me you're just that. You've been given a chance to improve the treatment of your people but you're too scared to take it because of what they might think of you."

Kaira feels her anger turn acidic in her stomach. She can't deny what he says; as much as she wishes her hesitation to work with him was because of who he was and what he stood for, she knows that's not the whole reason. "You're cowardly for having to have me do the work. Get off your high horse and do it yourself. Maybe if you were out in the field with your guards, you'd be able to keep them in line."

Kaira meets Forren's gaze, initiating a staring contest. Neither relent, though the red sand burns their eyes. Finally, the sound of another truck coming up the road breaks them up as they launch apart. Tuomas passes them to hop in the truck.

Forren looks at the approaching vehicle before turning to his truck and opening the door. He reaches in—somehow managing to reach the cab floor with how tall the truck is—and re-emerges with another lot of papers.

"I trust you snooped at the other paperwork I gave you. If you hadn't put it together, that's the number of guards we have on patrol and their schedule. This goes into more detail on some of the guards I want you to keep an eye on." Forren again glances at the truck that has almost reached them. "Make sure nobody else gets their hands on them." There's a threat in his tone of voice before he gestures with his head for her to return to the tents.

Kaira obliges without another word, taking the papers and tucking them into her clothing. Damn him for being so right about her being a coward. But she'll prove him wrong. She'll prove she can face her fears and lose the support of her people if it means bettering their treatment and giving them a future.

CHAPTER FIVE

Kaira is settled on her bed, her feet drawn up under her as she goes over the documents in more depth now that she understands them. Mostly, she's interested in the first document he'd given her; there's no point learning which guards to look out for if she doesn't know their shift schedule.

Previously, she hasn't been concerned with the schedule of the guards, unlike other prisoners who studiously study the rotations to find weak spots which might mean escape. Despite their attempts, nobody has ever found an answer in the rotations, leaving Kaira to assume the escapes that have been confirmed by Forren as being due to chance. This document explains the reason; they shift every few days to walk in new times, places and guards to make sure no pattern can be found. She's been given the next three weeks' worth of rosters.

Kaira pauses in her perusal of the documents as hushed whispers come from outside her tent. She cocks her head, listening closer so she picks up the gentle brush of sand. Kaira gathers up the papers, shoving them under her blankets and taking from that place a small metal scrap she's sharpened into a point. She never expected to use it against her kind, but guards certainly wouldn't sneak up on her tent.

Kaira's heart beats thunderously in her chest as she swallows, blocking the fear trying to claw out of her throat. The thought crosses her mind that she should leave the bed so they aren't suspicious of it, but then she worries whether she should stand in front of it to protect the documents.

She doesn't get the time to decide before the canvas door is pulled open, letting in a bright stream of sunlight and a cluster of men and women. Kaira turns on them, holding the weapon out to keep them from approaching.

"Stay back," she threatens, stepping back until her calf hits her bed.

She spins as one of the men moves to her left, taking another step towards her as if he believes her threat with holding the weapon is nothing. She raises the weapon at him and he meets her eye before stilling.

"What right do you think you have coming into my tent unannounced?" Kaira demands. "You know the rules as much as I do. Our tents are the only thing many of us have. They're sacred and it's wrong to barge into one."

One of the women tilt their head to the side, looking Kaira up and down. Kaira identifies them quicky: Deni. She's the one Kaira will have to get past if she wants to fend back this group.

"We have permission from two of the women sharing this tent. Besides, etiquette rules don't apply to traitors." Deni spits the final word like it's venom.

"I'm not a traitor," Kaira defends, taking a steadying breath as she feels her body shrivelling up, wanting to hide. All through her childhood, the lesson drilled into her above all else was respecting her community—her family. The lesson had only become more important as the wars had started, then with the conquest and all they were left with was each other.

"Then explain what you're doing with that foul golden boy," Deni responds harshly.

Kaira swallows. "I can't tell you what I'm doing with him, but I can promise you it's not what you think and it's not anything that'll hurt us."

"It really doesn't matter what you're doing with him; being in his presence is tainting enough. It gives a bad reputation if you ask me."

"You want to talk about my reputation? Let's talk about it, then. Do you really think I'd risk my reputation, my status and what it means to be my father's daughter? That should be enough for you to trust that I know what I'm doing and that my actions are informed by our best interests as Altairians."

The others in the room step back, as if the reminder of how important her father was to their community makes them return to their senses. Sure, he was no king or even an Elder, but he was their best scholar and that almost means more with how invaluable knowledge is.

Deni swallows, as if she wants to deny that Kaira's family's reputation is of any importance, but instead she lets out a forced breath. "Whatever. Not like someone like you can really do anything significant to harm us. All you do is chase children around all day."

"What I teach those children ensures the continuation of our culture. How dare you imply that it's not important? I do more—"

The door slaps open again and the woman entering comes to a halt with a startled breath as she takes in the scene before her.

"What do you think you're doing, Kaira?" her mother exclaims as she sees the weapon in Kaira's hand pointed at the others in the room.

Her sandaled feet rush across the space until she reaches forwards and knocks Kaira's hand holding the weapon away. She glares harshly at Kaira, ordering her to stay in her spot, before facing the others.

"I'm so sorry for Kaira's actions. I can't believe she'd do something like that," her mother says as if Kaira's not standing right behind her.

"It's okay, Mara," Deni huffs, turning up her nose. "We're done here. Ensure your daughter stays in line."

Kaira lets out an indignant hand gesture and rolls her eyes. They're judging her behaviour as if they haven't broken into her tent to verbally assault her.

"I'll be sure to, Deni. Again, I'm so sorry for this. I don't know what's gotten into her recently."

Clearly, Kaira's mother, Mara, has also heard about her meetings with the 'golden boy'.

The intruders turn around and leave. Almost before the tent flap has settled back into place, Mara spins around to face her daughter, her hand coming forwards to take the weapon from her.

"Hand over that weapon now, Kaira. Don't make me ask twice."

"No. It's mine. You have no right to take it."

"And you had no right to go pointing it around at those people. And Deni of all people? Have you officially lost your mind?"

Unlike Kaira's father, Deni is actually an Elder.

"They broke in here to attack me!" Kaira defends.

"Attack you? Are you serious, Kaira? Asking you questions is not attacking you."

"Really? You're going to deceive yourself into thinking they wouldn't have used physical force if I hadn't cooperated?"

Mara steels her jaw, her eye twitching in annoyance. "You would've deserved it. Meeting up with that golden guard? Just

34

what game do you think you're playing? We're prisoners, Kaira. *Prisoners.*"

"Stop treating me like a child, Mother," Kaira says, carefully tucking her makeshift knife under her blankets so her mother cannot see the papers.

"Then stop acting like one."

Kaira turns back around, facing her mother. "I know what I'm doing, Mum. And I think you'll find I'm finally not acting like a child. I'm doing this for us, for all of us. To make sure we're treated better."

"That shouldn't be your responsibility!" her mother shoots back.

"Well, nobody else is stepping up to the plate! I've got to do something; I can't just sit around and watch our people decay."

Kaira's mother shuts her eyes tightly. "You're certainly your father's daughter in that sense."

Kaira fidgets. The way her mother says that makes it sound almost like it's a bad thing, but that has never been how Kaira's viewed her father.

"You have two minutes to convince me that whatever you're doing won't get you hurt. Not like…"

"Not like Dad. I know," Kaira mumbles. "But I'm sorry. I'm not going to be able to convince you in that time. Why? Because I won't tell you much about what I'm doing as I don't want trouble finding you because of it."

Mara sighs before holding her hands out for her daughter, pulling her into an embrace. "You know what? From that alone I can tell you understand the seriousness of the situation and the risks. And if you can do that and still want to be involved, then there's nothing more I can say to convince you not to. I won't stand in your way, Kaira. Not after you've proven time and time again you can hold the reins to your own life."

Mara pulls back, still holding her daughter's shoulders to look her in the face. Her mother's composure is back to its usual hardness now. "You better not stuff this up, though, you hear me? If you step one foot out of line, I'll personally hand you over to Deni."

Kaira rolls her eyes. Her mother certainly grew up with the same teaching as her about putting their community first. Kaira looks up at her mother, her eyes softening. "It's going to be okay, Mum. I promise."

Kaira heads to the daycare tent earlier Monday morning, so the sun's just breaking over the horizon with eager arms to warm the day. Nora's already there, sorting out a new collection of rocks and sticks.

"So, you're alive," Nora says as she enters, looking up and smiling at her. "Finally, I can interrogate you about why those soldiers carted you off and then returned you. Case of mistaken identity?"

Kaira chuckles, settling down on the ground next to her friend. "Unfortunately, no. They know exactly who I am."

Nora sets down the materials in her hands. "What happened, Kaira? What do they want with you? The golden one, no less."

"I can't tell you much of what I know," Kaira sighs. "I'm sure you've got your own ideas, though, with how much my name is in the gossip channels."

"I'm worried about you."

"I mightn't be able to say much but I can say that there's no need for that. Or, at least, not from the golden guard. As you said, he returned me and, since then, has stopped guards from hurting me."

"So, who should I be worried will hurt you?"

"The rest of us."

Kaira knows that Nora's on her side; she expects no less from the only friend she's made since coming to the camp. But there's something comforting about the way that Nora still doesn't look at her differently from that answer—though she's sure Nora will have read between the lines: the other Altairians are casting her out.

Nora silently sorts the sticks for a while before saying, "Be careful, will you, then? I have your back too, always."

Kaira smiles. "I know." Her tongue wets her bottom lip as she figures out her own words. "Are you not scared I could be betraying us?"

Nora sighs, finishing putting away the last of the materials before standing. "I know you. I know you'd never do something that threatens what we have here, the family we've created."

Kaira stands and pulls Nora into her arms, hugging her tightly. "Thank you for believing in me."

"Always."

Kaira pulls back, gripping her friend's hands tightly. "I need you to promise me that whatever happens, you won't give up on the school. The children need it. They need you."

Nora nods, understanding what Kaira's saying. "Promise me you'll return and teach again one day."

"I will. Whenever I can, I'll drop by. I just..." Kaira puts her head back, blinking at the ceiling to stop the tears. "I don't want to bring you and the children into everything. Besides, the

Elders have expressed their displeasure at my choices and I don't want to be the reason why they stop sending the children here."

Nora nods again, pulling out of the hug. She knows she must do it or else Kaira never would. "Go," she says, gesturing to the door. "Go get us out of this place."

Kaira smiles at her, her eyes shining brightly, before she turns for the tent door and leaves. She pulls her headscarf low over her face, though there's for once no wind blowing up the sand. She pulls it up so when the tears begin rolling down her cheeks, they're not seen.

CHAPTER SIX

—— + ✳ ✴ ✳ + ——

Kaira finds herself pretending to be part of the wall repair group working closest to where guards patrol the road out to the logging area. It isn't that hard to sneak into the group, considering guards don't expect people to willingly join a team they're not in.

A few of the workers give her side eyes as she picks up rocks and fits them into the wall, but her glare is enough to make them look away. Has her picture been circulating along with the gossip about her because how else would so many people know she's the one causing all the drama? She's certain that even given the limited quarters they've lived in for the last four years that not that many people know her name.

She works away, placing rock after rock because they're forced to build the walls that keep them in. It's worth the tiring work, though, as a patrol of guards is only a few metres away. She can pick up most of their conversation, though it's not all that interesting, talking about upcoming parties, buying new uniforms and the weather forecast.

Kaira zones out, her mind wandering as she gets into the rhythm of the laborious work, until a sentence rings out clearly, breaking her focus.

"What do you think High Guard Arias is up to with that Altairian girl?" one of the soldiers questions.

Kaira spins around to see them more clearly, to see if they've identified her, but the soldier who spoke is looking away from her.

One of the other two guards shrugs. "You can make guesses. What else would he be doing with a girl—"

"Arias wouldn't do that," the final guard interjects.

"What do you think he's doing, then?" the first guard asks, cocking an eyebrow.

"He's earned the gold he wears. I'm sure he's using her for some reason that'll help shut down this place."

Kaira feels her heart leap at the thought of the camp being shut down, at the freedom that would mean, before the truth washes over her like a storm cloud as the second guard contributes again.

"It's about time. I don't know why the King hasn't ended their race already."

Kaira turns to the wall to hide her tears. She wants to leave, though she can't as the conversation morphs into another topic of interest.

"Did you hear about the logging incident yesterday? Do you think Guard Helos knew?" the third guard asks.

"Well, in a situation like that, either you were shirking your responsibilities or you purposefully put those workers in the fall zone," the second guard contributes, shrugging carelessly.

"I hope it was purposeful. That's the kind of dedication to our cause someone in our position should have. Only real leaders make decisions like that," the first guard declares.

"But it's not right, though," the third guard says. "Nobody deserves to die like that, even if they're Altairian."

"Well, we know why you haven't progressed through the ranks now, don't we?" the first guard replies snidely. Even with their back to Kaira, she can tell the disgraced look they'd be throwing at their fellow guard's forest green detailed uniform.

The third guard shakes his head, choosing to ignore the comment. He looks at his watch before gesturing to where Kaira and the other prisoners work. "Their shift's done; do you want to release them?"

The first guard faces the workers. Kaira picks up a rock to avoid being called out for shirking duties.

"Nah, if they work as slow as they do, they can stay back."

"We don't have the authority to keep them back."

The first guard once more turns on the third, shoving a finger into his chest. "You stay in line. Unless you wear a colour higher than mine, you do as I say."

Kaira waits until they're released from their duties, fearing what the guards would do to her if she's caught leaving before dismissal but also wanting an excuse to get a good look at the first guard's face as he finally lets them go.

The sun glares painfully into Kaira's eyes as she steps past the guards, keeping her head up and her headscarf back so she can take in their appearance. She meets their eye for as long as she dares, feeling a rush of power. For once, she'll be the one in control of their outcomes and it's all because of this partnership with Forren.

The line between the sky and the land is indiscernible with the sandstorm dousing them all in thick red dust that obscures the vision beyond a few metres.

Kaira stifles the coughs rising in her chest, not wanting her presence to be known by the inhabitants of the tents she passes. She's decided to watch another guard rotation that Forren had marked on the paperwork as of interest because of decreased responses to incidents recorded during their shifts. Kaira wonders how back to front their ways must be for lowered numbers of fights to bring bad focus to a group.

The three guards in this rotation are scheduled to be patrolling the cliffs near the path she'd taken the kids on. Given the weather, Kaira makes an educated guess that they'd likely be hiding out along the path to wait out the storm. There's always less need for the guards on days like this because even the prisoners aren't wanting to face the storm and, unless they're scheduled for work, won't leave their tents.

Kaira makes it to the sloping path earlier than the shift starts and begins the trek down along the cliff's edge. Her left hand is unfaltering in following the inside wall, making sure she doesn't stray from its offered safety as her hindered vision doesn't allow her to see where the path drops off to meet the sea below.

Slowly, the blown sand starts to thin enough for her to breathe without feeling it scratching painfully at her throat. She continues a while longer until she finds the cut-out that Forren and Tuomas had been hiding in the first day they met.

She slips between the rock walls, sliding down to sit as she settles in for the day ahead. Aside from the slightly squished quarters, it's the perfect place to conduct her spying so long as the guards don't know about the space.

There isn't much Kaira can do to pass the time, so she braids and un-braids her hair until she hears the tell-tale tread of boots. The noise is accompanied by quiet chatter, but this time it's not the contents of the conversation that freezes Kaira to the bone.

It's the language. Her own. Altairian. Spoken naturally.

The footsteps stop a short while away from her and her curiosity is overwhelming as she risks quietly standing to move towards the entrance. Carefully, feeling her heart thundering in her ears, Kaira leans around the opening, looking past the corner of the path.

The three guards are gathered in a circle, each with a sandwich in hand that they're eating. Kaira looks closer, her eyes attempting to gain visibility in the dust that still lingers. She doesn't really know what she's looking for given that either country doesn't have identifying features in appearance that can be trusted given how much diversity each country has.

But she needs not notice these things, because whilst they wear different colours of decorated uniforms, their thin builds are enough information for her. There's no denying that their figures are formed by starvation and hard work. They're not guards. They're prisoners dressed as them.

Kaira lets out a small gasp before shoving her hand over her mouth and falling back into the crevice as the soldiers spin around.

"Did you hear that?" one guard asks, as if it isn't a sign enough that the other two guards are peering along with him.

"Probably nothing," another replies. "Just the wind from the storm."

"Let's just check it out," the first responds. They're so close Kaira can hear them swallow before they speak again. "What if it's someone spying on us? What if they know—"

"Know what?" the final guard challenges, trying to get them to be quiet.

The first guard goes silent, but the second guard sighs loudly before adding, "Fine. No harm in looking."

Kaira's heart lurches in her chest as she tries to pull herself back, carefully shifting until her spine presses against the far side of the crevice. She holds her breath, her hand clamped over her mouth as she waits for them to find her.

"It's too dusty to see anything," one of the men moans.

"Yeah, even if somebody's here, there's no way they'll be able to see us. We're good. Let's just get back to our shift," another responds.

Slowly, the footsteps retreat, but Kaira stays hidden in her spot long after they go. When she finally works up the courage to run back to her tent, the sun is meeting the horizon. She slips out the bottom of the path before diving straight into the first row of tents unlike how she usually takes the main path as close as she can get to hers.

Her eyes dart around as she hunches over, attempting to hide herself behind her headscarf. She doesn't know if it's fear at what those 'guards' might do to her if they find out she'd been there, even though their shift will have long been over, or if it's fear at what the real guards might do if they find out she knows something of this scale and hasn't reported it. Because she can't, right? Not even to Forren.

No matter how much her actions have already been seen as betrayals to her people, she can't take that final step and call them out. Not when it might, no, *will* mean their deaths. Or can she? Can she really hide the bad things her people do when she's calling out the bad sides of her enemies? Can she be a hypocrite when equal treatment is the thing she's doing this all for?

44

CHAPTER SEVEN

The canvas door to Kaira's tent is slapped open with force and Kaira braces herself for the worst. She prepares for soldiers to storm the tent to take her away or the Elders returning to stop her betrayal or for Forren to show up again.

All she's met with, however, is Nora striding into the room, her face twisted in outrage.

"The children are gone," Nora exclaims.

"What?" Kaira shoots up from her bed. "What do you mean?"

Behind Nora, the early morning sun streams in the door.

"None of them showed up today." Nora paces the room. "I think the Elders had something to do with it, as, on the way here, I saw some of the kids and the look they gave me..."

Kaira lets out a frustrated sigh, running her hand through her hair before she digs into her trunk to find a change of outfit. "I'll go talk to those—argh! Why would they do something like that?" she questions more to herself. She looks up at Nora again as she finishes changing. "I'll sort this out, okay? I'll tell them I've left the school."

Nora stops her pacing, looking at her with downcast eyes. "The Elders are cutting you off like this?"

Kaira nods, taking a moment to calm herself before she responds. "They don't trust me, which is fair enough considering what I'm doing."

"But you're doing this for us!"

"I know but I need to show them that. I will, though. I'll show them I'm doing the right thing."

"I know you will," Nora says, giving Kaira a small smile before it fades, remembering her reason for coming here. "I hate that you must cut yourself off from the school. It only exists because of you."

Kaira smiles back at her friend, stepping forwards to brush a piece of hair out of Nora's face. "I may have established it but you're the one keeping it running. I'd never have been able to keep the children coming if it wasn't for how much fun you brought."

Slowly, Kaira steps back, giving Nora a once over. Her friend does the same to her.

Before Nora can say anything else, Kaira turns for the door. "Take today off. I'll talk to the Elders and make sure the children are allowed to go tomorrow."

Nora follows her from the tent, though they pause there, having to go in different directions. "Take care of yourself, Kaira. I know you know how to but make sure you know when to put yourself first instead of others."

Kaira nods in response, not knowing what else to say that won't end with the back of her eyes burning with tears. Her friend knows her well, knows what her downfall will be. The lessons from her father come to mind but she pushes them away. Keeping herself in mind first will be the only way she can truly put her community first.

"Go get them, girl," Nora says, giving her shoulder a light push to get her moving.

Kaira obliges, turning around as she marks out the route she'll take to the Elders' tent. Since they're family, they share two tents next to each other, so the number of them she can talk to at once will only depend on how many of them are on shift.

Once she reaches the tent Deni resides in, she announces her presence, only so she can convince herself she's above them regarding that. "Hello! It's Kaira Aziz. I've come to see the Elders."

There's no response and Kaira's on the brink of turning around and heading back to her tent when she sees the fabric moving at a seam, revealing an eye peeking out. It's quickly withdrawn as it realises Kaira's staring right at it.

The person inside is not foolish enough to pretend like Kaira hasn't seen them. Slowly, their footsteps approach and the flap is drawn open a sliver to allow Kaira to see that it's another one of the Elders that had visited her. Noha, Kaira identifies them as.

"What do you want, Miss Aziz?" they ask, though their tone is more exasperated than anything else.

"I want to speak to Deni and any other Elders available," Kaira says sharply.

"What business do you have?"

"I have concerns about the children being banned from attending the school."

Noha sighs and Kaira can hear whispering behind them before they respond, "Fine. Come in. Deni and Fletch are here and I'll go get the others."

They hold the tent open further for Kaira to enter and she does, feeling only slight trepidation. Noha leaves behind her and she wishes they'd have stayed because they were always her favourite whenever as a child she had to see them for their blessings.

Kaira stands awkwardly near one of the lounges that fill the space.

"You came sooner than I expected, I'll be honest," Deni says, smiling at Kaira, though it does the opposite of making her feel comforted. "Do you not have anything to do with your time but babysit children?"

Kaira's jaw clenches as she wills herself to breathe before replying, "Well, I seem to be getting up to quite a lot outside of *educating* the children. But I don't wish to elaborate until everyone is present. You aren't the only important person here."

Deni bristles but doesn't say more. It isn't long until the door is again opening and four more Elders enter, including Noha who holds hands with one of the others, a girl named Gigi. They file into the space, making the quarters feel cramped, and settle down on the lounge near Kaira, leaving her to stand before them.

"Everyone who's available is here now," Noha says. "You can say what you need."

"Thank you," Kaira says before clearing her throat. "Nora, the other girl helping at the school, came to me this morning to inform me that none of the children showed up for classes. She didn't know the reasons why, but I know that you had a say in it. That you banned the children from going to get back at me for what you see as my betrayal."

"Can you get to why you're here?" Deni questions, waving her hand in a hurrying manner.

"Sorry. Yes. Well, I wanted to assure you that I've given up my duties at the school and left Nora in charge. I—"

"What, to give yourself more time to dally with the enemy?"

"No, actually," Kaira interjects, staring harshly at Deni. "I did it to protect the children, in case things go sideways with the work I'm doing. Speaking of which, do you really think I'd agree to anything that threatens the children? I'm not in a position where I can openly talk about my role with the Keranian guard, but I want you to know that it's bringing reforms in how they manage their ranks. I'm an eye on the inside, someone to report the true conditions so that proof can be given of how we're treated. You might wonder how I can be doing such and, really, I'm wondering quite the same myself! But I've already seen changes being made and—"

"And you've gone off on another tangent?" Deni interrupts. "Please, get to the point. I'm not here to be a judge on what you're doing; it's your choice—your demise—at the end of the day. Return to the matter of the children."

"Right, well, all I want to say is that I'm leaving the school so you can send the children back. No matter what's happening, it's vital that the children have that space. They need it to keep from going mad and to have a safe place to connect with others and with our culture—"

"That's enough," Deni cuts in. Kaira fists her hands by her side, waiting for the rejection. Deni looks at the other Elders and they give her slight nods, though some are a little more hesitant than others. "We'll send the children back so long as you aren't anywhere near them. If we hear that you're close by, that'll be the end of the school."

"Thank you, thank you, thank you!" Kaira exclaims, her chest about to explode with happiness. "I can't thank you enough—"

"This isn't for you, Miss Aziz. Now get out of our sights," Deni says sharply. Kaira shuts up abruptly, feeling the reprimand.

"I'll show you out," Noha offers.

Kaira steps outside with Noha in tow, who lightly grabs her elbow to stop her before she can walk away.

"Thank you, Kaira. I don't know how Benji would cope without the school. He'll miss you, of course," Noha says, smiling warmly. "I'm sorry things haven't worked out with staying there. I know how hard you worked to get the school established."

"I'll miss him too," Kaira murmurs. "Nora will take good care of your son, though."

Noha smiles at her before their eyes go back to the tent still full of Elders. "You should go now. Take care, Kaira."

"You too," Kaira says before turning on her heel and walking away.

She doesn't make it far, however, before she hears another set of footsteps coming after her. She slows her pace, allowing her pursuer to catch up, before she pauses and spins around to face them. She shouldn't have been so silly as to believe it was another Elder with children attending the school.

"Those children were all much better before you set up that silly place," Fletch, one of the Elders who'd been hesitant to nod at Deni, says.

"What do you think will happen if they aren't given the scraps of intelligence this education offers? Do you really want to keep them in the dark?" Kaira says as Fletch steps into her personal space. Kaira fights the urge to back down. He might be an Elder, but he was only newly inducted into their ranks before The Fall at 21-years-old.

"If it means they don't know the truth about what's going on here, then yeah. It's unethical to teach children the ability to think about complex ideas when the environment they're in doesn't support that growth. It makes them feel trapped with their thoughts, imprisoned, even, as they already are."

"How is keeping children oblivious and ignorant to the truth of their world the wrong thing to do? Sure, it might make them more aware about the fact they're prisoners, but they'd have no hope of a future worth living for if all they did was walk around mindlessly, completing any tasks they're given."

"You're vacuous," Fletch seethes, spit flying from his mouth. "I'm going to shut that school down if it's the last thing I do."

"I dare you to try," Kaira shoots back.

Fletch loses it, swinging a fist in Kaira's direction. She lets out a cry of surprise, trying to step out of the way. She's too slow as she trips on a line of string holding up one of the tents nearby. Fletch's hand meets her shoulder, knocking her back further as she stumbles for her footing.

As she manages to right herself, Fletch has caught up to her, his hands reaching out to grab her arms, twisting her wrists sharply. Kaira cries out in pain before kicking one of her legs out, catching Fletch in the shin.

He releases her wrists, biting back an annoyed shout as he recovers and comes for her again. Kaira spins around, side-stepping a makeshift clothesline as she tries to run. The soft sand is impossible to break through and it slows her down too much as Fletch again reaches her, this time yanking her headscarf.

Kaira falls backwards, landing with an oomph on the ground, but she doesn't go down alone as she reaches back with both hands and latches onto Fletch's arm.

He lands on top of her, but she's quick to push up from the ground, throwing him off her before launching on top of him. She doesn't really know what she's doing then, given she has no training and, even if she did, she doesn't think she'd be able to hit an Elder, even in self-defence.

Shouts ring out around them as Kaira fends off Fletch's hands that still attempt to get a hold of her. Sand is thrown into their faces as the inhabitants of nearby tents come to see the drama, their feet stirring up the new layers that have settled since yesterday's sandstorm.

Kaira catches Fletch harshly with the bracelet on her wrist as she slaps away his hand and she winces as the metal cuts into his skin. He leaves a blow on her ribs as her focus breaks.

Suddenly, the noise around them goes silent and Kaira looks up, her body freezing as she sees a patrol of guards running through the rows of tents towards them. The other Altairians have retreated into their tents or otherwise fled to avoid looking like a guilty party.

Kaira feels a sharp sting alight on her brow. She cries out, falling off Fletch as he withdraws his hand, a stream of her blood running down his fist.

And that's her breaking point.

With a war cry, Kaira launches for him, her own hand coming out in a fist, screaming as she meets the bony flesh near his jaw.

She doesn't get the satisfaction of seeing if he's bleeding before arms wrap over her shoulders and she's pulled backwards. Her back meets the solid chest of a guard, but even that's not enough to stop her as she continues screaming at Fletch, attempting to wrangle out of the guard's hold to continue the fight. Fletch attempts to do the same, fighting his constraints as he's pinned to the ground by two guards. Another two guards stand between them with raised hands.

"If you want to keep your lives, stop resisting now," one of the guards demands.

It breaks through to Kaira as she calms down, becoming still in the hold of the guard, who slightly relaxes the grip he has on her in return. She hadn't noticed how hard the hold was, but she's sure she'll have bruises forming on her upper arms from it.

Fletch doesn't give up so easy, as he continues thrashing in the arms of his captors until one pulls a weapon from their belt. He looks up to meet the hard stare of the guard above him.

"Do it; I dare you," Fletch spits.

The guard lifts the sword, but Kaira speaks up before they can bring the weapon down. "I thought you were going to shut the school down first."

Fletch turns his gaze on her, glaring, but he softens his stance before turning back to the guard, lowering his head in acquiesce.

The guard hesitates, but finally lowers the sword, replacing it in its sheath at their side. They turn to the other guards and speak softly in their language. "High Guard Arias can decide on their punishments. Let's take them back to the interrogation rooms."

One of the guards still holding Fletch tightens his grip on the Elder. "This trash disregarded your orders. We have the right to serve out punishment."

Before the first guard can react, the guard pulls his own sword from his sheath and brings it down on Fletch. There isn't enough time for Kaira to shut her eyes, so she watches as it slices through his stomach. Of course, they won't just kill him in one fell swoop. They'd give him an injury that'd slowly kill him. The more suffering, the better, in the eyes of Keranians.

The guards let go of Fletch, letting him flop back onto the sand.

They spin, facing Kaira, as the guard who seems to be in charge turns to her. "Are you going to comply?"

Kaira nods, not wanting to think about what emotions might be running across her face.

She lets the guard holding her lead her through the tents, her gaze meeting the stares of a few eyes peeping out of holes. They rear back upon seeing her, no doubt recognising her as the girl the recent gossip has been centred on.

The guards take her to the only guard building located in the camp, on the far side where Kaira never strays. They reach a truck, one that probably used to be a cattle truck, and the back is lowered before she's forced to clamber in.

The ground is covered in a thick layer of gunk that Kaira doesn't even want to consider what it contains as she has no choice but to lower down into a corner and brace herself as the back is raised again. The guards load into the front two compartments of the truck before it starts up, shaking wildly in warning of what the trip ahead will be like.

Kaira sighs loudly, sinking further into her spot as the truck begins bumping over the tracks, leaving the camp. Her head rests back against the metal wall that meets with the cab of the truck as the putrid smell meets her nose. She shuts her eyes, trying to block out the view as the scenery changes around her, turning from the desert plains to the logged grounds of Kerani lands.

She's already defied odds in returning once from leaving the camp; can she really do it another time?

CHAPTER EIGHT

——— + ✴ ❋ ✴ + ———

There's a clock on the wall, ticking obnoxiously loudly. Kaira's foot taps against the table leg with each beat. A slow crawl of blood trickles down her face, though it's now drying in places. There's blood on her hands too; she hopes it's a mix of Fletch's and her own, even though she cringes at the thought of him being dead.

The door opens intimidatingly slowly and a guard walks in, a smirk on his face.

"Ugh, it's you," Kaira moans in his language, dropping her head onto the table upon seeing the golden details of his uniform.

"I'm starting to think you're obsessed with me, little birdie. What, with how frequently you seem to track me down," Forren replies, walking further into the room as he lets the door shut behind him.

"May I remind you that you're the one that's found me most of the time?" Kaira returns.

"Tsk, semantics," Forren pronounces before his gaze slides over the cuff on her wrist, linking her to the table. Slowly, he lifts his gaze and Kaira watches his shadowed green eyes slide over the blood on her face before he smiles widely. "I heard the other guy didn't come out so good."

Kaira presses her lips together sharply. "Only because your men intervened." She shrugs. "I'll admit he had me before that."

Forren stalks over to the table, pulling a set of keys from his pocket. He gestures with a tilt of his head to the handcuffs. "I'll unlock those if you promise not to attack me with your fury, little birdie. I know you hide a true fight in you and that I wouldn't come out the other side if you turned on me. As much as you tell yourself otherwise, I know you'd have had that man if my men didn't step in. The reports from my guards support such."

Kaira eyes him, trying to discern his intentions under his nice actions and confusing words. He doesn't know her at all. She'd hated every minute of the fight, winced every time she harmed Fletch.

She nods, flattening her palms to the table to show that she isn't going to lash out at him.

He leans in and puts the key into the slot. His hands brush hers as he unlocks the cuffs, letting her hands drop into her lap as they clatter onto the table. He steps back, settling into the seat opposite her.

"What happened out there, Kaira? Who did that to you?" he asks carefully.

"It was nothing," Kaira responds. "Just a little disagreement."

"About you working with me?"

"No. Not everything revolves around you, sunshine." Kaira laughs gently.

"Sunshine? That's a new one. I thought you were going to stick to calling me Forren."

Forren smirks when Kaira glares at him. She fires back, "Don't get used to it, *Forren.*"

"May I remind you that you're on my land now, little birdie."

Kaira huffs. "Semantics."

Forren smirks wider, his gaze boring into her. Her hand goes to her shirt, lifting it to her face to wipe away the blood. Forren's hand knocks hers away and he reaches into his pocket before offering forwards a handkerchief.

"Thanks," Kaira responds awkwardly, taking it from him. She dabs at the blood, feeling bad as it coats the fabric.

Forren huffs, standing to walk around the table. "You're terrible at that. Never gotten into a fight before?"

He takes the handkerchief before pushing it against her wound harder, brushing away the dried blood and the bits still running. Kaira stays silent as he does so, her stomach twisting with her mixed emotions ignited by the moment of kindness.

He hands her back the handkerchief. "Keep holding it to the wound to make sure it stops bleeding."

She obediently does as she's told as Forren returns to his seat. He leans his elbows on the table, his chin in his hands.

"So, what happened? Be honest with me. I'm a High Guard, after all. I have ways of knowing if you're hiding something or telling lies."

"I quit the school because people weren't happy with my choice in working with you and I didn't want how others saw me impacting the children. Then, the children were banned from going, so I went to the Elders to tell them I'd quit so they could send the children back and, well..." Kaira trails off, shrugging.

"They didn't agree with that?" Forren questions.

"No. Quite the opposite, really. They agreed to send back the children, but, as I was leaving, one of them followed and said they'd end the school once and for all and I challenged them to. They didn't take that lightly," Kaira elaborates.

"It takes a special person to be challenged by someone and not rise to the bait," Forren murmurs. He looks over her appearance again. "You didn't fight him immediately, did you?"

Kaira shakes her head. "No. He's an Elder. They're like royalty to us and, in our communities, you respect them above all else. It felt wrong to harm him."

"Even after he drew blood?"

"Yeah." Kaira looks about the room, her eyes lingering on the cuffs. "I suppose here's where I'd usually plead my case, say it was in self-defence, but it doesn't seem like you're interested in that."

"You're right. I'm not interested in torturing or killing my best source of intel," Forren agrees. "Talking about that, have you got anything for me?"

Kaira stays silent, gathering her thoughts. Does she tell him what she found out about that shift of guards? Slowly, she makes up her mind and says, "Shift four has a soldier devoutly loyal to you and one that loves nothing more than questioning you and your gold status. That latter guard also kept workers back after being informed time was up."

Forren nods, his gaze vacant as if he's somewhere else. "Yeah, I know that soldier. I'll be dealing with him soon enough. Anything more?"

"I'd advise you to crack down on soldiers who are disobeying shift leaders. Today, when they were breaking up the fight, the shift leader said to Flet—the man I was fighting that they'd be taking him here after he submitted, but another one of your soldiers took it upon themselves to...deal with him."

"Huh," Forren mutters. "I don't ever get reports of things like that. Is that everything you have to keep me busy?"

Kaira nods, feeling like the lie she's about to tell is clear as day on her face. "Yes, that's all so far."

Forren nods, either not seeing the lie or choosing to ignore it, though Kaira has a sneaky suspicion it's the latter. "Good. I knew you were worth taking the risk on."

He stands and gestures for Kaira to rise as well. She does and he leads her to the door. As he holds it open for her, his eyes linger on her upper arms, where bruises are beginning to mar her skin.

"The man you fought?" he asks.

"Your men," Kaira responds.

Forren swallows. "I'm sorry for that. They shouldn't have treated you that harshly if you were obeying them. As much as I like to have a hard hand on my soldiers, they shouldn't deal out that punishment to you, not when you're just regular people."

Kaira doesn't respond, instead stepping past him to continue out the door. Forren follows, gesturing to the taller truck he's been in the times she's seen him. He opens one of the cab doors for her and lets her in before walking around to hop in the driver's side.

"No Tuomas today?" she questions as Forren turns on the vehicle, letting it rumble to life.

"He's interviewing the guards that were involved in breaking up your fight."

"Do you do that for all the fights that happen?"

"Not all, I imagine, but I do for all the interventions I get reports of."

Kaira remains silent, watching as Forren pulls out of the complex and onto the road leading them back to the camp. The dry dirt under them slowly morphs into the red sand of her own land, but Kaira doesn't feel the same calming relief as she had last time. Instead, her body grows tenser until she can't keep quiet any longer.

"There are three men on shift seven. They aren't yours."

"What?" Forren asks, his eyes straying from the road to look at her briefly.

"They're Altairian," Kaira admits, swallowing harshly. "Prisoners. I don't know what they've done to your guards, but I'd advise you to try and find them."

"Thank you for trusting me enough to tell me that," Forren says quietly, returning his eyes to the road.

"Promise me you won't be too hard on the prisoners," Kaira murmurs.

She can hear Forren's swallow before he responds, "I can't promise you that, Kaira."

She looks over at him and he meets her gaze for a second again. She turns back to look out the front window, shutting her eyes tightly. "I understand."

CHAPTER NINE

The days after Kaira's second impossible return to the camp are a disaster. She's lost all ability to spy because she can't pass by any tent without people muttering rude remarks under their breaths, blaming her for the death of an Elder. Kaira hasn't come across anyone she's willing enough to ask if Fletch had, in fact, died and she isn't risking going to see Nora to ask her.

She debated asking her mother, but the only time she's seen her since is the one time her mother came back from work before the sun set. Her mother had wandered into the tent, seen Kaira and opened her mouth to say something, before her eyes had moved to the other women present and she'd shaken her head. Emotions had risen in Kaira's throat in that moment; even her mother didn't want to be seen associating with her. Kaira can't blame her for it, though; she doesn't know if she'll be able to continue with what she's doing if it starts to affect those closest to her.

"Just because you're up to something with the High Guard doesn't mean you can neglect your tasks," a female voice calls out behind Kaira.

Kaira spins, pulled out of her thoughts as she realises she's been scrubbing the same part of the bathing room floor for much longer than necessary. She gives a slight dip of her head in acknowledgement to the guard before turning to her work, scrubbing the ground faster.

It's unusual for a guard to be watching over basic chores within the camp like cleaning and Kaira wonders whether Forren has ordered it or whether the guards are just more closely watching her. It's clear from the whispers of "pampered golden girl" under their breaths that more are becoming aware of the fact that she has an arrangement with the gold-decorated High Guard.

Kaira finishes mopping before returning the cleaning tools to the shed they belong in. Then, she walks down the path towards the front of the camp, along the same side that the gate she's miraculously returned through twice sits. Where this wall meets the cliffs are open-stall stable-like buildings: the metal working buildings.

She passes the clanging and bashing noises, the open-flame fires and the hard-labouring workers. Sweat drips from their faces, their skin burnt red and tanned, as their backs strain from the effort of bending over all day. She makes it to the last stall, where a group of people stand around tables, files in hand as they sharpen the long blades the logging workers use.

Kaira picks up a file and settles herself at a far corner, just inches away from the terrifying cliffs. Here, the breeze coming up from the sea is cooling, a contradiction to the heat of the fires in the stalls at her back.

Her muscles strain as she runs the file over the blade. The soldier that'd been with her at the bathing rooms has followed her and leans a distance away on the front post of the structure. Kaira ignores her presence as she works, getting into the rhythm. Back and forth, back and forth, the movement monotonous as the sharp ringing vibrates in the air.

Nobody dares talk, but it isn't just because of the new presence of the guard. There's no energy to do so. No will, really. Everyone just wants to get in and out, as if talking will

62

make the work somewhat enjoyable and they'll do anything to make sure it's the opposite.

A sudden sound of scuffling outside has everyone looking up from their work, though their eyes quickly divert back as they remember the guard watching them. Kaira glances at the guard before rising from her seat.

She squeezes herself through the people working in her stall to make it to the low wall that separates them from the one over. Screams grow louder and clearer as she approaches, so it becomes clear it's only coming from one person.

Kaira can't see them as they aren't in the stall immediately beside her, so, with another look at the guard to see how she's so far reacted to Kaira abandoning her work, she pushes between the tables to exit the structure.

As she reaches fresh air, her eyes land on the commotion a few stalls down where a bunch of workers are running from the structure as guards converge from near the main gate and the entrance to the cliff path that's close to where Kaira is.

Kaira approaches, ignoring the dread growing in her stomach, until she can see into the open structure. There, in the middle of the action, is a man screaming above a knocked over drum of hot ashes. Burns have licked up his arms, leaving split raw red skin and blisters in their wake.

There are a few workers attempting to help him pull off his burned clothes but, as soon as the guards arrive, they're ripped away forcefully, ordered to get back to work. The small fight the workers put up is quickly shut down and the injured man is left to fend for himself.

As if sensing her presence, one of the figures that'd been trying to help spins around and meets Kaira's gaze. Nora. Her eyes meet Kaira's in fear, wide as her mouth opens and closes, though nothing comes out. Kaira doesn't need to hear it to know what's being said, though. *Papa.*

Kaira spins to face her guard. She guesses that she's one of the good guards, considering at the bathing house she'd asked her to continue working rather than using physical force. "Can't you go do something? Get the guards to help that man?"

It seems like her observations are correct as the guard hesitates, looking between Kaira and the drama unfolding. "That's not my responsibility," she responds carefully.

"But if I walked over there..." Kaira trails off.

"Then it'd be. I should warn you not to, though, golden girl. I know Arias well and I don't know how he's shown you this much patience."

"Well, that's two of us." Kaira sighs, looking over at the drama. Her body fights her mind, wanting to run forwards and help the man—*Nora's father*—as he falls to the ground in pain, but there's nothing she can do. The guards will hold her back and she'll only make things worse in escalating the drama. Kaira again meets her friend's gaze and opens her mouth, whispering quietly, "I'm sorry."

Kaira can see tears burning Nora's eyes as she steels her jaw, her hands fisting at her sides. Kaira only moves a few more steps before Nora is turning for the guards, viciously pushing them aside to get to her father. Her rage permeates the air as a guard falls, toppling another coal drum as they go down.

Kaira's breath catches in her throat as she reaches the back of the crowd, pushing them aside as she watches the ashes spill across the ground, scattering around Nora.

Her friend seems unaware of the burns marring her own skin as she continues to push forwards, screaming for her father. More guards crush the coals underfoot with their thick boots as they converge to keep her back.

A screeching noise pierces the air, causing everyone to freeze as, slowly, like moths to flame, their eyes are drawn to the PA system that's only on one other occasion ever been used.

"Halt!" The order comes out clearly in her language, making it clear which party it's directed towards. "Anyone who moves without a direct order will be subjected to immediate punishment."

Kaira shuts her eyes tightly, wanting to convince herself that the demanding voice isn't one she's become accustomed to.

There's a palpable energy of fear coursing through the crowd of onlookers as nobody dares to move. Kaira wonders if they're even daring to breathe.

"Anyone working in stall three who wasn't involved in the incident or harmed are exempt from work. Return immediately to your residences," the voice orders over the system. Nobody moves still, shock keeping them in place. "Now!"

The crowd around Kaira quickly dissolves, the sharp order spurring everyone into action. As she's left alone out the front of the stall, not daring to move, her eyes look around, hoping to catch sight of Forren. He must be near to be able to give orders as if he knows exactly what's happening.

"To the guards who have quickly jumped into the fray," the voice says, switching to Keranian, "will you do something useful? Provide first aid to the two injured prisoners before transporting them back to base."

The guards startle, looking around at each other before, finally, one steps forwards and spurs them into action. Kaira meets Nora's eyes as soldiers step towards her, one of them picking her up to get her off her burnt feet. She nods slowly and Nora returns it. It's an assurance that it's all going to be okay and an apology for not being able to do more.

"Kaira Aziz. If you please, would you step away and return to your own workstation," Forren orders.

The eyes of the guards nearby turn to Kaira as Forren continues her order in their language. She spins quickly to head back to her station as the guards put together that she can understand their language and it isn't an oversight on High Guard Arias' end.

"Be expecting me after your shift, Miss Aziz," Forren ends before the PA clicks off with another audible screech.

And, this time, given warning she's going to be meeting with him, Kaira feels her stomach clench with worry. Perhaps she's finally disobeyed one too many orders.

CHAPTER TEN

Sure enough, as her shift is finishing up, there's another guard who's joined the one watching Kaira. The details of his mask and the jewellery hanging across his brow are just as much of an identifying feature of who it is to Kaira as the golden detailing on his uniform.

Forren's silent as Kaira stops in front of him and he gestures to follow him. The female guard leaves them and they fall into step with each other as Forren guides her towards the main gate, where Kaira can see the towering truck he drives waiting.

The sun is setting as they reach the vehicle, making the sky a flaming mass of colours brighter than the red sand they cross. Forren holds open the passenger door, offering a hand to help her in which Kaira ignores as she climbs up.

He huffs before shutting the door and crossing around to the driver's side. Kaira expects him to say something as his door shuts, but instead he just turns the key. He puts the vehicle in reverse, backing it up before putting it in drive and pulling out of the metal gateway.

"So, you did order your guards to pay special attention to me," Kaira mutters as they leave the compound, feeling annoyance—it wasn't quite anger, yet—squeezing her chest. "Was I the threat or the damsel in distress?"

Forren sighs, pulling over to the side of the road once they're out of view of the camp. He drops his head to the steering wheel. "Neither. Both. I don't know." He's silent for a little, processing his thoughts. "Look, at the end of the day, it doesn't matter what I saw you as. What matters is that my role as the High Guard overseeing this camp is that I keep the peace and I made the decision to have the guards watch you more closely to do this."

"It matters to me what you think of me," Kaira responds before she can think about it. Did it really? That, she can't deny. But why?

Forren looks up from the steering wheel, meeting her gaze as he swallows. "Well, make of it what you want, but the reason I put the guards there wasn't just because I thought you might cause problems. I thought it might also give you a better chance at watching some of the guards, one-on-one, not just in their shift rotations, because you're the best chance I have at keeping—well, establishing—peace from what you're reporting to me."

Kaira's silent and, after a while, Forren turns the vehicle back on, the lights piercing through the darkness that's settled, and pulls onto the road.

Kaira swallows. "Did you find where your missing guards were?"

"They were found *alive* halfway down those cliffs. They'd hit a ledge in the fall. A team rescued them two days ago."

"Unfortunate," Kaira mutters under her breath.

Forren's hands tighten on the steering wheel. "May I remind you, Miss Aziz, that I'm still your superior. Don't think that my casual handling of your misconduct in the past means that I'll not enforce rules if it continues."

Kaira looks at him, pretending to pout as she clutches a hand to her chest in false concern. "Oh, but then who'll do all your dirty work?" Kaira breaks her face, sighing. "Well, at least you're stronger to your morals than me, not turning on your people."

Forren looks over at her with an indiscernible expression. "You're sorely mistaken if you think I subscribe to any sort of morals, little birdie."

"Why do you call me that?" Kaira asks, her brows furrowed.

"You were a flight risk when we first met. You tried escaping me and I thought you were going to throw us both off that cliff," he replies with a shrug. There's a little break of silence before he adds, "And because of your necklace."

Kaira's hand goes to the necklace pendant sitting under her shirt, which is indeed a little bird. A blue wren, to be exact. "You noticed?"

"Being a High Guard means you notice everything," he replies. "Though that comes with a lot of questions about those things. Like, who gave it to you? Why is it so special to you? Don't even try to deny that fact, because I see how much you play with it."

"Too bad we aren't in your interrogation room," Kaira responds. "I don't feel like answering your questions. Not when it means nothing to our partnership."

"Fair."

There's another silence, but this time it's not like the others. It's more...companionable.

Lights appear in the distance, the base, but the truck continues along the road, letting the base fall back into darkness behind them.

"Kidnapping me?" Kaira asks casually, though fear rises with the goosebumps on her arms.

Forren lets out a low chuckle. "You wish. I bet it wouldn't be long before you succumbed to Stockholm Syndrome." Forren shakes his head. "No, I sent your friend, or, at least, that's what I think she is, with the injured man to a hospital base in the next town. I thought you might like to see her."

"And in return?" Kaira asks.

Forren sighs and Kaira thinks he's annoyed at how well she can read his intentions. "Let's deal with that later," he says.

Kaira looks at him, weighing her options. What will he force her to do now? How much more can she betray her people? But she can't give up the chance to apologise to Nora, to make sure her papa's okay and that she isn't sitting in some damp jail cell awaiting punishment.

"As long as you aren't going to make me torture her, we've got a deal," Kaira finally responds.

"No, nothing like that," Forren responds. "Some would say it's much worse, but I don't think you'll mind it so much."

CHAPTER ELEVEN

Forren is true to his word and they pull off the main road at the next town, idling outside of a large building with a hospital symbol above the main entrance.

Kaira glances out her window, watching the streets that are teeming with soldiers even this late at night, though it looks like it's because it's late at night that they're out and about. Many of them stumble along as their friends guide them from buildings where loud music and flashing lights echo from. They wear more natural clothing, but their masks distinguish them from the citizens they mix with.

There are also groups of soldiers who are in uniform, strutting around with purpose, still on duty.

"Are you up to doing this?" Forren asks, noticing where her gaze is. She's amid her enemy, after all.

"My friend needs me," Kaira says.

Forren looks at her like he wants to debate the validity of her response as an answer, but instead turns off the truck and opens his door. "Come on, then."

Kaira breathes out heavily, pausing for a minute before she opens her door and clambers down. She shivers as the wind whips around them, pulling at her loose clothing and spraying her hair across her face.

Forren, who'd come to join her, reaches past her back into the truck, emerging with one of his gold-decorated coats. Wordlessly, he offers it to her.

"Thanks," she states uneasily, pulling it around herself.

She leaves it unbuttoned, as that feels more like a betrayal to her people than any of the others she's committed so far. Forren watches that decision knowingly but doesn't say anything as he spins on his heel and leads her towards the building.

The receptionist looks at them as they approach, their eyes flickering between Forren and Kaira in his coat. Kaira's a little surprised to see they also wear an eye mask like the guards and she wonders whether all Keranian hospitals are worked in by the army or only this one since it's so close to the camp.

"How can I help you?" the lady receptionist asks, her tone bored.

"I'm looking for the two prisoners who were brought here earlier," Forren answers.

The receptionist tsks under her breath as she shuffles through paperwork.

"Do you have a problem with my decision to send the Altairians here?" Forren questions, his voice lethally quiet. "Do I have to remind you who you're serving?"

The receptionist freezes and Kaira can almost see the shiver of fear that runs down her back. "No, sir. The prisoners are down that hall" —she gestures with a crook of her head to a hall on the right— "in the last room."

Kaira looks at Forren who gestures for her to go. She listens, beginning to walk that way before she hears continued whispers behind her. As she reaches the hallway, she spins back around, leaning on the wall to view the display of dominance as Forren hasn't followed her.

The whispers are too quiet to make out this far away, but Kaira doesn't need to hear them to make out the threat as

Forren reaches across the tall workspace to lean menacingly in towards the receptionist.

It isn't much longer before Forren pushes away, stepping in Kaira's direction. Kaira waits until he catches up before continuing to make her way down the hall.

"You know, I wanted to ask this before in the truck, but now is a good time," Forren says. Kaira's curiosity has her looking up at him as he continues, "What do *you* think about *me?*"

Kaira huffs, turning her gaze to the empty hallway ahead of them. Cobwebs linger in the corners and paint peels off the walls. She peeks in through the small windows on the doors, only to see that the rooms are empty, their furniture and equipment abandoned.

"I think that you're" —Kaira stalls, trying to decide how to word it— "kinder than you let yourself be seen as. I think the persona you put on around your guards is an act, one to make yourself feel better than them. But I think you're already better than them, just not in the way your country recognises."

"So, you think what I did back there was a show that I'm the stronger one?"

"No." Kaira is quick to disagree. "I fear you're stronger than any display I've witnessed from you. But I don't think you want to be; I think your duty to your country makes you put their expectations above your own feelings."

"What gives you the impression that I'm kind? Was it me giving you my coat or me not torturing you the times you've ended up in my interrogation room?"

"Neither. Call it a hunch."

With her gaze held forwards, Kaira feels Forren's burning into the side of her face. Kaira clenches her jaw to ensure no other silly things fall from her mouth.

Forren seems to understand her silence as he clears his throat, gesturing to the door at the end of the hall. "I'll wait out here if you'd like some privacy."

"Thanks," Kaira says, feeling slight annoyance tingling her fingers as she realises how much she's been saying that to him over the past few hours.

Kaira pushes ahead, breaking through the door to see Nora and her father on beds close to each other. She crosses the room to her friend, who's lying on her side, her gaze fixed on her father's face, whose eyes are shut in sleep.

"Hey," Kaira calls out.

Her friend startles and Kaira's reminded of the world they live in at that, knowing Nora likely hasn't slept a wink in the hours that have passed since the accident, too scared of what the Keranian soldiers and doctors might do to her if she lets down her guard.

Nora spins around, a slight smile pulling up her lips. "It's you," she says before her eyes fall to the coat Kaira wears. "Don't tell me you killed that High Guard to force your way here," she teases.

Kaira laughs her off. "Nope. You should know I'm much more skilled in blackmailing than murdering, dear."

Nora smiles again, but it's quick to pull into a frown. "Why are you here? Why are we here?"

Kaira presses her lips together. "I don't know," she answers truthfully. "I can only guess that Forren brought you here as a form of blackmailing me."

Nora laughs. "Forren? Is that his actual name?!"

Kaira laughs too. "Oh, no. That's just what I've been calling him."

Nora quickly sobers. "I don't want to be the reason why you're forced into something you don't want to do, Kaira."

"Don't worry about me," Kaira says, grabbing Nora's hands in hers. "I have a feeling that Forren won't hurt me."

Nora looks like she wants to respond something about the stupidity of trusting a feeling about him, given his position, but she doesn't. "I don't know what's going to happen once we're let out of here. Even if we're returned to the camp, Papa's not going to be able to work for a long time and who'll look after him when I must work?"

"I'll make sure you're both taken care of, okay?" Kaira says, squeezing her friend's hand tighter.

"I can't ask you to do that."

"You aren't; I'm offering. See it as my thanks for keeping the school running."

Nora smiles sadly but, before she can say more, the doors are being pushed open by Forren.

"We should get going," he says to Kaira, his eyes soft behind his mask.

Kaira leans over the bed to kiss Nora's forehead. "Take care, Nora. I'll see you again at the end of all this, I promise."

Kaira leaves before the tears burning the back of her eyes can fall.

"You shouldn't make promises you can't keep," Forren says once Kaira catches up in the hallway.

"So, where are you taking me?" Kaira asks in reply.

CHAPTER TWELVE

———— ···· + ✳ ✴ ✳ + ···· ————

"Nice fit," a voice calls out when they exit the hospital.

Kaira looks up from her feet, spotting Tuomas leaning against the truck as they eat a sandwich. "I'd disagree," Kaira says. "It reeks of '*god complex*'."

Tuomas chuckles. "I bet it does."

Kaira makes it to their side and they hold open the door for her to climb in. There's enough space in the vehicle that even with three of them along the bench seat, there's still enough room to not brush shoulders.

"Are you ever going to answer my question?" Kaira asks, looking over at Forren as he starts the truck.

Tuomas spins their head around to face him and, as if they know exactly what question Kaira's talking about, they exclaim, "You haven't told her yet?"

Forren clenches his jaw, gritting out from between his teeth, "Well, there wasn't really a good moment to, before now."

"Well, use this moment before we end up wherever we're going and I'm just as clueless," Kaira says.

Forren scoffs. "Yeah, you don't have to worry about running out of time. Hate to tell you this but you're going to be stuck with us for two weeks of travelling. Congratulations because you're officially going to be the first Altairian to see our capital, let alone go before the King."

Kaira freezes to the bone. "You're lying," she whispers, before adding more forcefully, "You're lying. You're lying!"

Before she even processes her thoughts, she's throwing herself at Forren, gripping onto him tightly and shaking him. He yells something about trying to drive as Tuomas launches across the seat to grab a hold of her.

Tuomas manages to wrestle their arms under hers, pulling her across the bench seat as Forren jerks the steering wheel, pulling them back onto the road.

"You take me back right now!" Kaira spits at Forren, weakly attempting to wrangle out of Tuomas' hold.

"If I'm going to take you back to the camp, I might as well drive us off this road!" Forren responds, anger prickling his tone. "Do you really think the King will be like me and disregard your transgressions?"

Kaira deflates instantly. Even she can't lie to herself and pretend like the King won't immediately order her execution for such actions. "Ugh! How do I keep doing this to myself?" she moans, slumping back in her seat.

Tuomas looks at her, as if making sure she isn't going to jump up and attack Forren again, but they seem quite sure she won't as they settle back into their own spot.

"I don't know why the King is summoning you. I mean, he could just be inviting you to tea?"

Kaira huffs. "Let's not pretend either of us are that silly."

"Fair point," Forren admits. "How about we don't know if he'll execute you?"

Kaira hums consideringly. "I could settle with that."

She lets out a yawn, her eyes fluttering shut.

"You can sleep if you like," Tuomas says. "I'll make sure Forren doesn't murder you."

Kaira looks over at them. "After the day I've had, I might just take you up on that offer."

Sure enough, only a few minutes later, her head has fallen onto Tuomas' shoulder as her soft breaths fill the quiet of the truck.

"Call in the cavalry to keep me in line?" Kaira jokes as she steps out of the truck, noticing the other vehicles that have joined them.

They're parked next to them in a clearing as the soldiers who have arrived in them set up their tents.

"Ah, if only I saw you as that much of a threat, little birdie," Forren sighs wistfully.

Kaira looks up at him and his expression confirms what she assumed from his return to her nickname: he's going to let her behaviour in the truck go.

Kaira looks around the flat piece of land they're on, where it stretches into the distance on either side as far as Kaira can see in the low light of the night that looms over them.

Forren huffs from her side. "Are you going to help me set up this tent?"

Kaira slowly roams her attention back to him, looking at the pieces of equipment in his hands. "Ah, so you've hired the cavalry to make sure that I don't run away in the night."

"I'm not concerned about that, considering you'll be sleeping less than a few metres away from me."

"What?" Kaira exclaims, dropping the poles she'd taken up.

"Do you think I pick up hitchhikers so often I have a spare tent?" Forren raises a brow.

"Well, someone with your looks wouldn't be unfamiliar with inviting people into their tent for a night, right?"

"You'd be surprised," Forren responds casually. "Watch out, you're in the way."

Kaira stumbles backwards. "Oh, sorry."

She watches as Forren goes about setting up the tent, moving with an ease that shows how familiar he is with the act of doing so. Kaira doesn't know why she's surprised or why she still expects him to be the posh '*I'm too good for sleeping in a tent*' kind. It's clear that he's as used to getting his hands dirty as any other Kerani guard.

Forren has the monstrosity of a thick fabric tent set up before Kaira can recover from her surprise and he holds the door open, gesturing her inside. "Milady."

Kaira bristles as she brushes past him. Inside, it's almost like magic has transformed the place as two thick sleeping mats are set out on either side of the tent, around the chunky middle pole that divides them. It's clear which side is Kaira's from the otherwise stark additions, whereas Forren's side has a large chest she imagines is full of clothes. There's definitely some sort of trickery going on as there's also a full-size dressing table and stool.

Kaira wordlessly sits on her bed, ignoring the urge to pick on Forren for the spread of beauty supplies that covers the table. She pulls off her sandals, placing them neatly beside the mat, before running her hands through her hair. The smell of smoke still clings to her clothes from the earlier mess in the metalworking buildings.

"Are you okay?" Forren asks.

Kaira looks up, realising she'd zoned out again, and abruptly startles. She can't help the loud gasp as she meets Forren's *unmasked* and bare face. His green eyes are brighter in the candlelight, his brow jewellery settled between their depths.

Forren turns around, his hands covering his face. "I'm sorry." He reaches for the mask that sits abandoned on the dressing table. "I'll sleep with it on, if it'll make you more comfortable."

"Oh, no. You don't have to! I was just startled. I...didn't know the rules relating to when you can take your mask off," Kaira says in a rush, feeling her cheeks heating.

Forren sighs, leaving the mask where it is, although he doesn't turn around to show his face to Kaira again, busying himself with fixing the blankets covering his sleeping pad. "We aren't allowed to take our masks off in front of anyone unless they're immediate family or partners. I don't really know what the rules are surrounding people that aren't Keranian. I...didn't think about taking the mask off; I'm not used to having someone else in my tent."

"How many people have seen your face?" Kaira asks.

"About six. I might have accidentally flashed Tuomas once or twice," Forren says.

There's a silence between them as they settle into their beds. Kaira berates herself for having made Forren feel awkward; she hadn't been offended by the sight—quite the opposite, really.

"Well, this is awkward," Kaira says when she's staring up at the dark black fabric of the ceiling. Closest to where the lantern shines in the middle of the room, she can pick out little swirls of golden pattern woven into the material.

"You could go to sleep," Forren says, though it comes out more like a question.

Kaira hums. "I could do that or you could find something to say to fill the silence."

"You were literally yawning earlier so I know you're tired. Just go to sleep."

"Aren't you a little bit intrigued by me, though? Isn't there something to find in that mind of yours to ask?"

Forren huffs. "Sorry, but unless I'm mistaken, this tent isn't an interrogation room. Looks like you'll have to sleep."

"Fair point," Kaira says, not being able to argue since she'd used the same excuse earlier that day.

She wants to keep pushing Forren, though, to use the opportunity to learn more about him.

More than that, she wants to convince herself that the reason she's so concerned with asking Forren questions about himself is because she wants to understand why he'd agree to work with her, not because she's intrigued by the boy who'd been given multiple excuses to execute her but had chosen not to.

Slowly, Kaira rolls over, tucking herself into the thick blankets that suffocate her. She doesn't want to give up so easily, but she gets the feeling Forren feels exposed enough for one day.

"Goodnight, Forren," she says into the dark as she hears him put out the lantern.

He makes another startled noise before replying, "Goodnight, little birdie."

CHAPTER THIRTEEN

———— ····· + ✳ ✵ ✳ + ····· ————

Kaira's almost bouncing on her feet as she helps or, more accurately, hinders Forren as he packs away the tent.

The sun is higher in the sky than Kaira thought they would've left the campsite at and as much as she wishes it's because of how late Forren had driven into the night, she has a sneaky suspicion that it's for her sake, given the whirlwind of a day she had.

"Ugh, do we really have to wait for your soldiers to be ready before we can leave?" Kaira huffs, looking over the collection of tents to see that the majority are only just beginning to pack away. "Can't they catch up later?"

"What? Are you wanting to get rid of the witnesses when you attack me down the road and steal the truck to drive away?" Forren responds, leaning on the truck beside her. Even he, with how much taller than her he is, barely comes up to the door of the truck.

Kaira tsks. "Damn, my plans have been uncovered."

Forren watches her carefully before gesturing his head towards the truck. "Come on. Tuomas will be finished soon and, once they join us, we can leave."

Kaira keeps in her squeal of excitement, but her smile says it all the same as she clambers into the truck, Forren hopping up behind her to leave the driver's seat open for Tuomas.

She stays silent once she settles into her spot, though she buries her hands under her thighs to keep her excitement in as she bounces, spying the supplies she'll need for her masterplan on the dash.

Forren watches her silently, assessing her. He looks so different with his mask replaced. Last night, it'd been even harder for Kaira to convince herself that Forren wasn't like her, that he was some strict, killing guard for her enemy. He'd just been...someone thrust into a war that they didn't start and didn't understand.

The driver's side door opens and Tuomas climbs in, glancing questioningly at the pair and the excitement permeating from Kaira before they shrug their shoulders and, with a smile, get the truck rumbling to life.

Almost as soon as they've made it through the crowd of soldiers that stand to attention as they pass, their middle finger pressed to the pendants on their forehead jewellery, Kaira reaches forwards and grabs the pen and paper off the dash. Quickly, she scribbles 'Interrogation Room' onto the paper before propping it on the dash, turning to Forren with a winning grin.

"So, ready to answer some questions?" she asks.

Forren dips his head. "Do I really have a choice? This is an interrogation room now."

Kaira smiles. "I'm sure you know what happens to people that don't subject to interrogation in interrogation rooms."

"Well, we have approximately two hours until our next stop for fuel, so go ahead. Ask you questions, little birdie," Forren says, leaning back in his seat like he couldn't be any less bothered by the prospect of her examining him.

"Okay. Why did you decide to ask me to work in this partnership?" Kaira asks.

"You're bilingual," Forren answers.

Kaira feels her brow furrow slightly, but she pushes on. "Why are you worried about your men not behaving now, when they've been doing the same things for years?"

"Now is a crucial time to demonstrate to my superiors that I have control over my men," Forren answers simply.

"Ah, so this is how it's going to be, hmm?" Kaira says. "You answer the questions but only as basically as is required."

"There's an easy solution: learn to ask better questions."

"Do you have any tips?"

"Yes," Forren says, technically answering her question which makes Kaira huff in annoyance. "Come on, you can do better."

Kaira presses her lips together, thinking about her wording before asking, "Share a tip you have for me that will improve the questions I ask during this interrogation."

"Expand. Once you get an answer, expand on that, asking something specific about it," Forren says with a smile.

"Before you said that now is a crucial time for demonstrating your ability, why?" Kaira fires back.

"The Golden Games are coming up."

"What are the Golden Games?"

"It's where all the gold status guards compete to see who is the best."

"And what does the person who comes out on top get?"

Forren swallows. "We're not allowed to tell outsiders."

"Even if you're threatened in an interrogation room?" Kaira asks, her eyes going pointedly to one of the knives sheathed at Forren's side.

"Especially then."

Kaira turns to Tuomas. "And do the same rules apply to you? Like, is it a whole population secret or can only the golden guards not say?"

"It's for all," Tuomas replies.

"Ah, dang," Kaira mutters.

Her next question is on her tongue, but it doesn't come out as her eyes drift to the changing scenery around them. They've passed out of the deserts completely and have emerged into dead drylands that Kaira imagines were once forests. The terrain is bumpy, going up and down little mounds and Kaira notices silver-grey smudges running parallel to them a while back from the road.

"What are those?" she asks, pointing to the masses on either side of the road.

"They're machines," Forren answers easily.

Kaira freezes as she notices they're moving. Like ground-burrowing spiders, they slowly creep towards them, their form becoming more and more noticeable.

"Okay, I don't care about this interrogation room stuff now, just answer my questions, please. What in the world are they?"

"They're war machines. Canons, tanks and carriers of other explosive weapons."

A wave of ice washes through Kaira's body as her eyes don't move from the massive machines. Their tracks functioning as wheels trundle across the ground, bringing them closer and closer towards them with each second that has Kaira's breath catching further in her throat.

She's heard about the weapons, about the tanks and the bombs and all that, but she'd never imagined they'd be like this. She'd never imagined that they were this huge, this *deadly*.

And there, lingering behind the monstrosities to their left, is a view far beyond what Kaira ever dreamed of. Climbing high into the sky are tall buildings in vibrant colours of purples and blues, with odd metal curls twisting around them. The whole city is lit up so bright it's noticeable even in the glare of the daylight. And, to add to all that, it covers a huge expanse of land, easily ten times the size of the prisoner-of-war camp that housed all that was left of her population.

"I never knew your capital city was this close to the old border," Kaira says. She can't find the words to say anything about the size of it or its look. Its design is utterly beyond her comprehension.

Forren lets out a disappointed noise in the back of his throat. "Oh, this isn't the capital, little birdie. This is just the beginning."

As they come closer to the towering buildings of glass and metal, Kaira notices that there's a huge river that wraps around the whole city, keeping it on its own little untouched island. The reason why is evident as a loud boom sounds through the air before a shockwave hits the truck so hard Kaira falls sideways, her head landing in Tuomas' lap.

"What is that?" she asks in shock, righting herself as her fingers cling to the front of her seat. Her eyes are caught to their right where a giant cloud of dust and debris rises into the air.

"That is the least of what these war machines can do. Training, if you will," Forren replies, looking over at her with unreadable eyes.

It's clear now why the land around them is the way it is: barren, bumpy and dirty. It hadn't been logged; it'd been mutilated by the weapons designed by the inhabitants of the land.

Kaira forces herself to look away from the sight to glance over at Forren. Any ideas she'd gained yesterday about him being like her are washed away. She can never be like someone who destroys their land in such ways, all in a show of their power.

Coiling in her gut is fear unlike anything she'd ever experienced. If this is what they can do to their own precious land, what will they do to her country?

By the time they're pulling into the city, Kaira hasn't yet torn her words from the fear keeping them hostage. She doesn't know if she wants to, not when she doesn't want to know the answers to the questions in her head.

They don't go far into the metropolis, sticking to the main road until they pull into an elaborately coloured building that must be where they fuel up. Tuomas gets out to do so and, in his absence, Forren's gaze burns holes into the side of Kaira's face.

"Don't tell me it's this that scares you after everything you've seen of what my people are capable of," Forren says.

Kaira presses her lips together, feeling her shoulders trembling with a rage she can't understand.

"Kaira—"

"Don't. Don't call me that," Kaira says harshly. "Not now."

She turns to glare at Forren, only to find him looking at her with a teasing smile.

"Do you hate that I know exactly how to rile you up?" he asks.

Kaira does, in fact, hate it. She hates that he only said her name to make her speak. At the same time, though, she can't deny that she appreciates him for it, for caring—if that's what you even call it—about her enough to bother to do so.

"How can you do something like that to the land?" Kaira asks. She waves a hand around the truck cabin to gesture to the city that encloses them. "And how can you have all this but then keep us the way you do?"

"I hate it as much as you do," Forren says, sincerity thick in his tone. "It's why these Golden Games are so important to me."

Kaira wants to push him further about these Games, but as she turns to face him, he's shutting down behind his mask. He's in no mood to answer her questions and, quite frankly, Kaira doesn't know if she's in the mood to ask them. How can he expect winning one contest to fix all this?

CHAPTER FOURTEEN

"Come on. We haven't got all day," Forren says as they pull up in a tight street that the truck barely fits down. He hops out of the truck and gestures for Kaira to follow.

Kaira looks at him questioningly, debating whether to ignore him, before she thinks better of it. This isn't the war camp or even its control base. She's in the heart of her enemy's country and Forren can't show leniency to her disobedience here.

Sighing loud enough for Forren to hear, she clambers from the vehicle, wrapping her arms around her body as the cold air meets her skin. She'd given Forren his coat back after the hospital visit as it seemed...unprofessional for her to keep it.

Even across the river, the loud booms and shockwaves can still subtly be felt, making Kaira unsteady on her feet.

Forren ushers her towards a narrow doorway shoved between two stores with windows looking into rows of colourful clothes and the masks soldiers wear. Tuomas follows behind them, looking over their shoulder like they expect others to jump out at them.

"You really are kidnapping me now, aren't you?" Kaira questions Forren once they're inside the building and only a long stairway going straight up meets them. Unlike the exteriors of the buildings within the city that'd been so bright they'd blinded Kaira, the inside of this one is so dark she must feel for the wall to have a grasp of where she is once Tuomas shuts the door.

Forren tsks. "Don't kidnappers usually take their victims to remote places rather than from them?"

Kaira tilts her head. "I suppose you have a fair point. But why are we sneaking around like criminals, then?"

Forren shrugs. "Well, in the eyes of some Keranians, you are."

"What? For being Altairian?"

"Exactly," Forren responds, taking the lead to guide the way up the staircase. "If the King says that you're the enemy, then it's safe to say that most people are going to blindly follow that. Very few people are brave enough to take on their own view and rewrite the narrative they believe."

"You know, for a soldier, you can be quite...philosophical. You should've become a social scientist. It might be more fitting considering you seem to be better at that than making people follow your orders," Kaira responds.

"Arguably being in the army is one of the places that best fosters social scientists. I mean, you do see the worst of humankind there," Forren says, his voice low with an emotion Kaira can't quite pick. Sadness, perhaps?

"Do you regret it?" Kaira asks, before elaborating, "Being in the army? Being a golden guard?"

"No," Forren says quickly. "Not with the possibilities it brings."

"Which are?"

"The Golden Games," Forren answers. "Come on, Kaira. You should be on to this by now. The Golden Games is the most important thing to Kerani and its citizens, even more so for us 'golden guards'."

Kaira goes to reply, but before she can, she runs straight into Forren's back as he draws to a stop. Her eyes have somewhat adjusted to the darkness so she can see the outline of something blocking their way. As there's a loud clinking noise before the object creaks open and they're flooded with unnatural light, she realises it's a door.

Kaira blinks blindly as Forren forges ahead, seemingly unbothered by the strikingly bright lights that make the room appear like they're walking straight into the burning sun. She feels a small shove on her back as Tuomas lightly pushes her forwards, urging her to emerge from the stairwell.

The texture of the ground beneath her sandals changes, going from hard stone to a soft rug. Slowly, like she's waking up from sleep and wiping the crusts from her eyes, the room comes into focus. It's been so long since Kaira's been in a proper house—a home—that it takes her a while to realise that's what she's in.

"Why are we here?" she asks, her eyes taking in the elaborate furnishings.

There are chairs and lounges everywhere, hundreds of pillows on each and just as many throw blankets. Tables line the wall, upon which sit little trinkets, though they don't look like the mismatched pieces one picks up on a walk and throws onto a table for safekeeping. They look carefully curated, like each piece costs more than what Kaira used to spend on food in a month.

"Welcome to my family home," Forren says with a wide sweep of his hand.

Kaira lets out a weird noise in her throat. "Okay, my question is even more important now. *Why* are we here?"

Forren turns to face her again, giving her one thorough look up and down. "If you're going before the King, I suspect you're going to want to wear something more...presentable."

"You expect me to dress up for a meeting with the King that I think it's fair to say I strongly dislike?" Kaira says, crossing her hands over her chest.

"Okay, well, how about if you plan on surviving the continued venture into our country, which is much colder than your desert gets even at night, perhaps you might like to have clothes that are a little more suitable?"

Kaira rolls her eyes, unable to find an argument. He's right, after all. She's already feeling the colder weather and, from what it sounds like, they still have a long way to go before they reach the Capital. "Well, I suppose it's in your best interests to keep me alive for whatever purposes you have of me."

"There you go. You really are getting it now, aren't you? Anything I do is for my own gain, is for cementing my place as one of the golden guards and, right now, you're my best asset."

Kaira huffs out an annoyed sigh. "So long as I don't have to wear your army's uniform, I'm free to dress up as you like."

Forren smiles wickedly. "Oh, you're going to regret saying that, little birdie."

Forren's once again right, as he always seems to be.

Kaira stands staring at herself in the mirror with a scowl on her face.

"What's wrong?" Forren asks, the smirk pulling up the corner of his mouth revealing that he knows exactly what's wrong.

Kaira waves her hands through the air, gesturing at the elaborate outfit. The base of it is a white satin-like gown that's fitted to her body but it connects to a fuller white overlaid skirt. Over her shoulders and fitted around her neck is a piece of gold chain jewellery that resembles feathers decorated with a thousand tiny jewels. It matches the gold jewellery that decorates her hair and falls on her brow, which, as pretty as it is, makes Kaira annoyed since it's clearly a matching piece to the one Forren wears. And, as if that isn't enough, there's a matching heavy red coat sitting on an armchair beside Forren.

"This is all too much," Kaira says. "Am I meant to be attending a winter ball or something?"

"Ah, unfortunately the ball comes later than the meeting with the King," Forren says. "Do you not like it?"

"I didn't say that," Kaira defends. "I just...don't want to draw too much attention to myself."

"In my opinion, it isn't the outfit drawing the attention. It's how you wear it: the confidence, the power, the..."

"Okay, you can stop with the compliments, if you can even call them that," Kaira says, feeling herself flush. She must agree with him, though. She does feel all of those things in the outfit.

Forren shrugs before heading back to his sister's wardrobe. Kaira might've made an embarrassing gasping noise that made her sound like a fish when he'd casually mentioned he had sisters. Her assumptions about him being an orphaned only child weren't correct, clearly.

"Don't worry; you'll only have to wear that for the meeting. Until then you can have something more casual," Forren offers, digging through the clothes within the humongous walk-in room.

"Thank the heavens." Kaira sighs, plopping down into the armchair as she waits for him to bring forth his next outfit. Surely, he can't put together anything worse than what she already wears.

It isn't long before Kaira again finds herself before the mirror, though this time her scowl is more a straight line of consideration. The outfit is composed of a pair of black fitted pants and a golden long-sleeve shirt with an almost invisible pattern of suns.

"Is the jewellery really necessary?"

"Aren't I allowed to claim you as mine?" Forren says with a teasing smile. He meets Kaira's frustrated expression before he adds, "It's formality more than anything else. Wearing the matching jewellery clarifies that you're with me."

"Right, so you can show everyone that you're so good at your job you managed to convince an Altairian to work with you." Kaira huffs out an annoyed breath.

"Is that not what happened?" Forren asks, tilting his head to the side.

Kaira can honestly not believe how right he always is. How is it even possible? Every human is bound to be wrong at some point; maybe the answer is that he isn't human.

"Fine," she says, "I'll wear this. I don't think it's going to solve the issue of me not freezing to death, though."

Forren tosses her a plain, brown wool coat before he gestures to a bag he'd placed on the armchair. "There's another two outfits like this in the bag so that you don't have to wear the same thing for the whole trip."

Kaira presses her lips together before stiffly saying, "Thanks."

Forren smiles rigidly. "It's my duty."

"It's not, though," Kaira says. "We both know that." She stays silent for a little, trying to gauge if he's feeling more open to inquisition now. After a while, she decides there's no harm in trying, so she asks, "Why is winning the Golden Games so important to you? I know you can't tell me what you win, but why is the prize important?"

Forren sighs loudly. "Because it gives me the best chance of achieving my biggest dream. Wouldn't you take any chance you had at achieving your greatest ambition?"

"Don't you think that's what I'm doing in working with you? My greatest ambition is to see my people freed. To re-establish Altair and see it prosper. This seems like my best shot at achieving that."

"Maybe we aren't so different from each other, then, in what our dreams are."

"Isn't your country prospering enough already?"

"I didn't say that was my dream," Forren responds curtly. Before Kaira can question him on what he means, he cuts in sharply with, "Anyway, ready to assume a new identity, little birdie?"

"What?" Kaira responds.

"You really didn't think the King would take enough interest in Kaira Aziz, did you? No matter how much I advocated that an Altairian could be beneficial to our goals, prejudices run deep and he never would've accepted it."

"What did you do, then?"

"I hope you don't mind pretending to be Keranian for a while," Forren announces.

Chills rack Kaira to the bone. She's come to terms with dallying with the enemy, but to play at being one of them? That's an entirely different realm.

CHAPTER FIFTEEN

They're back in the truck, trundling along the main road leading out of the metropolis. They'd spent the night at Forren's family home, but now the soldiers from the night before that are again following them in three vehicles.

Coming out the other side of the city is like driving into another world—though one more computable than the city itself. There are wide mountain ranges on either side of them with sweeping forests and snow-capped trees. Birds and other animals dart out in front of them frequently and Kaira can't help but miss the sight of them with how little she saw at the camp.

Forren's been silent beside her, though his eyes keep habitually travelling to her before he diverts them back to the road. Tuomas is with them again too, after they'd left the pair in the city to meet up with their own family. They're in regular clothes—well, as regular as one can get with the elaborate style that's the trend in the country—but their mask is still laid over their face, a more typical white compared to the golden colour of Forren's. It makes Kaira wonder if it's only gold-decorated guards that can choose a golden mask.

"Don't you ever wish you could take the mask off and just...blend in?" Kaira asks Tuomas.

Tuomas shrugs. "Doesn't everyone think that's what they want at some point in their life?"

Kaira glowers. Is half the education system in this country teaching people how to vaguely answer questions?

Kaira opens her mouth to ask Tuomas another question, but Forren cuts in sharply before she can do so, his gaze never faltering from the road ahead. "Kaira, will you shut your eyes until I say?"

Kaira doesn't know whether it's the sharp, low tone in his voice or the very casual use of her first name, but all she manages to do in response is look at him with her mouth gaping open.

Forren rubs a hand over his chin in exasperation. "I'll take that as a no."

At his annoyance, Kaira draws her eyes to the road ahead to peek at what could be so bad. She immediately wishes she'd listened to him.

Ahead, hidden within the deep valley, is an expansive stone wall towering above them, looking like it could be protecting a palace. The view beyond the metal gates reveals a setting from quite a different story.

A prison sits ahead, buried in thick snow as workers in even more thread-bare clothing than Kaira's community walk with chains around their feet.

They're led deep into tunnels with pickaxes, other groups emerging with wheelbarrows full of what's being mined. The bodies of the workers are beyond thin, looking lifeless as their dead eyes lead them unseeingly through the tasks.

Kaira presses her eyes shut to block out the view and, simultaneously, to hold back the burning tears. She feels a hand brush against her thigh and opens her eyes again. Tuomas gestures their head towards where a guard is emerging from an opening in the stone wall, approaching the driver's side of the truck.

They wear a pitch-black mask, but the colour of the buttons and stitching on their uniform freezes Kaira to the bone. Gold. They're the only other High Guard she's had the misfortune of meeting.

The High Guard is a heavy-set, broad and imposing figure who lumbers around in a manner that reveals just how aware of his position he is.

Kaira understands what Tuomas is saying in their movement to get her to open her eyes. She must act strong, unbothered. She must fit in with them; she can't seem like the powerless girl who wants to cry and scream at the sight before her.

With much force, Kaira manages to school her face into neutrality, though it's perhaps a bit on the scowl side as the guard reaches the truck.

"Passes and order of business," the guard demands without preamble as Forren rolls down his window.

"We're transporting a citizen to a meeting with the King," Forren explains, his voice hard in the tone Kaira's come to associate with his High Guard position.

He digs into one of the gloveboxes on the dash before emerging with two documents which he hands to the other High Guard. They peruse the document before handing them back and gesturing with a cock of their head to Kaira. "Does she have a pass?"

"Does she look like a guard to you?" Forren responds in the same bored tone.

"Well, you know the rules, Arias. Anyone who's passing into or through Akuma Prison must either present a pass or be subjected to questioning and frisking by a High Guard."

"Great," Forren announces, swinging open the door so fast it almost takes out the other guard. "Come on, Miss Aziz. I'll be conducting your relevant searches."

The other guard sighs loudly. "You know the rules, High Guard Arias. The guard must be on duty."

"Oh, yes. Thank you for reminding me of that specification, High Guard Gunner." Forren rubs his hands together before facing Kaira. "Wait here with Guard Koski."

Before Kaira can say anything, Forren strides off in the direction of the door in the wall. Kaira swallows deeply before turning to look through the metal gates that remain firmly shut ahead of them. Her stomach rolls as she pays closer attention to the bodies of the prisoners.

There are odd markings on their skin, though it doesn't take long for their origin to become clear as the distinct crack of a whip echoes through the air. Kaira winces, bile rising in her throat.

She spins around quickly, just in time to see Forren emerging from the stone building, waving a hand towards Tuomas and her. Kaira approaches him, welcoming any excuse to get away from the sight before her.

As she enters the warmer passage of the rooms carved into the thick wall, Forren points to a sign-in register hanging on the wall. "Now I'm officially signed in," Forren says, "I'll be conducting your interrogation and frisk search, if you consent."

"Please," Kaira says under her breath so he can hear her but the other High Guard—Gunner—cannot. Louder, she says, "That'll work for me."

Forren nods sharply before spinning on his heel and leading her through the hallways. Tuomas stays in the main area as they section off, but Gunner follows. Forren allows it until they reach a room that reads 'Interview Room'.

"If you don't mind, High Guard Gunner, I'd like to conduct this business so we can get on our way," Forren says, opening the door for Kaira before he spins his glare onto the other High Guard.

"If you don't mind, High Guard Arias, I'd like to witness this interview to make sure standards are upheld. If you have an issue with it, I can get in contact with our fellow High Guards to see their opinion on the matter."

Forren swallows harshly. "Kaira?"

Kaira spins back around from where she's just reaching one of the chairs at the table before shrugging casually. "No use holding up procedures when we have other matters to attend to."

Forren nods before entering the room, purposefully leaving the door swinging shut behind him instead of holding it for the other guard. He takes the seat opposite Kaira, but waits until Gunner has joined them.

"Could you state your name and business passing through Akuma Prison?" Forren asks.

"My name is Kaira Aziz and I'm passing through Akuma Prison as that's where my babysitters—sorry, entourage—have driven me to."

A smile pulls up the corners of Forren's face, but Gunner huffs impatiently. "You should be serious about this, Miss Aziz. It's a legal proceeding, after all."

Forren's quick to turn his glare on him. "I'm the one running this interview, thanks."

The High Guard offers up placating hands before leaning back in his seat, letting Forren take the lead.

"Miss Aziz, can you elaborate on why the guards in charge of your safe passage have you passing through the Prison?"

"I'm not sure. This certainly isn't my usual scene. I can only assume that it's because the Capital city or at least where I'm to be presented to the King is located," Kaira answers.

She can only hope that she's doing a good job at answering the questions how Forren wants her to. She gets the feeling that he's purposefully focusing on their destination to avoid asking her about where they're coming from and having to bring up her being a prisoner and not just a Keranian as she assumes the other guard thinks she is.

"You mention a meeting with the King? Can you elaborate on the reason for this, if it's not breaching the conditions under which you're meant to meet the ruler of this country," Forren carefully asks, his green eyes beneath his mask attempting to send cues to Kaira, though she has no idea what they mean.

"I'm under the belief I cannot reveal much to anyone who's not directly involved in the matter."

Forren gives the slightest nod of his head. "How about that, High Guard Gunner? Do you think that's enough, given there's probably little more she can reveal?" he asks, turning to face the other guard.

Gunner shrugs, though his face looks anything but careless. His brows pinch together. "Whatever. At least you're signed on as the one to interview her, so if it comes back that she shouldn't have passed... Let's just say it won't be me on the receiving end of the King's anger."

"Good," Forren says, standing up and clapping his hands down on the table. "Then we're done here."

He spins for the door and Kaira follows swiftly, fear nudging her along so that she isn't left alone in the room with the other high-decorated guard.

"I hope you don't think you're leaving without frisking the girl," Gunner speaks up, staying put in his seat.

"Of course not. Interviewees have the right to a private room for the frisking. I'm imagining that's what Miss Aziz wants," Forren says, turning to Kaira to prompt her to agree.

"Yes," Kaira says, feeling only the slightest trip over her words.

"Ah, I get it, now. She's your little pet, isn't she? Following you around like you have her so tightly wrapped around your little finger." Gunner hums, smug about the conclusion he comes to.

"Jealous, are you?" Forren says casually, though Kaira can see the tightening in his jaw.

Kaira scoffs at Gunner's suggestion. "Did you not get anything from that interview, *High Guard* Gunner? You know, I mightn't be used to this, but even I know the King doesn't invite many people to meetings. Do you really want to see why I was?" Kaira tilts her head, smiling in an intimidating way.

Gunner scoffs, though it lacks all power. Slowly, he turns his attention to Forren, swallowing before he says, "You might want to get to that frisking if you plan on making it out before nightfall. Your little princess might act all tough here, but in the face of the prison at night? There are reasons other citizens don't become guards: they can't stomach it."

Forren leaves a little pause for Kaira to defend herself, but, instead, she steps around him, exiting the room. She's done with wasting her time.

In her wake, she hears Forren say, "If you'd gone through what she has, you'd be the one cowering. There's only so many people who can survive where she's been for as long as she has."

Kaira waits outside the door as Forren closes it, leaving the other guard presumably seething inside. Forren doesn't say anything to Kaira and nor does she to him. He gestures her into another room.

This one doesn't have the table and chairs like the last room, instead barely furnished with a knee-height bench that leads to a square-shaped hole in the wall. There are two tubs sitting on the bench and Forren gestures at them.

"I need you to take off your outer layers and place them in one box. Then, in the other, put any objects you have that are designed to cause harm or might if I accidentally poke it, like hair pins," Forren says.

"And if I accidentally forget about one?" Kaira says.

"I'm not the one you want to hurt right now, little birdie," Forren replies instead of answering with the protocols of how she might be punished.

Kaira huffs out a breath, beginning to take off her outer layers and place them into the boxes. She shivers in the cold, but continues, wanting to get this over with.

"My jewellery?" she asks.

"Here," Forren says, holding out his hands to take them.

Kaira only hesitates slightly before handing them over. She pretends like she's busy trying to take the pins out of her hair as she watches Forren take the jewellery over to the box. He slips most of it into the box, but Kaira watches him skilfully slide a chain into his sleeve.

"What are you doing—" Kaira demands.

"I must inform you that the room is videoed. If you don't act accordingly, it'll be recorded," Forren cuts in, stopping Kaira from asking her question. He gestures to the clips in her hair. "Do you need help?"

Kaira nods. "Yes."

Forren steps closer and brings his hands to her hair, working to take out the pins. As he does so, he leans in, his lips close to her ears. "There are guards on the other side of that wall that'll check through the boxes for prohibited goods. Sometimes, things go missing."

Kaira swallows. "Thank you," she murmurs, knowing what he's implying. He'd slipped her bird necklace up his sleeve to make sure it didn't get taken.

Forren steps back quickly with the pins in his hands, placing them into their respective boxes before he pushes the tubs through the hole. He turns back to Kaira and gestures over her body. "I'll begin the frisking now," he says, before elaborating on the order he'll conduct the search in.

Kaira nods along obediently, knowing they can't avoid the search.

They both stay silent as Forren steps towards her and begins running his hands over her clothes, patting her down. It isn't as awkward as Kaira thought it'd be. His hands are careful, looking to the cameras like they're thoroughly doing their job, whilst Kaira knows he's holding back.

He stands up from where he kneels at her feet. "You're all good." In perfect timing, the tubs are sent back through the wall and Forren gestures at them. "I'll be outside. You can re-don your clothing and accessories and come out."

He leaves the room and Kaira quickly pulls on her coat and jewellery. She exits the room as she's still placing the pins in her hair. Forren watches the movement as Tuomas speaks to him from his side.

"You're right," Kaira says, gesturing to one of her wrists that now only has one bracelet rather than the three it had before.

Forren shakes his hand out subtly and the chain falls down his sleeve. He gestures for Kaira to spin around and lift her hair, which she does. Gently, he hooks the chain around her neck. "There you go."

"Thanks," Kaira says.

Forren adjusts the mask on his face before gesturing to the door at the end of the hallway. Sunlight peeks through it as it's held open by a red-decorated guard. "Ready to go?"

Kaira nods and follows him as he leads the way out. Outside, the wind whips wildly around them, tugging at their clothing. Kaira lets out a gasp as white flurries dash past her face.

"Not quite snow, but close," Tuomas says from behind her. "Once we get through the prison and climb the first mountain pass, it'll likely have turned into it."

Kaira nods appreciatively. She's used to cold nights in the deserts of her country, but it never got to the point of snow.

Taking her attention away from it in the hopes it'd stop her from feeling the cold of it landing on the exposed skin of her face, she looks over at the line of vehicles behind them.

The soldiers with them have been held up whilst Kaira underwent her interrogation. Now, they crowd around with steaming cups in their hands, slowly sipping at the liquid as quiet chatter arises.

It could almost have been an inviting scene if it wasn't for the shouts and whip cracks arising from Kaira's other side. She avoids looking through the gate as Tuomas leads her around the truck and into the passenger side. Forren signals to his men that it's time to go and they're quick to load into their vehicles.

The convoy rumbles to life and the gates ahead of them peel apart with loud groans.

Forren looks over at her before he starts rolling the truck forwards. "I'm going to say it once more, little birdie. I really would suggest you close your eyes."

Kaira shakes her head. "No. I need to see." See what, exactly, she isn't sure. Hasn't she got enough evidence of the harsh conditions the Keranian army imposes? Is it to convince herself that the life she knew at the camp wasn't so bad? Or is it to plan how she can continue working with Forren to improve the conditions here, too?

Forren either sees the determination on her face or hears it in her voice, as he nods and says simply, "I'm sorry."

To Kaira, the apology sounds like it's for a lot more than what she's about to see.

CHAPTER SIXTEEN

——— ⋯⋯ + ✳ ✴ ✳ + ⋯⋯ ———

The truck is awfully silent as it trundles slowly through the Prison. The sights that met them at the gate don't get any better the further in they creep.

Kaira's hands dig into the seat, keeping her firmly planted to stop herself from barrelling over Tuomas' lap and out the door to step in front of the harsh guards as their whips come down.

After they pass through the main area of the mines, it becomes clear that the few tents that had dotted the space that Kaira assumed were the sleeping quarters of the prisoners were not so. Set back into the mountains are wide cut-outs with bars running along the open fronts. Squeezed in tightly, hundreds of prisoners cower together to keep warm.

It's hard for Kaira to look at the prisoners, though not only because of the conditions they're kept in. It's hard to witness the clear distinction between the prisoners themselves. Some fall and don't bother with clawing their way back up or even protecting themselves from injury. They've given up hope, resigning themselves to this life, this prison. In contrast are the prisoners that fight. The ones that are whipped and punished as they use whatever is at hand—rocks and sticks—to throw at the guards, shouting obscenities. They refuse to let the guards break their spirit.

Kaira doesn't know how to react to that. She doesn't know how to react to the mirror it holds up to her face. The ones giving her hope are the ones fighting, yet she'd never been like that back at the camp. Maybe she couldn't compare her treatment to being here, but at the camp, she'd given up. She'd thought that she was fighting back by establishing the school and educating the children, but she was never fighting for her people's freedom.

As if following her train of thought, Forren says, "You were fighting, little birdie. Are fighting. Look at you now."

Kaira looks over at him, only now realising the tears in her eyes. "I wasn't, though. Not for a long time. I just accepted the fate I'd been dealt."

"We can't beat ourselves up for what we've done in the past. Sure, we can't forget about it, but we must reflect on how that knowledge of having been able to do something better but failing to do so will help us do better in the future."

"You say that like there's things you regret," Kaira fires back.

Forren swallows. "I don't regret things. Perhaps if I went back in time, I might change my decisions. But I can't. So, I accept that and do the best I can in the position I'm in now."

The truck comes to another stop and Kaira's attention is drawn to a second gate, this one their exit. The gate starts to rumble open, but just as quickly, it slams back into place.

"What the—" Kaira begins, looking to Forren as if he has an explanation.

He doesn't answer her trailed off question, so she follows his line of sight to the rear-view mirror. His hand goes to the sword sheathed at his side and he quickly spins around to face her.

"Stay in the vehicle," he orders before opening his door to jump out.

"No chance of that, buddy," Kaira murmurs as she follows him, her feet landing awkwardly on the damp ground. She hears Tuomas climbing down from their side of the vehicle but is distracted by the sight in front of her.

Facing them is a large group of prisoners, managing to run towards them despite the chains keeping them together. Each holds a weapon, whether it be a stone or scrap objects that have been carved to resemble knives.

Forren huffs in annoyance, noting Kaira's appearance. "Don't blame me for anything you witness. They're prisoners, Kaira. I can't afford to be nice, especially not when they're going to kill you."

"They won't!" Kaira exclaims, though the words are hardly out of her mouth before Forren tugs her out of the way, pressing her body against the front of the truck as the first rocks are launched at them.

They land with loud patters against the metal of the truck. Above the noise it creates, the yells of the prisoners moving in on them emerges as other guards exit their vehicles and shout orders for them to back down.

Forren looks past Kaira's shoulder and says, "Stay with her. Get her into the truck if you can."

Kaira follows his gaze to see that Tuomas has joined them. They nod, accepting the order.

Kaira quickly turns back to Forren as he pulls his body away from hers. "You can't just lash out at them for reacting to how they're treated here."

Forren steels his jaw, staring down at Kaira. "You're incredibly naive if you think you can simply drive through the prison and make those assumptions." Kaira rears back from the harsh comment, but Forren continues, saying, "You can follow Tuomas and get back in the vehicle or leave me to have to throw you in there, making the guards on duty step in to control this instead of me."

Kaira understands what he's saying in that. The guards would treat the prisoners much worse. She nods and Forren sees the honesty in her eyes as he returns the gesture before slipping around the corner of the vehicle.

Tuomas doesn't say anything. They simply gesture with their head to their side of the vehicle. Kaira follows them, climbing back into the truck.

She kneels up on the bench seat to peer out the back window, watching the action unfolding. She doesn't know how to explain the slight rolling that occurs in her gut watching it, as no matter how much she tries to convince herself it's because she's seeing prisoners treated how they are, she can't shake the knowledge that it's actually fear for Forren.

He works by himself, taking on the most determined prisoners. Kaira has the feeling that he refuses to raise his weapon because he knows she's watching, though she cannot prove it. Kaira doesn't know how he can do it, though. She doesn't know how he can resist the temptation of quickly sorting the onslaught with physical force, especially as weapons are raised against him.

Kaira watches, her skin pale and goosebumps rising on her flesh, as rocks are pelted at the gold-decorated guard and he's hit by them. As much as Kaira wants to defend the prisoners for this attack, for taking their chance of retribution, she doesn't know if she can.

As more Kerani soldiers pour from holes in the fortress wall, with even more joining from within the prison itself, Tuomas places a comforting hand on her shoulder, urging her to sit on the seat properly.

Kaira does, even if it takes a little convincing. Tuomas looks into the side mirror, as if they too want to join in, but they quickly turn back to Kaira. They pull a sheet of paper from the ground and place it on the dash.

"Up for a game?" they say as Kaira identifies the piece as the sheet she'd written 'interrogation room' on.

Kaira looks up at them. "Only if we can both play interrogator."

It feels like much longer than it should've been before Forren returns. Almost immediately after he's in the vehicle, the gates roll open.

Kaira glances in the mirror to see the remains of the attack, but there's no evidence left. Even the thrown rocks have been cleared. She turns back to Forren as the truck begins moving, followed by their entourage.

"You're bleeding," Kaira says, pointing to Forren's forehead where blood trickles down his brow.

"It's nothing," Forren responds, shrugging.

Kaira swallows before asking, "Are attacks like that normal?"

Forren again shrugs. "It's not uncommon. They probably recognised me—well, at least the gold I wear—and thought it was a good opportunity."

Kaira hums in consideration.

In the silence that follows, Forren's gaze goes to the piece of paper that still sits on the dash before he lets out a soft chuckle. "I wondered how you kept her in the vehicle," he says to Tuomas. Just when it's looking like he's moving into a better mood, it's quick to be erased as he clears his throat. "Since it's starting to get dark, we won't drive much further before pulling over." He adds for Kaira's sake, "It isn't safe to be out at night in these areas."

"Oh. What's out there?"

"People," Forren responds before adding, "and animals, I suppose. But mostly the people."

A shiver runs down Kaira's spine and she curls her fingers into the front of the seat. For the rest of the drive as they get far enough away from the prison that the sounds dull to nothing, Kaira stays silent.

"You can stay in the truck whilst I set up the tent if you like," Forren says as they finally pull into a spot just off the road and he opens his door to get out. The forest beyond creaks eerily in warning.

Kaira shakes her head as Tuomas hops down from their side of the vehicle. She doesn't want to be left alone.

She follows Forren as he exits the vehicle, but stops him before he can continue to the back of the truck where the tent is stored.

She digs into the pockets of the borrowed clothes she wears and presents forth a handkerchief. Awkwardly, she gestures with it to Forren's forehead. "You should, uh, clean yourself up?"

Forren accepts the offering and presses it to his cut. "Thanks."

He keeps the piece of fabric pressed to the blood as he pulls down the tent. Kaira steps in to help him.

"You tell me what to do and I'll be your arms, okay?" Kaira offers once she opens the tent bag and is again baffled at the array of tent poles and fabric before her.

Forren hesitates to agree but does so, giving her the first instruction. Kaira wonders how much he had to challenge himself to let up the power, even in something so simple as setting up sleeping quarters. How used to being the one in charge, unchallenged, is he from his gold status? How long has he held the gold ranking?

It doesn't take as long as Kaira expects for the tent to be set up. Her question from the other time they'd shared the tent about where the furniture comes from is answered as soldiers come over from different vehicles and silently set up the interior. Kaira has a feeling that they'd even set up the outside too, but that Forren stops them from doing so.

Kaira enters the tent first, hanging her jacket on one of the hooks on the centre pole. The breeze that comes through the door as Forren enters brushes cool hands down her arms, so she settles onto her bed, practically melting into the soft blankets.

She watches as Forren heads to his dresser, studying in the mirror sitting above it the cut on his forehead. There's a basin of water there, which he gestures to, looking up in the mirror to meet Kaira's gaze.

"You can wash first, if you'd like to," he offers.

Kaira startles, not having expected the kindness. She doesn't know why her prejudices still run so deep, why even after weeks of being acquainted with Forren and shown his true colours—not just the gold on his uniform—she still expects him to be the harsh soldier she was made to believe all Keranians were.

"Thank you, but I'm good," Kaira responds. She clearly isn't the one needing to wash up.

Forren nods before turning back to the basin, setting the dirtied handkerchief to the side. He lifts a piece of fabric that he wets to his face, washing off the rest of the dried blood before he sighs loudly, dropping the cloth back into the water and staining it a light red.

"I'm, uh, going to go over to Tuomas' tent," Forren says, leaning over his bed to rummage through a bag. He emerges with two piles of clothes, one of which he offers to Kaira. "I'll get changed there and you can get changed into this, if you like, whilst I'm gone. It should be more comfortable to sleep in."

"Thank you," Kaira says, taking the clothes.

Forren nods before exiting. Kaira stalls once he's gone, looking about the tent as if she doesn't trust she's really alone before she finally braves changing her outfit.

She's finished and returned to her bed, her old outfit hanging with her coat, when Forren re-enters. He looks over at her and a small smile appears at the corner of his mouth.

"I don't know why I didn't expect you to take the offering of clothes," he says. "I was surprised when you took my sister's outfit, too."

Kaira has surprised herself with both things. She shrugs, answering, "Like you said, the power and confidence are important. I need to show the King I'm...someone worth not executing."

"I wish it didn't have to be like this, little birdie. With me taking you to your possible demise. With you being a captive whilst I'm the captor."

Kaira looks over at Forren. "We can't help the hand we're dealt. What matters is what we do with it," she says, repeating a similar sentiment to what he'd said in the past.

Forren sighs heavily, turning back to the mirror as he pulls off his mask. After, he turns back to Kaira, his face clear and his emotions thick in his features: his downturned lips, his furrowed brows and sad eyes. "I fear more than anything now that you aren't going to like what I do with the hand I'm dealt."

Kaira stands up, moving to him and studying closely his naked facial features. He seems much younger without the mask, like he's been completely stripped back.

"I don't believe that," Kaira says. "I've seen you, Forren. I see you. You wouldn't have done all this if you had bad intentions."

Forren closes his eyes before stepping away, returning to his bed. Kaira stays standing, watching him move away with a sinking feeling.

"Only time will tell," Forren says as he slips into his sheets. "Just promise you'll hear me out after it all?"

Kaira's mind protests, yet she finds herself nodding. "Everyone deserves the chance to be heard. Besides, I kind of owe you after you listened to my side of the story instead of throwing me off the cliff the first time we met."

Forren lets out a sad little laugh before sighing again loudly. "We shall see how much you value your word, little birdie."

CHAPTER SEVENTEEN

The next few days pass by uneventfully. The convoy slowly passes through the forests, climbing the mountains to meet the snow that's falling. Rarely, large wolves and other beasts will cross in front of them. They traverse the path unhurriedly, looking up to meet the eyes of those in the truck in a show of dominance.

Summiting the tallest mountain, they stop at the peak, following a barely visible path away from the main road. It's only their vehicle that's there so far; the others have fallen behind, their vehicles, unlike the upgraded truck, not well suited to the snow.

"Want to take a look?" Forren offers, gesturing to the view that's peeking through the last line of trees.

Kaira doesn't have to be asked twice. She gestures with her hands for him to hop down and follows him, her feet landing awkwardly in the snow. After regaining her balance, she carefully negotiates her way past the trees, looking out at the view laid before them.

If she thought the city they'd come through was something from a different world, this is too. They stand at the furthest point of a semicircle, where water floods the bay cut out from the mountains.

To their left, climbing up the mountain with greedy hands, is a sandstone city full of arches and greenery. To their right, a towering castle climbs the mountain too, its tall turrets sticking out from where the mountain tapers into a peak. It's oddly shaped, with areas unsymmetrically pointing out over the ocean that creeps into the cutout.

"What do you think of your first look at the true capital city of Kerani and the Palace of Golden Kings?" Forren asks, leaning on a tree behind her.

Kaira hums. "It's not what I expected."

"What did you expect?" Forren asks, his golden mask shimmering in the sunlight.

"Destruction," Kaira states. "Something...hideous. It's beautiful, though. It's not something I'd expect from Keranians."

Forren takes a step closer, taking her hand in his. "What would you think if I told you I'd wished the same before I'd seen it for the first time?"

Kaira looks over at him, watching as the wind gently pulls at the waves in his dark hair. "I don't know," she answers. "If you thought that, you mustn't have approved of your ruler, right? Then why did you still want to become a golden guard?"

"It's the reason why. I saw the palace and thought that maybe there were parts of this country worth fighting for."

Kaira doesn't know how to respond, so she doesn't. She turns back to the mountain face, dropping Forren's hands to lift her arms up to the sky. She tilts her head back and soaks up the sunshine dancing upon her skin. Perhaps this is what freedom feels like.

Forren lets her experience the moment until the sounds of other vehicles passing by back on the main track meets them. He clears his throat before gesturing to the tree line, where the truck hides. "We should get going. I'd rather have us settled in the city before nightfall so we can be ready for the meeting with the King tomorrow."

"Is it that soon?" Kaira questions, feeling the happiness being torn from her. When she looks back out over the view, she can see the colourful tones lighting the sky, marking sunset.

Forren gently nods, like he doesn't want to verbally admit the truth. Kaira sighs heavily before following him back to the vehicle. There's no putting this off; it'd only more clearly spell out her demise if she didn't show up.

The capital city—Fairah, Forren called it—is even more beautiful under lantern light. It brings out the golden hues in the sandstone as they park the truck and exit.

Forren gestures towards a staircase wrapping around part of the mountain, where on one side are the roofs of houses from the level below whilst the other side is the ground floor of the buildings on their level. They're about halfway up and what's left of the sunshine highlights the long way down to the bay.

Even with the later hour, there are still people bustling about and, for once, Kaira doesn't receive any unwelcoming glances. It oddly feels like she fits in.

She follows Forren up the staircase, Tuomas at her side. She can't stop looking around: at the people, the view, the buildings that are more majestic than anything else she's ever seen but her own country's palace. Her fingers run over the rough sandstone and linger on the soft greenery climbing it. The smells are perfection as well: the salt of the sea below, the freshness of the air, the subtle flowery incenses burning in homes.

Her attention is drawn back to the moment as Forren diverges from the path and into an alcove that's the entrance to a building. Above the door hangs a sign saying, "Cozy Haven Accommodation".

Forren opens the door and gestures to Tuomas and herself to enter. Kaira does a full turn once inside, taking in the elaborate decorations from the rugs lining the floor to the chandeliers. There are lounges spread throughout the large room. The lack of windows throughout the back half of the room informs Kaira that the building stretches into the mountain.

A man carrying a child on his hip bustles out of a room that's set off to the side, meeting them at a desk in the centre.

"How may I help you?" he asks, flicking through paperwork on the desk.

"We're looking for three rooms for the night, please," Forren says.

"Of course. Are you looking for any particular size?"

"No, just whatever you can place closest to each other."

The man slides across three keys, iterating a price to Forren which he's quick to pay with coins he pulls from a purse.

After taking the keys and learning the directions to the rooms, refusing the man's offer to lead them there, Forren guides them up a narrow staircase. They exit the spiral staircase at the next level and stride down the hallway to the very end, where there's a large balcony they walk across. Also leading out onto the sandstone carved balcony are four arched doorways.

Forren hands a key to each of them, gesturing to their respective rooms. Kaira's is one of the edge rooms, Forren's right next to her. Tuomas enters their room, leaving Forren and Kaira alone in the night air.

"If you have any problems with your room or anything else, just come get me, okay?" Forren says, inserting his key into the lock on his door.

"Okay," Kaira says, moving to her own door.

Forren pauses as he goes to enter his room, looking back at her like he wants to say something more before he simply says, "Goodnight, little birdie."

"Goodnight," Kaira responds, feeling like she too wants to say more.

Forren shuts his door and Kaira enters her own room, locking the door behind her. She looks around the room, her vision slightly inhibited by the darkness before she finds a lantern. It isn't a normal one, though, with a button that tells Kaira it's electrical. She switches it on, her lungs constricting at doing so. It's been so long since she's had such luxuries that she can control.

She studies the space closer once the light enlightens the space. There really isn't much to it: a bed, a small washroom and a desk shoved into one corner. It's about the size of the tent she shared with the other women and her mother at the camp.

Kaira's chest constricts once more, remembering her mother. How long has it been since she last saw her? At least a week, maybe closer to two. A darkness swallows Kaira's mind; how can she not have been keeping track of how many days it's been since she left behind everyone important to her?

Kaira curls up on the bed, feeling the weight of her actions settling onto her as tears begin rolling down her face. How can she have so easily changed sides and not given a second thought for all that she's left behind?

A sob escapes her lips at the same time a knock comes at her door. Kaira pauses, feeling her throat tightening with the withheld sobs, but again the knock comes. Hesitantly, she makes her way to the arched window that looks out onto the balcony. She doesn't need to see any more than the golden mask to know it's Forren and open her door.

"Hey," he greets, holding out his arms with things laden in them. "I forgot to give you these. It's your outfit for tomorrow, some more sleeping clothes and dinner."

"Oh, thank you," Kaira says, taking the items as she cringes at the obvious croak in her throat.

Forren's about to step away, but he stalls. "Are you okay?" he asks.

Kaira nods. "Yeah. I was just thinking about...everything. But I'm fine."

Forren keeps looking at her before he nods. "Okay. Again, just let me know if there's anything I can help with, even if it's just being a shoulder to cry on."

"Why?" Kaira asks before she can think about it. "Why would you offer that to *me*?"

"Because I see myself in you," Forren answers. Seeing Kaira's confused expression, he elaborates, "I didn't offer to work with you because you spoke two languages. Well, not entirely. I did it because I saw the version of myself I wished I could be in you. I saw someone strong, someone willing to fight for what they cared about, someone selfless."

Kaira takes a while respond. "I think you're more like that person that you let yourself consider; you hide that person behind your mask and status."

Their eyes meet, a million unsaid things running between them before Forren finally breaks the contact. "See you in the morning," he says, turning back to his room.

Kaira shuts the door with her foot, depositing the items in her arms onto her bed.

Why are they like this? Why is she finding understanding and a place of belonging beside Forren when he's her enemy? Because that's what this comfort and familiarity is: belonging.

CHAPTER EIGHTEEN

The next morning, they walk down the sandstone stairways and along a flatter path that Forren says is the main street. Kaira can't help looking around in awe at the stone that shines under the morning sunlight coming up over the ocean.

She's fascinated, her eyes wide and mouth agape, as Forren leads her and Tuomas into a small cafe. It's decorated with green plants and purple flowers, whilst the walls are carved sandstone blocks that throw little patterns of sunlight in the shapes of stars onto the ground.

Kaira feels like she fits in with the outfit she wears—the first one Forren had dressed her in. She kind of likes the feel of the jewellery she wears in her hair too.

They sit at a light wood table. Immediately, they're delivered plates of pastries covered in powders of varying colours.

Kaira doesn't need an invitation to dive into the food, delighting in the delicacies. Forren and Tuomas join her and oddly the silence makes this moment feel like one of the most...pleasant they've had together. It makes it feel like they're friends catching up over breakfast.

Even with how pleasant it is, however, there's still an underlying tension. It's felt in Forren's cold stare, in Kaira's shaking foot and in Tuomas' hand constantly running through their hair.

No-one seems willing to bring up the impending meeting with the Kerani ruler, but Kaira's desperate to find out more about what to expect.

Finally working up the courage, she takes a deep breath before asking, "What time is the meeting?"

"Just after midday," Forren answers stiffly.

Kaira presses her lips together before saying in just as tight of a tone, "Look, I don't want to play the interrogation game. Just give it to me straight: what's going to happen?"

Forren's jaw hardens. "The meeting is mid-afternoon, but Tuomas and I must check-in at the guard quarters, so we'll head over there before midday. We'll take the ferry. There'll be heavy security clearance for us, but it shouldn't be so bad for you. Once it's time for the meeting, you'll be taken to the throne room, a reception room usually for receiving international guests or an interrogation room, depending on what assumptions the King's already made."

"Wait," Kaira says as he goes to take a breath, "you won't be accompanying me?"

Forren looks up at her and his eyes are swirling pits of emotions that Kaira can see her own feelings reflected in. "Likely not. There's no reason for me to be involved."

"But you found me in the camp and have brought me here. Doesn't that mean anything?"

"No. It doesn't," Forren responds. "As soon as I deliver you to the King, our partnership is over. It was the moment I took you from the camp, really."

Tears prick the backs of Kaira's eyes. She should've come to the same conclusion, but...she'd expected that they'd continue working together. That for some reason the King would find use in her continuing to work with the army.

She pushes back from the table, feeling the overwhelming urge to get away from the reality presented so bluntly before her.

Kaira leaves the cafe, not knowing where she's going as she wanders the sandstone streets. She passes a few people, but all they do is nod at her and carry on.

It doesn't take her long to pass the archway houses and shops and meet the bottom of the mountain. The sandstone slowly fades into plain sand and beyond it is the bay. The water shimmers gently in the sunlight, like the sun has personally come down to grace its skin.

Kaira walks until the water laps at her toes and she bends down to run her fingers through the surface. After all the years of looking at the water from the cliff, it feels disappointing to be touching the ocean now. She'd thought when she finally got the chance to do so, it'd be because their time of freedom had come.

A little part of her resents Forren for what he's done. Sure, he might've wanted the best for her when he took this opportunity to allow her access to greater things, but he'd taken away everything of importance to her in claiming she's one of his people.

"Kaira."

Kaira startles at her name being called. She spins around so fast her feet don't move, instead becoming stuck in the shifting sand so she loses her balance. Arms come around her waist, steadying her against a solid body.

"Sorry," Kaira says, stepping back from Forren as she looks over his shoulder expecting to see Tuomas. They aren't there, however, so she turns back to Forren. "You scared me."

"I apologise," Forren responds, letting her go once he's sure she's found her footing. He swallows and looks past her, watching the waves gently coming in. "I...came to find you."

"I didn't mean to run away," Kaira responds.

"No, that wasn't the problem. I understood that part. I actually..." Forren pauses, playing with the pendant resting against his brow. "It sounds stupid now, but I had somewhere I wanted to show you. Before we went to see the King and..."

"This was all over?" Kaira supplements.

Forren nods, playing with the jewel on his brow.

"Do we still have time?" Kaira asks.

"Are you sure?" he asks. Kaira nods and a grin lights up his face in response. "We should go, then. It's not too far away."

He grabs Kaira's hand and leads her from the water. Kaira expects them to walk back up the mountain, but instead they travel around the side of it, bypassing where the houses end and the mountain turns into unrestrained forests. The trees are large, their stumps wider than any others Kaira's seen before.

They pass from sand onto rocks the height of them that they traverse over.

"Wow," Kaira responds, dropping down onto the soft sand on the other side of the rocks. They're in a secluded cove and when Kaira looks out over the ocean, she can see where it meets the horizon.

Forren settles down onto the sand, just out of reach of the lapping water. Without hesitation, Kaira takes a seat next to him, running her hands through the tiny granules.

Forren lets out a gentle sigh and lifts his hands to his mask. Kaira swallows deeply, her heart racing as he pulls it from his face. Somehow, there's something so different with him doing it this time than any other time. It's the first time Kaira's seen his face revealed in the light of day and there's no denying that he's pretty.

His eyes hold layers upon layers of emotions behind them as he turns with slightly blushed cheeks to meet her gaze. Kaira knows what this is: him laying himself out in front of her, unhidden.

"Why are you doing this?" she asks, hoping he doesn't take it meanly. She doesn't want the question to scare him and make him put the mask back on.

"I want to give you something honest to remember me by. This place, my face, everything. They're all the truest parts of me—the only parts left untouched by my position."

"Why?"

"Because it's going to be over soon." Forren tears his gaze from her.

"Because of this meeting with the King?"

"In part, but not for the most. I..." Forren trips over his words and takes a minute to swallow. "It'll all make sense sooner than I wish."

More questions burn in Kaira's throat, but she knows that's all he'll give.

"Kaira, can I ask something big of you?" Forren probes, looking over at her with an un-fakable sincerity. "Will you call me by my name, my real one, just once?"

"There'll be plenty of time for that in the future, Forren," Kaira says. Even though she denies it, she tests the shape of it on her tongue, silently trying out saying *Mikko*. She doesn't know why she hasn't used it; it really doesn't make sense to have kept calling him Forren when she's the one in his land.

"What if this is the last chance we get?" Forren asks.

Kaira looks over at him before pushing to a stand. "I promise you, Forren. There'll be a time in the future that I call you by your proper name, High Guard *Arias.*"

Forren snorts as he stands, though his eyes glisten before he pulls on his mask. She can't identify what it is clouding his eyes, but it's almost enough to make her cave and say it. Instead, she turns and heads back the way they came, his name silently repeating on her tongue.

No matter what Forren implies about the meeting with the King not being the only thing that'll tear them apart, she's going to make sure that they're stuck together. There's going to be another time when she can say his name; she'll make sure of it.

She'll not let his country take the very last thing she has: his friendship.

CHAPTER NINETEEN

Kaira fiddles with the jewellery hanging on her brow, her fingers playing with the coloured gems.

"Ugh," she sighs exaggeratedly. "Where is he?"

Tuomas looks over at her, their face a mix between annoyance and humour. "Hopefully, he's left early and is at the training yards; we can't afford to wait any longer."

Forren had left Kaira soon after they returned from the cove and Kaira hasn't seen him since. Tuomas met her down at the docks at midday like they'd planned, but the golden guard hadn't turned up.

Sighing, Tuomas gestures to the boat pulling up at the wooden platform they stand on. It comfortably fits them and the other clusters of people—mostly guards—that pile on with them.

There's an inside area, but Kaira chooses to walk out to the front where bench seats face the water. She takes a seat, pleased to see that it's only her and Tuomas that have come out here. It isn't long before her pleasure grows as, when they pull off the dock, a long-furred brown dog wanders over and settles at her feet.

Kaira pats it affectionately as it smiles up at her, its tongue hanging out of its mouth. It helps settle the anxiety churning in her stomach, which is only contributed to by Mikk–*Forren*'s lack of presence.

"Mikko won't let anything bad happen to you, you know," Tuomas says, a smile lighting their face as they watch her petting the dog.

"Even if he's randomly allowed in the meeting—if he's even at the Palace—there's limits to his position. I know he won't have the power to disobey what the King declares," Kaira says. "The whole reason I know how to speak your language is because my dad was a scholar; he taught me things about your country other than the language." Kaira feels compelled to add, "I suppose nothing he could've taught me would've prepared me for" —she gestures her hands around the air— "all this."

Tuomas runs her words over in their head before they say quietly, like admitting a secret, "There's a way you could make sure Mikko is at the meeting."

"Let me guess: cause a scene and force the King to keep a collection of guards on me or something?"

Tuomas chuckles lightly, shaking their head. "Sometimes tradition is more powerful than brute force." They swallow before tilting their head to hers, their eyes locking on the jewellery she wears. "Use that to your advantage. He told you it shows you're...connected and displays he's assuming responsibility of you. In return, it also means you're assuming responsibility of him."

"I'm not following," Kaira says, her brow furrowing.

"When a Keranian shares a matching piece of jewellery, like the ferronnières, it means they're...partners, in whatever definition that looks like to them. Like how mine also matches his." Kaira's eyes go to Tuomas' jewellery and, for the first time, she notices that it's similar, the gems the same colour. "According to our law, partners are extensions of one another. Following with this, if you announce that you want him to be present, it can't be refused because he's a part of you."

Kaira thinks that over before she finally asks, "What does that mean if my execution is ordered, though? Can't he be killed too?"

Tuomas grimaces. "All that interrogation training is making you too quick for your own good. You're right in that, yes, normally that's the case, but Mikko has an extra layer of protection given the Golden Games are coming up. Nobody, especially the current King, can harm him. If the King orders your execution, thus Mikko's with it, he'd be annulled."

"Why are the Golden Games so important?" Kaira asks to distract herself from the slight blossom of hope rising in her chest.

"Because the winner becomes the next Kerani King and, now, the new ruler of Altair," Tuomas says.

Kaira's breath escapes her. This whole time Forren has said that working with her would help prove his worthiness for the Golden Games but that means he's been using her for the chance to not only be the next enforcer of the current state of her people, but also the first ruler of her country since the conquest. He's vying for the position that essentially erases everything that's left of her country by handing over its control officially.

Kaira presses her eyes shut tightly. She should've listened to the Elders—they're Elders for a reason, after all. They were right when they claimed she was going against them.

The boat docks at the shore on the other side of the bay and Kaira can hardly get her feet moving as she's frozen looking up at the Palace. It looks like the town with its sandstone archways and climbing vinery, yet it's impossibly more elaborate with the chandeliers that glimmer inside the arches and the painted mosaic floors and ceilings.

Tuomas guides her from the gently swaying boat, leaving the dog behind, and it's only once they're on solid ground that Kaira comes to her senses. Behind tall metal gates sits a huge courtyard swarmed with training guards. Even in all the fights she's seen the guards break up at the camp, she's never seen anything like the sheer force and training demonstrated here.

"Oh my," Kaira gasps as the gates slide open and Tuomas ushers her forwards.

Kaira's eyes greedily take in the colours of the uniforms: reds, blues, greens, two or so of gold. There are even levels Kaira has never seen before: purples and a brown. She sticks close to Tuomas' side as they follow a path around the central free-for-all fighting, yet their other side is also surrounded by fighting. The danger feels even more alive in the close quarters the stall-like rooms cut into the surrounding fortress wall force.

"Ah, here he is," Tuomas says, leaning against the wall of a stall as they watch the fighting taking place within.

Kaira pauses next to them and her lungs burn as her breath leaves her body.

Forren is shirtless, fighting with his bare hands against a wide-shouldered female guard with golden buttons lining her chest. The power in them both sends chills down Kaira's spine, where they curl around the base and linger. The punches and dodges are controlled, trained to be deadly. Both guards aren't holding back, even though one wrong move could easily spell a serious injury or death.

"Are they training for the Golden Games?" Kaira finally finds the words to ask, her eyes not lifting from the display of the two golden guards.

"Mikko, yes. His sister, no. She could easily win it, even against Mikko, but she doesn't want kingship," Tuomas responds.

"That's his sister?" Kaira feels her jaw drop as she takes in the female guard again. Sure enough, their looks are similar, at least from what she can see behind the female guard's white and golden thread mask. Her eyes are a similar green to Forren's, her hair the same black.

"His twin, to be exact. Mila is a boss in everything she does."

Kaira turns her head to briefly look at Tuomas, witnessing the admiration that shines on their face.

The fighting comes to a quick end as Forren looks up and meets her gaze. He calls out something that Kaira can't understand and Mila, his twin, pulls up short from landing another blow.

The female guard spins around to them as Forren approaches.

"Hey," Tuomas says in greeting.

"Hey," Forren answers, facing his sister to gesture at Kaira and then in reverse, "Mila, meet Kaira. Kaira, meet Mila, my weaker, younger sister."

The smirk on Forren's face reveals that he's purposefully antagonising Mila and Kaira can't help but smile at the antics.

Mila smiles at her, holding out a hand. "It's nice to see that the person my brother has dressed in my clothes can wear them with the respect they deserve."

Kaira's cheeks heat in the face of the compliment. "It's nice to put a face to the owner of them. I was beginning to think Forren had made you up to disguise his actual passion for cross-dressing."

Forren chokes with laughter. "Sadly, the sister isn't made up; I can't deny, however, that I like dressing up sometimes."

"Good. I like men that are comfortable enough in their masculinity to not be frightened off by the idea of dressing in clothes traditionally seen as feminine."

Kaira smiles at Forren, who returns the gesture, before Mila loudly clears her throat from beside them.

"Mikko told me you're a prisoner he's escorting. I think he's been just as vague with your existence as with mine seeing as you've got a nickname for him," Mila says.

"Oh, the nickname is far from revealing of how close we are. It means foreigner in my language," Kaira says. "It felt fitting considering he's responsible for keeping my people locked up in their own country."

Mila laughs loudly, causing a few guards close to them to look over. Her following glare is quick to scare them off.

Forren clears his throat. "Luckily for me, I don't have to be worried about you both getting along too well as you've got a meeting I have to deliver you to, little birdie."

Kaira looks up at him, properly meeting his gaze for the first time since they'd left each other at the cove. "I'm calling on the partner thing, for the jewellery," she says, gesturing at the gems on her brow.

She'd thought about it long and hard on the boat ride, concluding that even though she's mad at Forren for having used her to secure his position as the next ruler of her country, she'd rather have him by her side. She tells herself it's only because his presence safeguards her from execution, but even she doesn't believe that.

Forren looks at her, his brows pulled together, and Kaira wonders if he's going to refuse. Tuomas and Mila are silent too, shock written across Forren's twin's face in her dropped jaw and wide eyes. Eventually, though, Forren just nods at her and says, "Good."

"Good? That's all you're going to say?" Kaira utters in outrage.

Forren shrugs. "What do you expect me to say? You have the right since I made you wear the jewellery. If I'm using you, why not use me too?"

"That's not why I'm doing it."

"Then why is it?" Forren asks, his green eyes meeting hers in a way that says he's all too familiar with the reason.

Kaira swallows harshly. "It doesn't matter."

As she says it, she feels the truth of the words settle into her, becoming a reality she can't ignore. Even if she does admit that it's because his friendship means a lot, it's not like anything can come from it. Whenever the approaching Golden Games are, he'll have finished using her in his bid for power and their partnership will be over. They'll go back to the way it was when they didn't know each other—when Kaira was a prisoner and he was the guard keeping her locked up. Only, he'd be something even worse.

Tuomas clears their throat, looking pointedly at their watch. "Well, I've got to go sign-in and...do other things," they say, gesturing vaguely around the facility. "I'll catch up with you after the meeting."

"I'll come with you," Mila adds.

Before Forren or Kaira can say anything more, the pair are hurrying away, whispering furiously as they go. With their departure comes a wave of worry washing over Kaira as she realises there's nothing left between her and the meeting.

Forren clears his throat. "We should get going. I can take you to a room to freshen up first if you'd like?"

Kaira shakes her head, running her hands down the sides of the dress she wears. "No, it's okay. Well, I mean, do I look fine? I feel fine, but if I look like I need to, then—"

"No, you're all good," Forren cuts in, giving her a once over.

Without saying anything more, he spins sharply on his heel and leads her across the courtyard towards the entrance of the Palace.

CHAPTER TWENTY

The loud echo of footsteps against the mosaic marble floor is the only thing to break the silence as Kaira's led through the main hall of the Palace of Golden Kings.

Three guards follow them as Forren keeps pace at her side. The guards wear golden decorations and heavy body armour. Two have long spear-like sticks whilst the third has a shield.

Ahead are two towering wooden doors. Every step towards them has the pressure in Kaira's chest increasing tenfold.

The doors glide open soundlessly into the room beyond. Kaira stifles a gasp. The throne room is magnificent as coloured pane glass windows douse the room in yellow.

Sitting on the throne is the King of Kerani, dressed in flowing golden robes that drape delicately from his dark-skinned body. His beauty takes Kaira's breath away before she remembers who he is: her suppressor.

Following Forren's lead, who's comfortingly placed his hand on the small of her back, she bows her head and bends her back once they reach the base of the throne.

"Your Majesty, I present you High Guard Arias delivering Kaira Aziz."

Kaira startles as one of the guards, who'd stopped at the door, announces their arrival.

"Thank you," the King responds before looking at the pair before him. "Everyone but Miss Aziz may leave."

Kaira looks across at Forren and he nods, urging her on.

"Your Majesty," Kaira says, not knowing how to address him. She'd planned to go along with how he led the conversation. "I'm requesting for High Guard Arias to stay in the room by rules of partner rights, given I'm wearing a matching piece to his ferronnière."

The King startles, looking closely at her jewellery before nodding. "Very well."

The other guards leave and the anxiety clogging Kaira's throat settles minorly.

"Miss Aziz," the King says, drawing out her name in a way that has her shifting on the spot. "I see it's not just rumours that you speak our language."

"No, Your Majesty. I speak both Keranian and Altairian."

The King waves his hand about. "Please, call me Kyles. Arias has said that he found you in the camp?"

"Yes, Your Majesty. He located me after finding out I spoke the language."

"Yet he claims you're Keranian? What were you doing in the camp?" Kyles says.

Kaira recalls what little Forren has shared with her about the story he gave the King. "I initially snuck into the camp on my own free will. I'm naturally a curious person and wished to understand why the camps were necessary. After that—"

"Was the word of your ruler that the Altairians were to be controlled not enough?" Kyles' words are ice-cold, his stare just as much so.

Kaira swallows, stammering over her words. "No, that's not what... I wasn't questioning your authority; I just couldn't understand placing people in camps like that and it seemed a little ridiculous to—"

"Ridiculous? You have some nerve if you think you can come in here and call decisions I make ridiculous." The King looks her over disgustedly before glancing at Forren. "As I'm sure you know, I can't do anything that affects High Guard Arias, but there's still options. You were interested in the camp, so why not order you to be kept there? If you feel pity for those feudal, archaic animals, you're no better than them."

Pressure grows in Kaira's mind as her thoughts spiral, wondering how she could've spun this meeting around so much. "Your Majesty, just let me explain. I simply meant that it seemed ridiculous to not eliminate them entirely. I mean, who's to stop you? You've eliminated their rulers, their country; who's going to fight you to protect them?"

She's going to be the one to fight him.

"You're foolish if you think your accent is deceiving anyone," the King shoots back. "I don't know what business you have pretending to be Keranian, but I can only trust it's something worthwhile considering you have the most prospective High Guard at your side."

Kaira doesn't know how to react to that, feeling like the rollercoaster she's on that'd felt like it was heading for rock bottom is suddenly climbing again. She nods once, keeping her gaze downcast.

Kyles tuts, his age showing as wrinkles crease his forehead. "Tell me. How has this country been? Is it what you expected?"

Kaira knows this is a test more than anything else she's been asked so far, yet she can't decipher the answer she's meant to give. Forren's stuck on the same puzzle beside her as his eyes move with his racing thoughts.

"It's not at all what I expected. The people here have surprised me and...I've come to understand why you've formed the views of my people—of Altairians—that you have. We could've never dreamed of the technological advancements that your country is leading, let alone accepted them."

"So, you understand why we've had to conquer your country; is it not a worse crime to have left you in the old world whilst this change is coming about?"

Kaira swallows, clenching her fists at her side. "I don't agree with that," she says sharply. "The technology might be inspiring and impressive but look at what it's doing. I don't think it's right to force people into a new world if their 'old' world's serving them fine, just as they're serving it."

The King is quiet, stunned, Kaira guesses, from her outright rebuttal of his opinion. "Well, Miss Aziz. I must give it to you: you're head strong." He hums, before he adds, "It's lucky for you, because you know what we most like to foster? Strength and perseverance. We don't want people that too easily submit." He lets out a harsh chuckle. "I think you'd fit in well with our kind."

"I fear that too," Kaira says, her voice lacking the power she'd had before. She refuses to acknowledge the words—the offer—that linger beneath what Kyles says.

"Perhaps you wouldn't if it's what gets you out of this room alive," the King says softly. Suddenly, he turns to look upon Forren. "Tell us, boy. What potential did you see in her?"

Forren isn't startled to have been called upon. Easily, he answers, "She's one of the only people alive that's Altairian and can speak both languages; she'd be a great intermediary."

"An intermediary... Did you intend for her position to be openly known?"

Kaira zones out. She would've thought her stress would've kept her focused but that's not the case. Her attention is only drawn back to the situation as one sentence rings out particularly strong around the room, echoing around the vast expanse of the vaulted ceilings.

"Miss Aziz will be placed under state-ownership until the next ruler is announced. If that happens to be you, High Guard Arias, you'll be free to do with her as you wish. If not, well, that piece of jewellery isn't going to do much to protect her—or you, for that matter. As for right now, Miss Aziz will be placed under the supervision of someone not involved in her situation."

The supervision of someone other than Forren? "No!" Kaira cries, before attempting to rein in her emotions. "I refuse to be parted from For—from High Guard Arias."

"It's okay, Kaira," Forren says from her side.

Kaira turns to him, her face flushing red with anger. She opens her mouth to tell him that it really isn't, but something in the way that he isn't even looking at her has her words falling dead on her lips.

This was his intention all along, wasn't it? Using her to secure his position in the Golden Games before letting the King toss her aside. She should've known better than to trust him and his slimy people.

"I hate you," Kaira mutters under her breath in her own language.

Forren simply laughs at her statement.

Kaira turns harshly back to face the King.

"High Guard Arias, you may escort Miss Aziz down to the guard's quarters where you can place her under the care of High Guard Freja. She's proven herself capable of handling Altairians," the King says, dismissing them both.

Kaira spins around, not waiting for Forren to demonstrate the correct way to leave the King's presence, and charges from the room.

"Kaira!" Forren calls out as he catches up to her, the doors to the throne room sliding back into place behind them. "Let's talk about this, okay?"

The guards that'd delivered them to the throne room don't follow, staying by the heavy doors. Walking back through the halls they'd come through, Kaira can't see any of the beauty in the place. All she sees is flamboyance and a display of money and power hiding the truth of what's happening at the border: where 'prisoners' are kept in labour camps and the natural landscape is being destroyed in the name of progression.

"I don't have anything to say to you and your traitorous ways," Kaira spits back, refusing to look at Forren.

"Kaira, please—"

"No," Kaira states harshly. "Nothing you say will make up for anything of what was done back there."

"What are you so mad at?" Forren says, exasperated.

He stops abruptly and Kaira has no choice but to stop too, slightly ahead of him. Despite how angry she is at him, she isn't going to go wandering off alone in the castle.

"What am I mad at?" Kaira responds, fisting her hands at her sides. "Maybe that you led me to believe I had a chance at saving my people. Maybe that you're going to let the King give me away, because you never really cared for me, did you?"

"Kaira," Forren says. Kaira almost breaks at the way her name falls from his lips. He shouldn't be allowed to say her name that gently. "I do care for you. You know me better than to think I'm just going to turn into someone like our ruler when I become king."

"So, it's true, then. You really are going to," Kaira returns. Perhaps she hadn't believed the words coming from Tuomas and from the King; only now are they feeling true as Forren says them aloud.

"If I win the Games, which I'm sure Tuomas revealed to you is how we decide the next ruler."

"How can you know Tuomas told me? You haven't had the chance to talk to them alone since you left us to make our way here." Kaira huffs, crossing her arms over her chest.

"I could see your anger, little birdie, when you saw Mila and I fighting. And, talking about my sister..." Forren trails off, gesturing to the hallway behind Kaira.

Kaira spins, seeing the gold-decorated girl coming towards them with a smile. Kaira gets the feeling that she'd been listening to their conversation and flushes.

"Kaira, it's my pleasure to deliver you to the care of High Guard Freja," Forren says.

The remaining fight slumps out of Kaira, falling in a puddle to the ground. Her shoulders drop, her fists uncurling.

Forren flicks the jewels on Kaira's brow before stepping back. "We'll talk later, okay? I'll come find you." He turns to his sister and, with a flourished salute, says, "She's all yours."

He's out of sight before Kaira can recover from the fact his sister's the guard she's being put under the supervision of.

"So, what should we do?" Mila asks in Altairian.

"Anything to get my mind off all that," Kaira responds.

Mila laughs, wrapping an arm around Kaira's shoulder to guide her down the hallway. "I know just the thing."

143

CHAPTER TWENTY ONE

It turns out Mila really did know just the thing.

Kaira doesn't have the energy to think about everything going on with Forren as she lifts the bow once more, feeling the strain in her arms as she tries to fire the arrow. It falls pitifully to the ground closer to Kaira than the target—a haybale—she's aiming for.

"Closer," Mila says from beside her before lifting her own bow and firing it at a smaller target way beyond Kaira's. The arrow sinks perfectly into the middle.

"Do you have working vision?" Kaira says. Her shot was definitely worse than the other ones she'd attempted—not that they were really any better, though.

"What is it that they say in your country? It's the trying that counts or something like that." Mila gives Kaira an apologetic look.

"You don't have a saying like that? What do your parents say when they're trying to make you not feel bad about being terrible at something?"

"You think they say anything to encourage someone who fails?" She shrugs, like she wants to show it doesn't bother her, but Kaira can tell in the steeling of her jaw that it does. "You don't even get congratulated when you place first."

Kaira sets down her bow, turning to face Mila. "Is that why you became a golden guard? To get their approval?"

Mila's about to fire another arrow but pauses. Her teeth chew at the inside of her cheek as she considers. "No. I don't think so. I think it was more to spite them if anything. I'd bet the same is for Mikko."

There goes Kaira's distraction as the conversation loops back around to Forren.

Mila must see it on her face as she puts down her weapon, taking a seat on another haybale. She gestures for Kaira to join her, which she does, looking back over at the training yard they're in.

It's set off from the main courtyard and is a long, narrow area out in the open. It's quite brisk, so Kaira's glad for the layers she wears, even if the fancy dress and elaborate accessories aren't the best for target practice.

"Why are you upset with Mikko for wanting to become king?" Mila asks.

"Why don't you want to become king—well, queen?" Kaira asks instead of answering. "Tuomas and your brother have said that you could easily win the Games."

"I might be physically strong, but I'm too quick-tempered to push through the judgements. I'd need another person on the throne with me to balance that out and there's only so many people I like sharing with."

"Judgements?" Kaira asks. "From my people for upholding the conditions we're kept in?"

Mila shakes her head. "Quite the opposite. It'd be the turning from my own people when I declare I'm bettering the treatment of your people. I'd be terrified of what your people would do too. Even though I'd hold the best of intentions, they'll still cling to beliefs about who my people are."

"Do you really think that's what Forren wants to do? Restore my people to their land and repair what's been damaged with your country?" Kaira asks.

Mila meets her gaze. Her eyes are so similar to Forren's that it's unsettling. "I think you need to find it in yourself to trust that. I know you know him well enough to judge his character."

Kaira looks up, her response dying on her lips as the gates to the arena open and Forren strolls in. He gives his sister a small nod and, seeming to understand something in it, Mila stands and turns to Kaira.

"I'll catch up with you later, okay?" she says.

Kaira nods and watches her leave.

Forren looks around the arena, chuckling. "I hope my sister wasn't too hard on you."

Kaira shakes her head. "Not at all. It's nice to try something new, even if I'm particularly good at it."

"Yeah, there's a reason I stick to swords," Forren laughs. "Besides, nobody can look good at archery when Mila's in the room."

"I don't think anyone can look good at anything when she's in the room," Kaira responds. Though she hasn't even known Mila for a day, she can tell that about her.

"Anyway, enough talk about my sister when your favourite Arias is in the room," Forren says, pointing dramatically to himself.

"Yeah, sorry to say but I think that title's going to be taken from you. Besides, I thought she wasn't an Arias since she's High Guard Freja? It goes off your last name, right?"

"Usually, yes. But by the time Mila decided to start training to be a guard, I was already climbing the ranks. She decided to go by her middle name as if she knew we were both going to become High Guards and be fighting for the name." Forren clears his throat, sitting next to her. "Can we pretend for the moment that we're at the cove again? I have more that I want to say that I didn't then."

Kaira looks over at him, judging his intentions. His hands twiddle together as his head hangs low. "Sure."

"Are you a person that believes in giving second chances?" Forren asks, though the way he says it, the depth he says it with, makes it seem like he already knows.

"I don't think there's a limit to how many chances you should give someone, so long as there's hope that it might make a difference."

"Do you think there's hope I can prove my intentions align with yours?"

"Is this you asking for me to give you another chance at proving I should support you in becoming king?" Kaira asks.

"Not exactly. I don't need your forgiveness to become king. I need your forgiveness for the Golden Games themselves; you don't know what they're like, little birdie."

Kaira reaches out and grasps Forren's hand. "Well, right now, you're still my best chance at freeing my people, so I guess you're in luck." Kaira pauses before adding, "I still don't like that you used me, though."

Forren stands up abruptly, keeping hold of Kaira's arm so she's forced to follow him. "I need to show you something."

He runs to the gate, pulling Kaira with him. Her stomach pulsates with excitement.

After running a long way, passing by other guards and going through hallways and open-air rooms, Forren finally draws to a stop in a passageway that's built into the stone of the mountain. Before him is one of many dark wooden doors.

He pulls a key from a chain around his neck and inserts it into the lock, opening the door.

Inside are two bunk beds, one on either side of the room, with large dressers lining the far end of the room. There's a young female soldier sitting with Tuomas on one of the beds and they look up as the pair enter.

"Could you make yourself sparse for a little?" Forren asks them.

The female soldier, wearing a light blue fabric mask that pairs funny with the green of her uniform huffs but stands. "Is that any way to treat your little sister?"

Kaira's eyes widen. Another sister?

"Please, Malin?" Forren asks, softening his tone.

Malin turns her attention to Kaira, looking her over curiously. Malin seems to be a few years younger than Kaira—about fourteen—and it turns Kaira's stomach thinking about how she's already a soldier.

Malin hums, turning back to her brother. "Only if you let me meet your friend afterwards."

"It's up to her if she wants to meet you or not," Forren replies.

Malin turns eagerly back to Kaira, who shuffles awkwardly at the attention.

"Uhm, okay?" Kaira responds.

"Yay!" Malin exclaims, clapping her hands together.

Tuomas wraps their arm around the girl before she can launch at Kaira for a hug. "Come on," they persuade. "Let's leave them so it's less time before you can meet Kaira."

Tuomas guides Malin from the room as her dark curls jump around her head. As the door shuts back into place, Forren strides to the back of the room.

"I didn't think you'd be the kind of person who lets their sister join a war at such a young age," Kaira says as Forren buries his head in a trunk, riffling through its contents.

Forren shrugs as best he can in the position he's in. "It's the safest place for her to be; at least here Mila and I can look after her. Besides, it would've been harder for her to stay at home, trying to live up to the expectations we've set." Kaira can hear Forren tsking before he adds, "I'm making her drop out after the Games anyway. If she doesn't accept it, well, hopefully I'm the king and can enforce it."

Kaira can't understand where he's coming from, though she tries. Her position had been the exact opposite in a way, with the kids she taught having no choice in being part of the war.

"Ah-huh! Here it is!" Forren emerges victorious from the trunk with a fat notebook clutched in his hands.

He sits on the bottom bunk opposite to the one Tuomas and Malin had vacated and gestures for her to join him. Slowly, he hands over the book after using a smaller key on the chain around his neck to unlock it.

"What is it?" Kaira asks, though she only needs to read the first page she opens to know the answer. It's his journal.

"I don't write in it often, but it's everything that's made me who I am." He swallows before continuing, "The first entry is from the first time I saw how we treated your people. I was only six and, even then, I knew it was wrong."

Instead of saying more, Forren gestures for her to start reading. At first, it's hard to decipher his writing that demonstrates how young he'd been but, given her experience with the school children, it doesn't take her long to pick up on the little quirks of his writing.

Forren's mostly silent as she reads, at times skipping over chunks and at others lingering longer on entries. She reads about the first time he'd seen an Altairian beaten. She reads about how through their schooling they were shown videos that depicted her people as nothing more than scavenging animals. Tears prick her eyes imagining the first time he'd run away from home and ended up in Altair, badly burnt from the sun, yet despite him being Keranian her people had taken care of him and shown him the way home.

She really feels her emotion splatter all over the place as she reads about his realisation that becoming a guard would be the best chance at helping her people. It tugs at her to read about his debates with his morals when he was involved in forcing her people into the camps; he'd been a young guard and knew it was the best way to prove his worthiness to climb the ranks.

By the time Kaira hands the journal back over, her eyes are red and puffy and the lamps have burned so low she can't make out his face. She doesn't need to see the little details, though, to tell when he pulls his mask off and brushes a hand over his eyes that he's wiping tears from his own cheeks.

"Even at the time, I knew what I was doing was wrong, but I still did it hoping that someday I might be enough to make a difference," Forren says, his voice cracking.

Kaira leans over and wraps her arms around him, letting him bury his head into her chest. "I believe you."

"I've thrown away so many of my morals in this bid to gain power, but I don't know if it's worth it. What's this all going to mean if I don't win the Games?" Forren takes a shaky breath, pulling back from Kaira to say, "That's what really drew me to you. Despite everything thrown your way, you still held onto your morals."

"Not now," Kaira says. "Not since I agreed to work with you and come here. That was throwing away everything my people believed in."

"Sometimes, morals and cultural beliefs don't align. What made you seem so powerful to me was that you could see when your people were wrong and knew when it was best to choose the bigger picture."

"You were choosing humanity, Forren," Kaira says. "Even though" —she swallows harshly, feeling her heart stammer— "you may have...hurt people, you were choosing humanity and trying to save our future."

"I want to say that I hope you'll stick to that view in the future, but I won't be so selfish. I want you to stick to whatever views you believe in and if that turns you against me, then I understand. I promise, I do."

"Why do you keep speaking like you're going to become a completely different person? Like you're going to become the very thing I thought your people were?"

"Because I am," Forren answers. "I have no choice but to when I've come this far. The Golden Games..."

But, like always, he manages to avoid the conversation as a timely interruption appears in the form of Tuomas and both of Forren's sisters entering the room.

Kaira pulls away from Forren as if she's been caught colluding with the enemy.

"Can I meet your friend now?" Forren's little sister, Malin, asks excitedly, sitting down on the bunk opposite Kaira.

Kaira agrees that they can get to know each other, even as she wishes they'd stayed away longer. She feels like she's on the brink of finally uncovering the depths of Forren and, as she watches him sneak away to replace his journal, she can't help but feel like he also regrets them not having more time to talk. Will they ever get the time to talk before the Golden Games are upon them and they must face how much they really trust each other?

CHAPTER TWENTY TWO

The five of them had slept in the room that night—once they finally got to sleep, that was, since they stayed up late sharing stories of what it was like growing up in their respective countries. Kaira had taken Forren's bed as he'd shared with Tuomas.

They eat breakfast in a hall filled with wooden tables and all-you-can-eat buffets lining the walls. It makes Kaira queasy in the stomach being surrounded by so many Keranian guards, especially with the looks they give her. Clearly, it's going around that she's Altairian now that the King has assessed her. It doesn't help that she's the only person in the room who isn't wearing a mask. Plus, add to that the fact that Forren isn't right beside her, given she's squished between a still over-excited Malin and an apologetic Tuomas.

As if on some secret signal, the whole hall stands and makes their way towards the entrance.

Panic rises in Kaira before Forren's familiar presence arrives at her side. It doesn't last long, though, as he says, "Stick with Mila, like the King wants. We can talk after dinner."

Then, he's heading in the opposite direction, pushing through the crowds, before she can respond.

Mila pauses at Kaira's side, cocking her head to the open archway that leads into the main training quad.

"Want to train more?" Mila asks, following Kaira's gaze to where her brother departed to. Kaira can read the question beneath it: do you want to train to keep your mind off my brother and his avoidance?

"Sounds good," Kaira responds, letting Mila guide her through the crowds. Tuomas follows as Malin slips out of sight in the direction of her older brother.

They make their way back to the archery area, but once Mila sees the people there, she scowls and leads them away. They end up in one of the small stall-like cut-outs in the main quad.

"Done much sword fighting before?" Mila asks.

"Guess you can tell not," Kaira responds as Mila goes immediately past the real swords and the wooden practice ones to the foam ones right at the back. She hands one to Kaira before taking one for herself.

Mila huffs. "I know our country fosters a lot of violence which is looked down on by your people, but self-defence is important."

Kaira feels like letting the comment go but she can't help but defend her people. "It's not like knowing how to use a sword or fire a bow would've helped us when your people wouldn't let us keep our kitchen knives when you sent us into the camp."

Mila pauses from where she's using her foot to draw a smaller circle towards the edge of the room, standing within it to face Kaira.

Instead of arguing back, Mila shrugs. "I was never one for verbal debate. Let's fight it out."

Kaira doesn't get any more of a warning before Mila launches at her, skilfully wielding the foam sword. Her paths of movement look like well-rehearsed dances as the golden details on her outfit glimmer in the sunlight and her green eyes flash with determination. Her hair is cut harshly around cheek length, giving her a fierce look that shows Kaira how daunting it'd be to face her on the battlefield.

It's not like Kaira needs to be shown that as she feels it when the sword comes down on her upper arm. The foam edge means it doesn't cut her, but the sharp sting signals the bruise that'll form later.

"This isn't a very fair fight," Kaira huffs as she steps out of the way of another focused swing from Mila.

"Life's not fair. What're you going to do about it?" Mila responds with a smirk.

Kaira tightens her grip on her sword. She isn't going to let Mila get under her skin. Besides, she knows what Mila's doing; she's using this fight as a replacement for the debate about her people not taking up physical defence. If she refuses to fight, she might as well be shouting that her people simply take what comes their way. She isn't going to let Mila use this as a chance to make her people seem like they're to blame for the conditions they're kept in, even if Kaira knows Mila doesn't entirely feel that way—the girl said so herself.

It turns out that Kaira's as bad at sword fighting as archery. The bruise on her upper arm isn't going to be the only one lining her body. Kaira wouldn't have a chance against any Keranian guard, let alone a gold-decorated one, but she isn't going to admit her weakness.

"You can fight better than this, Altairian," Mila comments, hitting Kaira in the upper thigh.

Kaira can't respond with how heavily she's fighting for her breath, each one wheezing past her lips.

"Tell me, Kaira," Mila says, causing Kaira to brace for what's coming. "When you were in the throne room with the King, did you think about slitting his throat? Did you think about killing him and seeing how much that could change?"

No. The answer comes fast to Kaira's mind. She hadn't.

Mila tuts, lunging at her again. "What did you achieve in that meeting, then? Would you have made your people proud?"

The answer to that isn't so simple to come. Would she have? The Elders hadn't wanted her anywhere near the Kerani Army or their King, but would they have liked her to end his reign given she was that close? Probably.

"You've betrayed your people, Kaira. Don't lie to yourself," Mila says.

Kaira breaks.

She cuts with her sword across to Mila, her anger only growing as the gold-decorated guard easily steps out of the way. "I didn't betray my people. Everything I've done has been for them. Sure, I didn't murder the King, but I didn't submit, either."

"And where did that get you, hmm? Where has your kindness gotten you?"

"Stuck with you, obviously," Kaira spits back. "It kept me with your brother. Kept me alive."

"Ahh, Mikko," Mila sighs. "And do you think when he becomes the next ruler that your words will be enough to keep him in line? You know he's been using you to win the Games. He'll turn on you straight away."

"Mikko won't do that." Kaira jabs at Mila, realising she believes her words. Mostly. Of course, there's still part of her that worries, but with everything that he's shown her so far, she owes it to him to trust him.

"But let's say he does. Do you think a little talking will get a guard like him to change his ways? He's Keranian, after all. Have the words of your people and their persuasions ever been strong enough in the face of our physical force?"

Kaira doesn't know what Mila's trying to get at. Already in the short time she's spent with Mila she knows that she wouldn't do something without having a clear goal. Kaira just doesn't understand her enough to decipher what that is.

"Are you really going to have blind faith that Mikko's going to do what he promises or are you going to make sure of that fact?" Mila says sharply, landing one final blow that knocks the sword out of Kaira's hand and makes her lose her balance, falling to the ground.

"Enough, Mila," Tuomas calls from the side, coming over to them.

At the same time, a siren pierces the air, echoing around the quad. Kaira's heart rate spikes as the soldiers training around them are quick to place their weapons back in racks.

Tuomas reaches her, pulling her from the ground as Mila puts away their weapons.

"What's the siren for?" Kaira asks, watching as more soldiers pour from the quarters cut into the mountain, coming to line up in the open.

"The King is calling a meeting," Mila responds. "Perhaps he's going to put an order out for your execution."

Kaira pales, feeling her legs shake.

Tuomas rolls their eyes. "Mila, don't you think you've tormented the girl enough for one day?" Mila huffs out a soft laugh before Tuomas turns back to Kaira. "She's playing with you. The King wouldn't bother doing something so elaborate to murder one of your kind. I bet it's announcing when the Golden Games will be hosted."

That news scares Kaira even more. How long will it be before her country really is no longer hers? Before Altair is erased from any maps, the land given a new name and ruler?

She follows Tuomas and Mila as they exit the stall and park on the edge of the gathering crowd. Sure enough, at the far end of the site, beneath the towering palace, a stage-like structure is being erected.

The crowd murmurs in excitement, the energy in the air tangible. Kaira steps closer to Tuomas as her eyes scan the crowd for Forren, but she can't see any gold-decorated guards aside from Mila.

The animated whispers die down as a figure steps forth from the shadows. There's no doubt, even from this distance, that it's the King with the heavy drape of material that covers his shoulders. In addition to that is another tell-tale sign in the number of guards—all gold—that form a protective circle around him.

He moves across the stage with a terrifying confidence. His stride and posture are one of a man used to having people bow down before him. It's startling for Kaira to witness as the guards in the courtyard, even Tuomas and Mila, fall into a bow before him. Watching hundreds of powerful warriors seamlessly fall before him makes Kaira realise just who she'd been in discussion with the day prior.

The King of Kerani is not one to be messed with.

Kaira follows the lead of her friends, bowing too, before straightening as the King gives a gesture that must mean to stand back to attention. A chill runs down Kaira's spine as the King scans over the crowd, searching for something—or someone, as it becomes evident as his eyes land on her and his lips curve into a smirk.

"Good morning, my devout people." The King's voice booms out over the crowd, needing no extra assistance to reach even the far ends of the courtyard. "As I'm sure you've realised by now, I'm here to announce the specifics about the much-anticipated Golden Games, so I shall not bore you with a grand speech."

Kaira gets the feeling that boring them with a grand speech is exactly what he's about to do and she's proven right as he delves into how excited he is to be hosting the Games. When he clears his throat loudly, Kaira promptly jumps back into her body, realising she'd zoned out.

"And now, with much pleasure, I'm thrilled to announce that the 21st Golden Games will be held in a fortnight," the King says, the tone of his voice breaking into Kaira's ennui.

Mila startles, letting out a quiet, "What in the world?", as Tuomas follows it up with a similar sentiment.

"What's wrong with that?" Kaira whispers.

Mila turns sharply to her. "Normally, they're given at least a month—even up to a year—to prepare once the date is announced. Something must be wrong for the King to be springing this upon them now. We knew it was going to come up eventually, but not this quickly."

"That's not all." The King draws their attention back to him, breaking through the confused chatter of the soldiers before him. "I'm delighted to also reveal that for the first time, the Golden Games will not be hosted on Keranian soil. Given this is a particularly special event with the title for the new ruler of the land once known as Altair up for grabs, it seems only fitting for the Games to be hosted at the Royal Fortress of Erasme."

Kaira's blood curdles under her skin. How dare they have the audacity to host the Games declaring their new sovereign at a place so sacred to Altairians?

Kaira can't focus on her anger for long as flashes of shining gold in her peripheral vision catch her eye. She hadn't noticed that beyond the guards protecting the King the rest of the golden ones had come out, lining up to be gazed upon by the crowds below.

Almost as if drawn by some greater force, Kaira's eyes immediately land on a mask now so familiar to her. Forren's jaw is gritted as if he too is unsettled by the news. He spins from the stage before being dismissed by the King and returns to the shadows of the Palace.

Kaira slips from Tuomas' side, beelining for the entrance to the sleeping quarters. She hopes that Forren is heading back to his room so they can finally talk. Now it's even more important than ever.

As she reaches the carved-out hallways inside the cave, her eyes blink rapidly, adjusting to the sudden darkness enclosing her. Once Kaira adjusts, she can just make out the form of a figure running down the hall, about to slip around the corner and out of sight.

"Forren!" she calls out. "Wait. We need to talk."

The figure doesn't stop, skidding around the corner.

Kaira doesn't give up hope, pushing into a run as she follows them. "Forren!" she again shouts as she nears the corner, barrelling around it.

She slams straight into a solid mass. As she pulls back from them to be met with their golden mask, relief floods her. He waited.

"What are you doing here?" Forren demands sharply.

"The announcement. The Games—" Kaira begins, only to be cut off.

"I know, Kaira. I was there." He rolls his eyes. "I asked you what you're doing here."

Kaira pulls back sharply from him. "What is your problem? I only came to see if you wanted someone to talk to. I wanted to see how you're feeling."

"Like crap, obviously. In only a few days I'll be fighting for my life and to be the next ruler of my country. Do you know how much pressure that is? What if I'm not enough?" Forren's body posture is harsh, clammed up as he crosses his arms over his chest.

"Then we'll find another way," Kaira says, stepping up to Forren as she places a hand on his arm, hoping to comfort him.

"When will you realise that there is no 'we', Kaira," Forren says, pulling from her grasp. "If I don't win the Golden Games, you have no future. The King will execute you. There will be nothing left for your people. Nothing left worth fighting for anymore."

The words hit Kaira hard, bringing tears to her eyes. But she's past her days of crying over her problems. Steeling her jaw, she replies, "Then we fight. We fight until nothing is left. We still have a chance at winning this, Forren."

"There is no 'we'!" Forren repeats. "I'm the one that must win."

"Well, obviously," Kaira responds, smiling to lighten the mood. "But I'm still here to support you."

"I. Don't. Want. You. To. Be," Forren grits out.

Kaira's face falls, but walls go up inside her mind. "Why? Are you so quick to write me off as an asset as soon as my Altairian position is of no more use? I'm more than just my nationality."

"Can't you see, Kaira? I don't want your support. I don't want to be around you. All you've done is made this about you. All I wanted was to see your people treated how they should be, but now? Now you've invaded my mind and made it so all this ends with you being treated how you should be."

Even if it should be heart-warming, this admission that he cares about her, it's anything but. He's disgusted by these feelings towards her. And he has every right to be.

"I'm sorry," Kaira responds, her tone emotionless. "I'm sorry you don't see me as being worth that."

She leaves before the tears can fall.

CHAPTER TWENTY THREE

Forren doesn't say anything to Kaira—or anyone in the room—when he returns late that night. His clothes are dishevelled, suggesting he'd been training.

Kaira mulls over being the first to say something, but what would she say? If he no longer wants to work with her, then she'll find a way without him. She can't give up when she's come this far. As much as the argument had hurt, there's truth to it: what will be left for her in the wake of her betrayal if it sees no improvement in her people's treatment?

With those thoughts swirling in her mind and taking her mind off the person in the bunk above her, Kaira manages to drift off. That doesn't equate to her getting much sleep, though, as she tosses and turns all night, dreams throwing her mind into overdrive with visions of the tanks and weaponry they'd seen moving in on the camp.

Stark in her mind she sees screaming in terror the people she'd left behind: her mother, Nora, Benji, the other children. Did she really think her alone—just one girl whose only strong suit is being able to speak two languages, as if this isn't something most Keranians can do—could make a difference?

"Want to go for a run?" Kaira hears whispered in the dark.

She rolls over and looks vaguely into the darkness where she knows Mila's on the other bottom bunk. "How'd you know I was awake?"

"Do you really have to ask? It'd be impossible to ignore your fretting," Mila says.

Kaira winces. "Sorry if I kept you awake."

"Eh, not like I was missing out on anything sleeping."

Kaira hears Mila stand and a moment after something soft hits her in the face. A jumper. Without having to be told more, Kaira gets up and pulls it on.

She follows Mila out the door, moving down the hallway until they break out into daylight—well, break out into the outside because she can't call the small fingers of sunlight peeking above the horizon daylight. They'd taken a few turns that Kaira hadn't been down before, so she's surprised to find that they're about midway up the mountain, with a path that trails along its side in front of them.

Mila moves into a jog and Kaira follows, stumbling on the roots of the trees surrounding them. She isn't exactly used to running in forests. A sudden sadness washes over her at that thought. She misses the feel of her sand beneath her feet—not the sand of the beaches, but her thick, orange sand. She misses only having to put on one layer and not be freezing. She even misses struggling to breathe during sandstorms.

As if sensing she's overthinking, Mila picks up the pace.

By the time they pull to a stop on a small cliff face overlooking the shimmering green and blue sea, the sun has blossomed in the sky. No mirror is needed for Kaira to know that her face is bright red as she bends in half, hands on her knees, to catch her breath.

Mila, looking like she's just divulged in a feast to make her energised and not like she's run a marathon, moves into a few light stretches. Kaira watches, wishing she had even the tiniest ounce of physical ability left to copy her.

"Kaira..." Mila approaches hesitantly.

"Mhmm?" Kaira responds.

"You're not mad at what I said yesterday, right? Yes, we may have different views, but neither are wrong. I didn't anger you during our fight to dig at your beliefs, but to get you feeling something. You needed the harsh love to show you what you needed to know."

"Don't worry; I'm not holding something against *you*," Kaira responds, smiling despite the reminder of who she's actually holding something against.

"Well, if it isn't me, I'm assuming my brother got on your bad side."

"You could say that," Kaira mutters.

"He's pretty good at that," Mila offers. "It's because he's too scared to say what he actually means, so he reverts to what he's expected to say as a soldier."

"I don't know about that," Kaira responds. "I think saying what he did would've been scarier than anything else."

Mila shrugs. "Okay, but if he manages to get over his sulk, just ask him about it. Though I'd like to say to fight it out in the ring, most people would probably say that talking is the best way to put it all out in the open."

"Oh my god, you're so right," Kaira exclaims.

"See, talking helps!"

"No, not about that. The fighting. I'll kick his butt; let's set it up."

Mila's eyebrows almost touch her hairline. That's saying something that Kaira can see them at all considering Mila has her mask on. "Are you sure about that? Did you not see yourself with the swords yesterday? Or with the bow? Do I need to remind you that he's also a High Guard?"

Kaira raises her own brows. "He might be able to beat me in those instances, but I've survived a prisoner-of-war camp for four years. Give me a weapon I'm more familiar with and I'll show you—and him—what I can do."

It'd been hard to track Forren down, but Mila managed it, using her High Guard privileges to gain access to the special training rooms equipped for them.

Now, Kaira stands opposite the golden masked warrior in one of the training rings lining the central quad.

"Do you really want to do this?" Forren asks, his eyes a tumultuous storm. One of his hands plays with his jewellery.

"Don't antagonise me," Kaira responds sharply.

"Don't say I didn't warn you, then." Forren shrugs, sinking into his position as he raises his double swords.

"Likewise." The smirk on Kaira's lips grows.

With that, Kaira leaps forwards. She mightn't have swords of her own but hidden up her sleeve is the one weapon she's ever needed: a piece of trash fashioned into a knife. She didn't make it sharp enough to harm Forren—despite everything, she couldn't bring herself to put him in that danger—but he'd still feel it.

Forren half-heartedly swings one of his swords out towards her, though it's clear it isn't intended to land. Kaira sees the shift in his expression as she lithely slides under the blade, standing up to shove her elbow into the small of his back in her own warning. Forren catches himself from sprawling on the ground and, as he spins back to face her, Kaira can see the growing interest on his face.

They're doing this.

Again, Kaira stays quicker than him. She'd thought that being under the eagle eyes of Tuomas and Mila—as well as the those of the other guards they're quickly drawing the attention of—she'd find it challenging. She'd thought that being in a new environment would put her at a disadvantage. Instead, it feels like she's moving through air, not weighed down by sand, not having to dodge tents or keep an eye out for approaching guards. It's a walk in the park, really.

It doesn't take her long to find out that Forren's mask creates blind spots in his vision. She keeps herself moving in those areas, making Forren continually move to see where she's coming from. She knows her only advantages are her smaller size and her speed. If she gets pinned or cornered, it'll be over in a blink. He has the skill, the size, the muscle, the training.

They circle each other, not getting anywhere but sussing out how the other moves and their weak spots. Kaira just has to wait for him to underestimate her again, for him to get accustomed to her avoiding his onslaught before she meets it head-on.

Kaira's body strains, her muscles trembling with exertion. She should've waited for another day to do this; wasn't going on a run this morning enough? But life doesn't always let you pick the time and place of your battles.

The atmosphere is electric as their onlookers grow. The tension is palpable as the guards realise what she can do. From the corner of her vision, Kaira keeps an eye on Mila's face, seeing the pride there. It's that that gives her the confidence that she can do this.

Kaira startles, almost tripping over her feet as she rears back to avoid a fast blow from Forren. She can hear the blade slicing through the air and Kaira looks down to see where it's grabbed the loose hem of her shirt, tearing through it easily. That was close. But it's also her opening.

Forren freezes as his eyes move from her to his blade, checking for blood. Kaira pounces. She moves in from the side, using her foot to collect him in the backs of the knees, simultaneously wrapping an arm around his body to grasp his wrist, digging her nails into the skin so he drops one of his swords.

Then, just as he's realising what's happening, they fall to the ground as he loses his balance. Kaira lands on top of him, straddling his waist with one hand holding down his that still holds his last sword, as her other hand holds her makeshift knife to his neck.

Their spectators are silent. Kaira's heart roars in her chest as it catches up on everything that happened. She can imagine Forren's heart is racing under the layers of his guard uniform. He meets her gaze and Kaira smiles at the look there.

It's not annoyance, like she expects, or vexation. It's not a look that reveals he feels challenged by her or that he's embarrassed by having been beaten by her. It's pride and satisfaction.

His lips curl up in a smile as his green eyes dance with delight. "You've got me," he says.

Kaira leans forwards, adjusting the fall of the pendant over his brow so it sits right, before standing, holding out her hand to him. He accepts it and lets her pull him to his feet.

"Let's hope that teaches you a lesson for underestimating me," Kaira says.

Forren takes a step closer to her, brushing his hand over the pendant across her brow. "I never underestimated you, little birdie." Stealthily, he reaches forwards and takes from her grasp the knife she still clutches. Holding it up between them, he says, "I'm keeping this as a keepsake, if you don't mind, dear."

And, with that, he spins away from her with a confident stride in his step, as if he knows exactly what confusion he's left her with. Maybe Mila was right; fighting really doesn't get you answers like talking does.

CHAPTER TWENTY FOUR

"I've got something to show you," Tuomas calls out cheerfully as they enter the dorm room where Kaira has been lying for the last few hours.

Kaira moans, rolling over in the bed as her body protests. "What?" she asks.

"You'll have to come and see." Tuomas leans over to pull the blankets off her.

"I don't think I can move," Kaira groans. Every part of her body aches, but more than that her mind does. It feels clouded with the events of the last few days.

"It'll help you feel better," Tuomas wagers.

"Yeah, that's what Mila said about the running, but look where that got me."

Tuomas doesn't respond. Instead, they reach over and grab her arms, dragging her towards the edge of the bed before grabbing her legs and throwing them to the floor.

Kaira has no choice but to clamber to her feet to avoid falling to the ground. As much as it feels like she's hit rock bottom, she isn't quite ready to admit that, yet.

Moaning and complaining, she follows Tuomas through a series of maze-like twists until they break out into a carved-out room under the mountain, where the walls have been left bare so the clear rock face is displayed.

Soft green and blue lights decorate the vaulted ceilings to illuminate the natural wells of water that line the floor. Little lights run around each pool, each a different colour to signal the temperature of the water as they range from a deep, cold blue to a red that surrounds a lightly bubbling pool.

"How do you make the lights different colours?" Kaira asks.

"I show you a cave full of natural pools of water and magnificent displays of quartz and your focus is on the lights?" Tuomas laughs before explaining, "You've seen Mikko's hometown, the city of innovation. Science has brought us a long way."

Kaira hums in fascination as she moves between the pools and towards the far end of the room where little wooden rooms are segmented. Peeking into each, Kaira attempts to discern their purposes. Some have beds sculpted to the shape of the human form, whilst others have benches around pits of marvellous smelling steam. Even though there are so many lights, they're all quite dim, lending a certain calming atmosphere to the setting.

"What is this place?" Kaira asks.

"Simply put: the centre of relaxation and rejuvenation."

When Kaira turns around, Tuomas is smiling at her, as if joyed at her speechlessness. She's never seen anything like it and already she can feel the energy of the place sapping away her stress. Tuomas was right: this *is* just what she needs.

Tuomas steps back towards the light that shines through the open door they entered through. "Well, I'll leave you to enjoy yourself; take all the time you need. I'll be right outside if you need anything and will make sure no one disturbs your peace." They get to the door before they add, "Oh, there's bathing suits available over on that shelf or you can go naked if you want."

"Eww!" Kaira exclaims, hearing them giggle as they shut the door, closing her in.

A deep breath passes through Kaira's lips and, for a moment, she simply shuts her eyes and soaks in the air, feeling condensation greet her face. Yep, this is exactly what she's been needing.

Dragging her feet—this time not because she doesn't have the energy to, but because she wants to savour every moment—she makes her way to the shelves and selects a pair of swimmers. She pulls them out of the wrap they're in and changes, leaving her clothes and jewellery neatly folded in the cubby she'd taken the outfit from.

Then, she spins back around and lets out another sigh. Where does she start?

A door clicks open not far from Kaira's head and she launches from her seat, crossing her arms over her body as if she's undressed.

"Just me," Forren placates, entering the room.

Kaira's jaw drops. Not only is he not wearing his mask, but he's also shirtless, displaying the expansive length of his toned, tanned body.

"Watch out: if you keep looking at me like that someone might think we aren't enemies," Forren remarks as he slips onto the wooden bench running parallel to Kaira's.

A long, thin basin runs between them, out of which steam rises. Kaira blames the smells rising with the steam for her having drifted off to sleep before. Kaira lies back down, bringing her arms under her head as a pillow.

"Hmm, enemies." Kaira hums in consideration. Her voice is only a whisper. "And yet here we are, doing whatever this is."

Forren huffs in laughter.

"Why are you here?" Kaira questions. "I thought you didn't want to be around me. Something about me making you realise you had feelings, like any other human."

Forren sighs, fiddling his hands. "I'm sorry about that. I shouldn't have said anything I did earlier. I was caught up in the moment after the announcement and I just needed someone to take my anger out on."

"Did it work?" Kaira asks, raising a brow.

"No. It made me feel worse," Forren admits. "But having you beat me in that fight? That put some things in perspective."

"And what would those be?"

Forren peers around the room, a smile lighting his face. "I didn't see a label for an interrogation room on my way in."

"Aren't we beyond the prisoner and guard relationship?"

Forren bows his head. "You're right." He takes a deep breath. "When you fought me and showed that you weren't going to give up just because your best chance had been taken away, I realised it wasn't your morals that had drawn me to you, but the fact you cared so deeply about things. And yet there I'd been, pushing you away because I cared for you."

"So, you came here to tell me that?" Kaira asks.

"You know me better than that; I wasn't raised freely speaking what I thought and felt. So, I came to show you that I cared and, through that, ask to be reaccepted into your plans to repair humanity." Forren's face drops at the end of the sentence as he begins twiddling his fingers again. He lets the silence grow between them, keeping his eyes diverted from her.

"What?" Kaira asks. By now she's figured out his tells; he always goes silent whenever he's thinking about things.

"We begin the march in the early morning," Forren says, not needing to elaborate.

Kaira freezes. Is it really going to be so soon that everything's going to fall apart? Two weeks had felt like a short amount of time, but now this seems to have been snatched from them. "How...how long will it take to reach our destination?"

"It'll take about a week to reach Erasme."

Kaira hears Forren roll over onto his side to face her and does the same.

"I'm sorry, Kaira," he says softly.

"You have nothing to be sorry for," Kaira responds instinctively.

"We're taking over your country again," Forren responds sharply. "That isn't going to be easy for you."

"I won't be there, so it'll be easier this time."

Forren winces. "Yeah, about that... The King's making sure you stay close by his side. He doesn't want you getting up to any mischief."

Kaira rolls her eyes. "I'm flattered he thinks so highly of me."

Again, they lapse into a steady quiet of understanding, letting the atmosphere of the room lull them into a feeling of ease. It feels much easier to be having this conversation here than somewhere else, like they can't get angry at each other when surrounded by such calming energy.

"I—" Forren says suddenly, breaking the air before he stops abruptly. It's a little while later that he finally continues, "I didn't underestimate you earlier. I just...was trying to delude myself into believing you've never had to fight. I didn't want to admit that I played a part in...making you have to learn to protect yourself in that way. But I'm ready to accept responsibility for that, now."

"I'm glad I've learnt how to," Kaira responds. "Sure, the circumstances mightn't have been ideal, but that doesn't remove the value I gained from knowing how to take care of myself."

"I'm thankful you know how to as well, but we're going to make a world where you don't have to. Where nobody has to."

"Don't get too ahead of yourself. Even if you become the next ruler, the camp will still remain a dangerous place."

"Not if we remove the camp."

Kaira's eyes shoot up to Forren, not processing his words with the casual tone he'd said them with. "What?"

"Let's remove the camp. Return your people to their country."

"You mean that? You really want to?"

"Yes, princess." Forren smiles, his face bright and carefree.

"Ugh, princess is even worse than little birdie." Kaira slides to her feet as she runs her fingers through her hair.

"How do you think I feel being called Forren?" Forren exclaims, standing as well. He takes a step closer to Kaira, so there's just the low stone basin at their knees separating them. "Please, just once can I hear you say my name?"

"Maybe once you win my country back."

With that, she turns on her heel and strides from the room.

CHAPTER TWENTY FIVE

Kaira had enjoyed her impromptu therapy session with Forren yesterday, but she's even more grateful for it with the chaos that's thrown at them the following morning. The preparations for the Golden Games are officially in full swing.

Mila was adamant that Kaira be her shadow, so Kaira's been following her, sticking to the walls and out of the way as Mila prepares with the King. Kaira knows what Mila's doing; she's having her visible to the King to show she's taking her role supervising her seriously.

She hasn't seen Forren since their spa day—or any other gold-decorated soldiers but Mila at that. She's been hoping to catch up with him before they reach Erasme. Whilst she tells herself it's to make sure he's following the plan and is dedicated to winning the Games, the uneasiness in her stomach warns her of her growing fear about how violent the games might be.

Shoulders brush past Kaira in their hurry, though they don't seem to realise it's her—as she'd noticed after the show with Forren in the quad that the other guards had been drawing back from her even more.

Kaira presses her lips together, drumming her fingers against her leg. Can this day get any more boring? She can't take much more of this state of doing nothing as the King stands on his podium, Mila steadfast and unmoving at his side.

As the sun reaches its peak, a figure breaks from the crowd in front of them, approaching. Mila tenses before identifying who it is from their blond hair. Tuomas.

They whisper for a few moments with Mila, before the gold-decorated guard spins to the King and swiftly says a few lines. The loud clatter of the preparations prevents Kaira from making out what is said.

"Ready to get out of here?" Tuomas asks as they reach her side.

"Please," Kaira mutters in response, quick to follow them as they lead her from the shadows of the Palace.

As Tuomas shows her onto the ferry to head back to the other side of the cove, something switches in Kaira's head. This is it. This is the moment that begins history being made.

Worry niggles at her, reminding her of everything she could've and should've been accomplishing whilst at the Palace, lounging around as her people suffered. She's quick to push those thoughts away; she can't change the past and all she can do is focus on the now and the future. That sounds a lot like Forren in her head.

As the ferry hits the dock, Kaira gets the sense Tuomas needs a reprieve from her. She'd spent the whole trip interrogating them on the ins and outs of the Golden Games. With how many laws are in place protecting the sacred event, she didn't get much out of them except that it's a series of tasks—usually between three to seven—eliminating guards until only two are left for the final showdown.

Tuomas practically javelin vaults Kaira into the lifted truck they'd travelled here in from the camp. As her butt hits the bench seat, she's pleased to find a golden masked, black haired warrior in the driver's seat.

"I didn't think you'd be travelling with us!" Kaira exclaims as Forren starts up the vehicle.

"Yeah, don't tell anyone I'm here," he replies with a laugh.

"You're not meant to be?" Kaira says as loudly as before, though this time it's more in shock than...excitement, if that's what one would call her emotion at seeing him.

Forren grimaces. "Well, there's no rule saying I can't be, but it's tradition for the guards to travel together to be shown off."

"I should've expected that," Kaira retorts. "Your people live for fanfare and bragging."

"You know us so well."

Forren eases the truck into a slow crawl, heading past the sandstone buildings as they climb the mountain at a pace one could've jogged faster.

"Is it fear at what's to come or fear at leaving your country behind?" Kaira asks in response to the slow pace.

"I think we've established, considering I've been the High Guard in charge of the camp for the last four years, that I'm not afraid of leaving my country," Forren responds. That's as close as Karia's going to get to him admitting he's apprehensive of the journey ahead.

"You've trained for this your whole life, Forren."

"Exactly. What if it all comes down to nothing?"

Kaira looks over at him, her eyes boring into the side of his head until he turns to face her, meeting her eye. It's not like they're at risk of falling off the mountain as he takes his eyes off the road—with their pace they'd be lucky to even roll half a centimetre off track.

"I believe in you, Forren. I know the kid that wrote those journal entries won't let you lose this fight and the you that you are now is the same. You'll not give in and you'll not give up."

The words inspire the confidence in Forren that Kaira had intended them to, given how his shoulders relax. The same can't be said for Kaira as she seems to soak up the tension he let go. Him not giving up is exactly what she's afraid of; he'll keep fighting, even if he knows there's no outcome but death. He needs to know when it's time to drop the dream they hold.

Kaira has another striking thought that feels like lightning shooting through her body.

"Stop the truck!" Kaira calls out, barely giving Forren the time to stop, even with their snail's pace, before she's clambering over Tuomas' lap to exit the vehicle. Promptly, she walks to the cliff and deposits the entirety of her stomach over the edge.

Her body shakes as it fights for breath between the heavy heaves. Someone follows, holding her hair back for her. Nothing is said, which comforts Kaira but also makes her embarrassed.

The dry heaves finally cease and she straightens, wiping the back of her sleeve across her mouth before feeling remorseful, given it's one of Mila's beautiful—and expensive, no doubt—dresses.

Forren lets down her hair. "Are you okay?"

Kaira nods, feeling her chest wobbling as she opens her mouth to explain herself. They haven't been in the vehicle long enough to say it was travel sickness.

Forren's green eyes pierce into her before he nods compassionately. "It's okay. Do you feel well enough to continue?"

"There's no other choice," Kaira mutters, pulling herself together enough to make her way back to the vehicle.

Forren returns to the vehicle behind her. "Tell me what's wrong, Kaira," he says, worry creasing his eyes.

Kaira presses her eyes and lips shut, leaning heavily against her seat. "Later," is all she has the energy to mutter before overwhelming exhaustion washes over her body, pulling her into the land of nightmares as one thought takes over her mind. How can she rather Forren stop fighting to save his life when giving up spells doom for her and her people?

CHAPTER TWENTY SIX

———— + * ✳ * + ————

Kaira wakes with her head against Tuomas' shoulder, her hands fisted in their shirt. She pulls away, muttering apologies.

A tense silence fills the vehicle, alike nothing it'd been before, even when they were a prisoner-of-war and the two guards assigned with their transportation.

Forren breaks it by reaching over to his door and pulling out a water bottle, offering it to Kaira. She takes it readily, realising the gross taste clinging to her mouth.

Forren waits until she's finished drinking before he asks, "Do you mind grabbing that pen and paper from up on the dash there?"

Kaira, with only a little hesitation, does so. "What do you want me to do with this?" she asks.

"I think you know where this is going," Forren responds.

Kaira debates acting like she doesn't know, but she knows Forren isn't that gullible. Sighing exasperatedly, she scribbles on the paper 'Interrogation room'.

She props the paper up on the dash and, for the first time, bothers to pay attention to how the scenery around them has changed from the snow-laden peaks to flatter ground Kaira remembers from the other side of the Prison. She isn't surprised that she somehow missed passing through it entirely—if they even have as perhaps there's another way around—considering she's also missed the point where they joined the procession of vehicles.

As far as the eye can see both forwards and backwards vehicles—all smaller than Forren's truck but still quite big—line the road. If she squints, she can make out the back of the golden guards' procession leading the queue given the flags and streamers decorating the open-backed trucks.

Forren seems to have been waiting for her attention to return to the vehicle because, once it does, he's quick to fire the first question. "What was that back there?"

"Me sleeping," Kaira responds, avoiding, like he's trained her to, what he's really asking.

"Before that, Kaira. On the side of the cliff." Forren's voice already sounds exasperated.

"Oh, of course. That was me vomiting." Forren spins to glare at her but Kaira shrugs, adding, "You'll have to be more specific with your questions to get the answers you want."

"Why were you vomiting?" There's no doubt this time that he's exasperated with her.

Kaira's tempted to respond with it being because she was sick in the stomach, but given everything that depends on her remaining pleasant with the Kerani guard, she decides not to test it. "I had a thought and it...unsettled me." Kaira pauses and Forren must get the sense that she isn't just leaving it at that and is just trying to find the strength to keep talking because he waits for her to continue. "I...realised that I'd commit the biggest betrayal against my people if it came down to it."

"Which is?" Forren probes.

"I'd rather you back down in the Games if it isn't looking like a good outcome rather than keep fighting and putting your life at risk for even the slimmest possibility of my people getting their freedom." The words come out in a rush and Kaira presses her lips shut tightly. She stares out the front windscreen, avoiding meeting the gazes of the two soldiers in the vehicle.

A hand tightens around Kaira's, coaxing her to let go of her tight grip on the front of the bench seat as they hold her fingers steadily. Kaira moves her gaze from the bleak sky overhead to the golden masked guard at her side.

"It doesn't make you any less of a person for thinking that, Kaira. We're all prejudiced when it comes to protecting those we care for. It's part of being human." Forren glances at her, making sure to meet her eye with his next sentence. "I'd do the same if it was you in that position."

Kaira mulls his words over. She doesn't know how much she really sees it as being a justifiable reason for her actions but, for simplicity's sake, she chooses to believe it.

That night, Kaira's summoned by Mila to her tent. Kaira obliges her wishes, even though part of her wants to stay with Forren like she's become accustomed to.

The next morning, as she treads through the rows of tents to where she knows Forren has set up, disappointment racks her bones as she stares at the empty plot of land. Has he left so early to avoid her? The thought passes through Kaira's mind before she even realises she's feeling that way but, once it comes by, it's hard to shake.

Kaira makes it back to Mila's tent to see the other girl still sleeping. Being as quiet as she can, she rummages through her clothes bag, finding an outfit to change into for the day. Her nose scrunches as she pulls out a dirty brown article resembling a rag before she realises with a start what it is. It's the outfit she'd accompanied Forren from the camp in.

As quickly as that, her disappointment morphs into resolve.

"You woke me with all the thinking going on over there," Mila says from behind her.

Kaira spins around. She can't help the smile drawing up the corners of her lips as she watches Mila sprawled out on her bed, yawning unabashedly. "You can hear thinking? Do you Keranians have superpowers I'm not aware of?"

Mila chuckles. "No, you're thinking is just loud enough that I'm sure the Olikans on the other side of the earth can hear it."

Kaira tilts her head. "Do you have much involvement with other countries? I've heard that your trading systems are much more expansive than what ours used to be."

"We have too much involvement with them in my opinion," Mila responds. "But, if you want to learn more about them, you'll have to ask Forren. For now, I'm more interested in knowing what had you thinking so loudly."

"It's really nothing interesting," Kaira mumbles, pushing other items she'd taken out into the bag, burying her clothes at the bottom.

"Kaira."

The sharp tone in Mila's voice has Kaira's brows drawing together. "What?"

Mila studies her before sighing loudly. "I should've known it. You're planning on running away. Back to that camp."

Kaira's stomach sinks. She wants to deny it but if it hadn't just been demonstrated, Mila can see right through her. "Are you sure you don't have superpowers?" Kaira asks.

Mila tilts her head in an unimpressed look. "If you want to make grand plans like running away from the Kerani King and his best guard, if I may say so without being too self-absorbed, you can at least find the courage to admit to your plans when they're thwarted."

Kaira swallows deeply as she steels her spine. "Fine, yes. I was planning on running away but only temporarily. More like a brief departure, really." Kaira crumbles, her voice shaking. "Don't say anything about this to the King, please. I promise, I'll throw away all plans if you promise me that."

Mila huffs. "You think you can bargain with me?" Slowly, a smile takes over her face. "Come on, haven't I taught you anything about sticking to your guns? Don't give up so easily; I know you're stronger than that, Kaira."

Kaira bows her head, feeling red overtake her cheeks. How can she make such a fool of herself in front of Mila? She's like the very definition of what Kaira wants to be; confident, valiant, loyal.

"So," Mila says, "what's the plan for sneaking away?"

"It really doesn't matter, now. I've thrown them all away."

Mila tsks. "I hope that's to make way for the new plans that'll involve my help."

Kaira's eyes shoot up from the floor. "Really?"

Mila nods, smiling widely at Kaira.

And, with that, Kaira dives into the plans.

Working with Mila is even better than Kaira had planned. Not only does it make the mission a lot easier in taking away one of the hardest obstacles which was going to be avoiding Mila's sharp gaze, but the girl also has a lot to contribute.

By the end of the day, they have a solid plan for the following morning, which involves Kaira getting up a whole heap earlier than she would've preferred.

As the sun begins its descent, Kaira paces the tent. Mila doesn't seem to notice her or can't be bothered to, as she sits on her bed, looking in a small hand mirror as she braids her hair out of her face.

"What if the tent-bearers don't actually go a stop further?" Kaira asks, feeling her stomach coiling tightly.

"They must unless the King submits an official change in schedule. If he does, I'm the first person to hear about it," Mila responds monotonously.

"What if…" Kaira stops her pacing, pressing her eyes shut tight. She's asked every possible question there is and Mila's answers haven't changed. "What if everyone I need to see at the camp has been killed since I left?"

Instead of saying something comforting as most probably would, Mila simply says, "Well, you won't know until you get there, will you?" And, somehow, that's more comforting. It's just what Kaira expects from the girl who she's come to consider a friend.

"And if they are?" Mila continues, finishing the last braid and tying it off with a band. "There's only one thing to do: fight harder with Mikko for the future."

Kaira flops down onto her bed, sighing heavily. "How can you be so casual about this?"

Mila shrugs, standing from her spot as she smooths out the creases in her uniform. "Well, in situations like this, second guessing our plan will only result in a plan that's less thought out and more prone to oversights. It's best to stick to the plan we have whilst we know it's strong."

Mila spins around to Kaira, sending a giant white ball in her direction. It slams right into Kaira's face, who laughs as she pushes the pillow away from her.

"Go to sleep. Be ready for when I return in the morning," Mila says strictly.

"Yes, ma'am," Kaira responds formally, causing Mila to laugh before the guard slips from the tent.

Kaira rolls over in her bed, left alone with the noise in her mind and the task of falling asleep.

CHAPTER TWENTY SEVEN

The morning dawns bright and early, heat seeping out across the wastelands as they're closer to the desert lands that mark Kaira's country. Kaira wakes with the sun, tumultuous nerves hiding beneath the exciting prospect of seeing her family again.

She dresses swiftly, layering her clothes under the borrowed cloak from Mila. She looks at herself in Mila's mirror, her eyes lingering on the jewellery resting against her brow. She doesn't pause to consider why she keeps it on as she busies herself with her hair.

Once she finishes, she quickly leaves the tent. A little way away, three wagons are being loaded with supplies, folded tents piled high on the trays. Kaira hesitates momentarily: should she approach with confidence that she's meant to be there or sneak her way onto the wagons?

Clenching her jaw until her teeth ache, she settles on the first option. It seems like the only plausible option given the quantity of guards that surround the vehicles, decorated in green and purple.

Kaira fists her hands at her side and storms forwards. Her gaze is unwavering, so much so that she doesn't notice the guard walking perpendicularly to her until she crashes straight into their shoulder.

"Watch where you're—" The guard she'd run into cuts off abruptly as they look her over. "Oh, it's you."

"It's you," Kaira responds to Tuomas, rubbing a hand over her face that'd hit them so hard she wonders if her features are imprinted on their shoulder.

Tuomas watches her carefully before letting out a sigh that sounds eerily like Mila's when she'd discovered her plans. They look away from her to the direction she'd been heading before a smile pulls up the corner of their mouth.

"I hope you're causing trouble for Mikko whilst he isn't around," Tuomas teases.

"I wouldn't have thought I was becoming predictable. I haven't been that misbehaved it's expected now, have I?" Kaira responds.

"Quite the opposite, really. You've been too well behaved that sometime soon you'd have to rebel."

Kaira huffs, pretending to be annoyed. "Well, if you don't mind, I should probably be getting going. You know, trouble to cause and all," Kaira says, stepping past Tuomas who easily spins around to fall into step beside her.

"Sign me up. What are we up to?" Tuomas asks merrily.

"You aren't going to dob me in to Mikko, are you?"

Tuomas manages to cover their surprise at Kaira's use of Forren's real name, the only sign being the slight raise of his brows. "Nope. Even if I wanted to, I wouldn't be able to get close enough to him. The High Guards are being kept under lock and key."

They nod their head over to a brief gap in the row of tents and Kaira catches a group of guards in their black and golden uniforms jogging around a field. On-duty lower-level guards surround the area, making sure no one disrupts them.

Kaira's eyes instantly seek out a golden mask but can't find it in the sea of uniforms. Disappointed, she turns away, focusing her attention on the loaded vehicles beginning to rumble to life. Knowing Tuomas is likely going to hold her up until they know what she's up to, she decides to indulge them.

"I'm heading out with the tent-bearers to move ahead of the group. I'm" —Kaira swallows, knowing how absurd the idea sounds— "going to head to the camp."

"Loose ends you need to tie up?" Tuomas asks.

"You could say so." Kaira shrugs. "I can't..." She swallows harshly, working past the block in her throat. Somehow, it feels harder to admit her fears to Tuomas than Mila. "What if Mikko doesn't win?"

She leaves the rest up to Tuomas. If Mikko didn't win, she'll have gone against the wishes of the Elders for nothing. If Mikko didn't win, her life might be threatened. If Mikko didn't win, the last hope of winning back her country will be lost.

"As long as you're there to support him, you have nothing to worry about," Tuomas says. Kaira knows the question in their answer. They're wondering if Kaira's going to stay at the camp until the Games are over.

"I'm still coming," Kaira answers. "I'll catch up after you pass by the camp. Mila helped me make the plans; no matter what, I'll be there for him."

"Good. I'll tell Mikko to pick you up from the camp, then."

"I thought you didn't have contact with him?" Kaira raises an eyebrow at Tuomas, watching their reddening cheeks.

"I'm his second-in-command; nothing can stop me from getting to him. You just wouldn't have spilled the beans otherwise and I was too curious as to let that opportunity pass."

"You're such a—"

"Oops!" Tuomas calls out, cutting her off. "Would you look at that? Quick, you better go before your ride leaves."

Kaira spins around to see the first of the vehicles she's meant to be in pulling out of the campground and, muttering curses at Tuomas who stands laughing at her back, she hurries to catch the last of them.

The tent-bearers don't question her presence as they make their way over the wastelands, being jostled around by the deep crevices created by the bombs.

Kaira bites at her nails as she watches the passing scenery—well, it's more just scorched dirt and ditches. Last time when she'd passed through here, she'd felt a deep hatred and disgust that it was possible for Keranians to do this. Now, the sight fills her with motivation. They're going to end this. They're going to take back both lands from the hands of the Kerani king, because all this time, it hasn't just been her country fighting for survival.

"Sometimes you've got to wonder what the King was thinking when he decided to take this dump," the driver of the vehicle Kaira is in mutters, gesturing loosely with his hand at the road ahead, where the wrecked land is beginning to morph into the sandy plains of Altair. Kaira doesn't know exactly when they cross the border given there's no clear markers.

"Yeah, it's not like there's much to the place except for sand, sand and, hmm, more sand," another guard replies, distaste curling his face into a scowl.

"Sand is not all we have," Kaira butts in before feeling herself pale. Her insides twist as her hands bunch into the fabric of her coat, wishing the seat will swallow her up. But there's no way she can leave her statement at that as all three guards in the vehicle turn to look at her, their faces in various stages of shock, perhaps more so from having forgotten she's there than at her having said something.

"Well," Kaira adds, "it might look like it's only sand because you'll have only ventured into the areas of dunes close to the border. The further you go, the more you see. There are salt flats and all different natural features. That's not even considering the diversity of flora and fauna we have; they're quite fascinating in how they've adapted to survive the climate."

The guards share a look between themselves before breaking into laughter. Clenching her fist, Kaira turns to stare out the window.

Luckily, as Kaira's chest wobbles with dejection with every bump they ride over, it doesn't take long for them to pull into the space that'll be the next campsite. Before the vehicle has finished rolling to a stop, Kaira opens the door and jumps out, landing awkwardly on the uneven and soft grains of sand. The sun's just above the horizon, its light too weak to properly illuminate the ground.

Looking over her shoulder, she judges if anyone in the vehicle is paying attention to her, but they still seem busy laughing at her as their obnoxious cackles break the silence.

The second the headlights go off, Kaira bolts.

She mightn't be able to see much, but she'll always know her way home among the dunes. Her feet are fast and sure as they pick their way along the uneven sand. Sinking into the soft first layer feels like coming home, the sand welcoming her as if she's a part of it.

This is why it'd never be her people that'd enact the destruction creating those wastelands.

Kaira doesn't stop, even when she's sure she's out of sight of the convoy. Her legs carry her up and down the dunes, rarely stumbling. Her lungs expand and contract, taking in the fresh, dry air surrounding her as it intwines with her very being, breathing life back into her soul.

Darkness sinks down upon her, but it's not a suffocating presence. It's a warm hug that encloses her in a blanket of safety. The stars light the way home and she follows them; Mother Earth will always make sure her children find their way home.

Kaira doesn't let herself pause to consider the tiredness that weighs down her bones or the dryness in her throat that pleads for water. Her body will get what it needs after her soul gets what it needs: being back among her people.

And there, settled amongst the dunes on the edge of a cliff, is the camp. Bright spotlights illuminate the complex, casting shadows over the thin fabric tents that quiver in its presence. Even in the dead of night loud noises emerge: lively chatter, the shouts of guards, the deafening clang of workers, the squeals of children.

The sight's enough to finally draw Kaira to a stop. All this time she's been wrong about life at the camp. Not a single person has given up, like she'd thought when they weren't doing anything to escape. They're still living, still surviving, still pushing on. Sure, life is nothing like life in the Kerani's advanced technological city or the lazy, homely life in Fairah, but it's still life.

Kaira's knees hit the sand. Tears roll down her cheeks as weighty sobs draw themself from her body. Her fingers draw small granules of sand between them. Her toes kick off her shoes to bury themselves in the grains. *This* is home.

"Kaira."

Kaira freezes, her chest putting a fast halt on her next sob. That voice shouldn't be here. That voice should be back at the last campsite—or back in the capital city if that much time has passed.

Slowly, Kaira sits up, pushing her hair from her face to meet the boy standing opposite her.

"What are you doing here?" Kaira asks Forren.

"I'm here for you," he replies easily, taking a step towards her.

How long has she been out here in the heat even though it's night. It's still the first night, she thinks.

"Why?" Kaira asks, her voice barely more than a whisper. She looks away from him; maybe when she looks back, he'll be gone.

"Because I want to be here for you," Forren replies.

"Are you real?" Kaira asks, looking up at him to meet his gaze again. "Is any of this real?"

Open your eyes, she tells herself. *Open your eyes and see that this is all a dream. Open your eyes and see that you're not the hero you think you are. How could you ever have believed this? Believed that out of everyone in that camp, you'd be the one to take a chance, be the one with the strength to make a change?*

Kaira squeezes her eyes shut tight. "No, no, no, no, no," she mutters furiously under her breath. Her hands tighten in her hair, pulling it sharply until little strands give up, snapping off into her fingers. This is all too good to be over. This can't have just been a dream. It can't be.

"Kaira, open your eyes," Forren says, sounding closer this time.

"I don't want to," Kaira responds with a hiccup.

"Why don't you want to?"

Why does he keep saying her name like that? It's too caring, too familiar.

"Because I'm too scared to," Kaira responds. She's too scared to admit that she's given up, that she's succumbed, that she's nothing but one of the lifeless bodies moving about in the camp she sees in the vision before her.

A weight settles down beside her. Kaira keeps her arms wrapped around herself, her eyes pressed tightly shut. She's even too weak to let go of this vision of what hope could be out there.

"Do you trust me?" Forren asks, his voice near her ear.

Kaira nods.

"Then open your eyes."

Kaira does.

Before her is still the same sight, this time doused in a brilliant sunlight that highlights the forms moving within the embrace of the stone walls.

"Take it in, little birdie, because I promise you: this will be the last time you'll ever see the camp like this again," Forren says from beside her.

Kaira turns to him, her heart feeling like mush in her chest with the emotions warring in it. Fear, joy, surprise, disbelief, scepticism, doubt. Slowly, she smiles. "I think that sounds more like a threat than what you intended."

Forren's shoulder nudges hers before he lets go of her hand to wrap his arm around her shoulders. "You know what I mean."

Kaira turns her head in his embrace, pushing her cheek to his chest above where his heart beats. "Gods, is this really real?"

"Well, I mean, I'm not one of your gods, but I'm pretty sure it is," Forren mumbles into her hair.

Kaira takes a deep breath, looking once more over the camp, this time noticing the vehicle sitting a little way away. There's a figure within it that's watching them, but they're quick to duck away as they catch Kaira's gaze, pretending not to be there.

"How are we going to accomplish this, Forren?"

Forren shrugs. "By believing in ourselves. We've gotten this far together."

Letting out a deep sigh, Kaira says, "I need to go see my family and my Elders."

"We've got to," Forren corrects.

"I can do this myself," Kaira responds.

"I have full faith you can, my dear," Forren responds, pushing her away to clamber to his feet. "But I also have business with your Elders. I hear it's custom to go to them for approval to be adopted into your people?"

Kaira's breath leaves her chest, making her sway on the spot as she stands. "What?" she asks. "You...you want to join my people?"

Forren shrugs. "Well, if it means I get to roll around on the ground as you were and call it connecting to my origins, I'm all for it."

"Hey!" Kaira shouts good-naturedly, pushing Forren so he falls over laughing. "That was rude." She can't stop the smile pulling up the corners of her mouth, though, even as she asks, "Are you sure? It's not a decision you make on the spot."

"I've only been surer about one other thing in my life and that was helping you get your country back," Forren says. "Through you I've gotten to know so much about what it means to be Altairian: fighting for your people, your country, connecting with your origins, valuing life above money or luxury. I mightn't be ready to completely give up my identity as a Keranian—"

"You could never. It'll always be a part of you," Kaira adds.

"Precisely. So, when this fight to free your country is over, I want to fight to free mine, too. I want to make being Keranian something to be proud of, something I don't want to hide," Forren finishes.

"Well, looks like we have big plans on our hands. We better start checking things off the to-do list," Kaira answers.

When she looks over at Forren, she can see hope glimmering in his eyes and she imagines the same is in hers. How have two people from completely different backgrounds come together to give each other hope that things can be better?

Linking their hands together, Kaira leads them down the last sand dune and to the entrance of the camp.

CHAPTER TWENTY EIGHT

Even with the regular morning noises of the camp washing over them as they enter, the air seems tense and silent. Eyes peer at them blatantly, lingering a moment too long.

Kaira presses her lips tightly together, ignoring the whispers swirling around them, making her once more doubt herself.

Traitor. Kerani slave. Viper.

Forren looks at her from where he walks a pace behind her, letting her set the tone in being the leader. In his eyes, he asks whether she wants him to do anything, but Kaira subtly shakes her head. She can handle whispers when she knows it's only lies falling from their lips.

There's a clear space around the tent they're heading for, like it's a rock in a river parting water. It leaves a bad taste in Kaira's mouth. The houses of the Elders had always been somewhere to go when you needed anything; it's wrong for it now to be a place avoided out of fear.

The flap to the tent opens before them when they reach its untouched orbit. Easily, Kaira steps inside, keeping her chin high. She'll not let the Elders look down upon her, not when they deserve no more respect than others. What have they done that places them above anyone else other than be conceived by the parents they have?

The air in the tent is suffocating, the fabric holding in the heat of the day. Kaira blames the sweat beading on her forehead on it, not the fear coating her skin.

"I didn't think I'd be seeing you back here," Deni says.

It's clear the Elders had warning from one of their many eyes around the camp that Kaira was on the way.

Kaira glances at who else is in the room: Noha, Gigi, a few others.

"Looks like you aren't the only disappointed one, then. I had hoped I wouldn't be seeing you again, too," Kaira returns.

Forren's choked chuckle is swallowed by the gasps that reverberate around the room.

"Why bother, then? Stay away; it's not like you'd be missed. You can't take back the betrayal you've committed," Deni says, recovering herself.

"If we're talking about betrayals, I think it's worth discussing the betrayals every Elder here has committed," Kaira spits back. "How can you sit here and call yourselves Elders when you've done nothing to protect your people? What happened to the vows you took at your appointment? 'We stand to protect the ones who cannot protect themselves. We stand to safeguard humanity and all that comes with it. We stand as mothers, fathers, sisters, brothers, carers and guardians of those needing guidance and a loving hand. We stand as protectors and to this cause we devote ourselves.'"

Kaira leaves a lingering silence to fill the air, her eyes slowly landing on each Elder that had taken the public vows, renewing them every four years. It'd once been one of their biggest celebrations, but now it's nothing more than a band-aid placed over a fatal wound. It's the assigning of a role to make others feel secure in that someone else will take charge in the hard moments, yet that control is never demonstrated.

"I'm not here to tell you how to do your job, but to tell you that you might want to consider what your job will mean in a new world. What role do you want to play when a new dawn comes around?" Kaira continues.

"Right," Deni chuckles dryly, her tone demeaning, "and this is where you come in with your whole save the world attitude once more. You're here to tell us that it's going to be you bringing around this new dawn, aren't you?"

"Don't be silly," Kaira says in the same demeaning tone. "One person isn't enough to lift the sun. Some of us still believe in supporting each other, however. In a few days' time the Kerani ruler will be changing and Altair is getting a new ruler. I don't expect you to do anything considering none of you have worked up the courage to make a difference in all the years we've been here, but, if you have a change of heart and remember what it is to be Altairian, then perhaps you'll prepare and tell our people we're going home."

Kaira's words make herself reflect on what it means to be Altairian. She's always felt a strong connection to her people and to her culture, but, after this adventure she's been on, it's only grown. A lot of that has to deal with the company she kept. As much as Kaira's shown Forren about her country and him to her about his, he's also shown her about hers too, making her realise beliefs she once took for granted. Now, she can admit being Altairian is something she actively chooses, not just something she was born into believing.

There's nothing else that needs to be said, so Kaira leaves. She doesn't need their approval to continue with what she's going to do. If they were so afraid of the consequences, they would've written the future themselves, not waited for someone else to.

"I suppose I'll have to wait for another time to get approval to join your people?" Forren asks, following behind her as she picks her way through the trash littering the ground.

Kaira hums. "You know what? I'll make you a deal. You become the ruler of Altair and promote me to be your equal and then I'll promote you myself."

Forren looks over at her, his green eyes meeting her brown ones. "Deal."

Kaira gives a steady nod in response as her mind dances with thoughts. Never in her wildest dreams did she think she'd casually be making deals about being a ruler with her people's enemies. Oh, how things can change if one is open to seeing other perspectives.

Kaira can't see her mother.

Even if it's just a 'see you later' rather than a final 'goodbye', it's too hard to face. She tracks her mother to the metal-working stalls, but she stays in the last layer of tents, hidden from view.

"I can't do it," Kaira mutters to Forren, who stands beside her. "Does that make me a bad daughter?"

"Nothing could ever make you a bad daughter," Forren responds. "Not wanting to face seeing her only shows how much you care about her."

"I need to do this, though. She needs to know." Kaira wills herself to work up the courage, schooling herself through breathing. "I can't trust anyone else will truthfully tell her what I'm doing."

Forren watches her for a while as she moves her body around, antsy as she tries to build the determination. Kaira ignores his inquisitive look, wondering how he could understand her situation. What was his relationship with his parents like?

"Wait here," Forren states suddenly.

Before Kaira can question him, he's stepping around the tent they're hiding behind and crossing the dirt track to the stalls. It's too late for Kaira to call him back as he strides confidently up to her mother, waving off the guards that step forwards to offer him assistance.

Her face draining of blood but her heart warming with appreciation, Kaira watches, unable to move as Forren pulls her mother away from her work. Kaira's mother, Mara, doesn't react with the same fear to Forren's presence that other prisoners around them do. She just follows him away calmly, like she knows he's the one Kaira's working with and trusts him from that alone.

Kaira picks at her fingernails, her eyes intent on the distant conversation playing out. There's too much noise coming from the workers to make out anything of what's being said and, other than Mila, Kaira wonders if she's ever met more stoic faced people.

"Hey."

Kaira startles, spinning around as she clutches a hand to her chest.

"Nora!" Kaira almost shouts, before remembering she's hiding from her mother.

Kaira steps forwards, pulling her blonde-haired friend into a tight embrace. Nora hugs her back just as tightly.

"Look at you," Nora states, stepping back from Kaira and holding her at arm's length. Her eyes linger on Kaira's figure that's filled out since she's been gone. "Freedom's served you well."

Kaira's lips twist, her eyebrows drawing together as she ponders whether her friend is resentful that she got out, but there's no sign of bad feelings in the light blue of her friend's eyes.

"So," Nora says, pulling Kaira's thoughts back, "how's everything going? They haven't ditched you here, have they?"

"No, nothing like that. I made them bring me back." At least, that's easier to say than that she ran away and was caught doing so. "I wanted to come see you all before, well—" Kaira stalls. Before what exactly? Before they got a new ruler? Before the prisoner-of-war camp was a thing of the past?

"I'm just happy you're here," Nora says, rubbing Kaira's shoulders.

Kaira gives Nora a once over, only for guilty feelings to rise in her gut. Heavy bags hang under Nora's eyes as her thin frame is draped in torn clothing.

"How's your father?" Kaira asks gently.

Nora smiles wider. "He's great. Honestly, I need to find myself a friend like your guard. Papa's still in the hospital, but I get taken to him every second day to visit."

"I'm so happy for you both." Kaira pulls her friend into a hug.

"I don't know how I'll ever repay you," Nora says. Before Kaira can reply, she adds, "And no, don't even bother saying that it's enough for me to run the school and look out for your mother. I'd do that regardless of owing you or not; that's what friends are for. Talking about that, though, the school's doing amazing. I imagine it's your guard friend's doing that the older kids haven't been put to work, yet."

All the breath is pulled from Kaira's chest. How is it possible that Forren's already doing so much for her and yet he's doing so much more behind the scenes? And he isn't just doing this for her sake—he would've been sure to tell her of all the things to win her favour. He's doing this because he wants to.

"I know, he's great," Kaira sighs.

"So, is he over there asking your mother for your hand in marriage, then?" Nora teases.

Red overtakes Kaira's face as her blush grows. "Nora!" she cries out in reprimand before breaking into laughter. It's interactions like this that she's been missing most since leaving the camp.

"Oh, would you look at that? Mister Loverboy is making his way over. I better get going and leave you two to each other," Nora says, peering around the tent.

Kaira copies her, seeing her mother heading back to her stall as Forren makes his way back over in their direction. She tears her eyes from the sight and the emotions that threaten to rise knowing this is possibly one of the last times she'll see her mother if things go wrong.

Nora pulls her into one last hug before stepping back. "I've been telling the children you'll be back soon. You better not make me a liar."

"Never," Kaira responds, forcing a smile.

Nora looks over Kaira's shoulder as Kaira feels a familiar presence appear. Then, with one nod at Forren, Nora slips back between the rows of tents without a goodbye. It's a safeguard that they'll see each other again.

"I'm glad you caught up with your friend," Forren says, falling into step beside Kaira as she moves into action, knowing she can't stay in the camp any longer or else she'd never be moving on.

"Me too," Kaira responds, trying to keep her tone light. She opens and closes her mouth a few times, unable to find the words to ask how her mother's doing.

"She's doing well," Forren supplies, following her thoughts. "She's proud of what you're doing and says your father would be proud as well. She isn't so keen on the idea of me marrying you—"

"What?" Kaira barks, tripping over a pile of trash. She spins around as Forren catches her to see his expression. "Oh, you heard what Nora was joking about?"

Forren smiles, his eyes dancing in the sunlight as the rays glint off his golden mask. The sight of him so carefree twists Kaira's stomach into knots.

Shaking her head, Kaira spins back and begins walking.

She doesn't once look back at all she's leaving behind as she exits the camp. She'll either return to see it freed or she'll not return at all.

CHAPTER TWENTY NINE

The convoy sneaks their way through the billowing clouds of the sandstorm, the red dust swirling around them unforgivingly. A slight detour from the main roads and they'd be lost amongst the dunes and sandstone mountains forever.

"How often do you get these?" Mila exclaims as she peers over the steering wheel, attempting to gain an extra metre of sight.

"In the warm months, several times a week," Kaira answers with a shrug. "Sometimes they last a few minutes, other times they go for days."

Mila shakes her head in disbelief as she creeps the truck forwards, making sure the vehicle ahead of them stays in sight. She brushes a hand over her forehead, wiping away the sweat from the suffocating heat filling the vehicle.

The thin fabric and loose design of the outfit Kaira wears keeps her a lot cooler than the guard uniform Mila wears.

Mila comments, "Not long now."

Kaira knows what she refers to. "You said we should be reaching the city in a day or two?"

"Yep. At least, if this sandstorm doesn't get any worse," Mila says, again peering up into the sky as if she can read the weather forecast in the gatherings of the clouds.

"Will the Games go ahead in this weather?" Kaira asks.

Mila shrugs. "I imagine so. The Games have never been cancelled or postponed. The next leader of our country should be able to face any conditions, no excuses."

Kaira nods. She'd expected as much. "I hope the storm stays."

Mila's brows furrow as she bites her lip. "You wouldn't worry about Mikko fighting in it?"

Kaira smiles. "He's been the High Guard in charge of the camp since it was established. He's spent more time in these conditions than anyone else."

Mila hums. "You've got a point. And all this time I thought Mikko was putting himself at a disadvantage staying there. You know, I really didn't expect Mikko to—"

Kaira squeals as Mila tears left, avoiding the vehicle in front of them who slams on their brakes as ahead a massive fireball launches into the air. The shockwave hits the vehicle, shaking it wildly. The sound of brakes locking up permeates the air as Kaira jumps out of their small truck.

"Kaira!" Mila shouts, scrambling across the seat to follow her out the passenger door given hers is blocked by the vehicle that'd been ahead of them.

"Put something over your face!" Kaira calls out instead of halting, pushing into the red clouds towards the billowing black smoke.

Kaira slips her headscarf over her hair, bringing the sides around to cover her mouth and nose. She keeps a distance from the disaster zone in case of a second explosion, but her eyes track over the twisted metal of two intertwined trucks before moving further on. None of those trucks have as many modifications as Forren's.

A flicker in the corner of her vision brings Kaira to a halt, spinning sharply back around to the flaming wreckage. There, amongst the burning metal and limbs, is a proudly waving Keranian flag with a crown printed over the image.

"Oh god," Mila mutters as she rushes forwards, screaming orders as guards from other vehicles join them.

Frozen in place, Kaira can't do anything but stare wide-eyed as the flames are wrangled under control. The scene is a flash of colour breaking through the red clouds slowly releasing them from its clutches as guards of every level swarm the scene. The orders are shouted with cracking voices, fear clinging to the cries.

"Kaira," a voice calls from her side before a warm hand lands on her shoulder.

"The King," Kaira answers, her eyes intent on the scene before her. Those vehicles didn't have anywhere near the modifications of Mikko's truck because they weren't trucks at all. They were the King's personal cars.

Tuomas steps further into Kaira's view, their eyes watching one form moving amid the mess—Mila. She's the one person not swept up by the chaos, a clear leader keeping order. With a collected ease, Mila oversees the flames being extinguished before, after assessing the likelihood of a second explosion, she lowers herself to the sand. She shimmies her way into the wreckage, navigating over smashed glass and twisted framework until only her knees down are visible.

The waiting is tense. Nobody moves as Mila conducts her search and the silence continues as she makes her way back out and stands up. By now, the dust has left them in a clear circle that reveals as far as four vehicles on either side, the space between them filled with soldiers. Mila's eyes meet Tuomas and Kaira's with a telling look before she spins around to face the soldiers.

"The King is dead!"

Bodies fall around them as Mila's voice rings out. Guards lower to their knees, pressing their fingers to the jewels on their brows before lowering their heads to the ground. Kaira's spared the trouble of deciding whether she should follow their lead as her gaze is caught by another figure standing to the side of the wreckage. Forren.

His gaze is heavy, looking upon his sister, as she tilts her head down, pressing her chin to her chest. Forren spins away, though not fast enough for Kaira to miss the glassiness to his eyes. Her mouth falls open as she sees the same look mimicked on Mila's face as the golden guard girl spins around to face her and Tuomas again.

Kaira spins to face Tuomas too, a question on her tongue. She doesn't need to ask it, though, as his expression already answers it.

"Oh, Gods," Kaira mutters, because that's not the look siblings give each other when their suppressor is pronounced dead. That's the look siblings give each other when a disliked but still cared for parent is pronounced dead.

Forren is the King's son.

He's the son of the ruler who'd taken her country and placed her in a prisoner-of-war camp.

209

CHAPTER THIRTY

Kaira leaves the Keranians to their mourning as she shows herself away from the wreckage. In a daze, she makes it to the safety of a vehicle. She's already climbed into the front seat before she realises it isn't the vehicle she's meant to be in, Forren's instead of Mila's.

She flops down across the bench seat, burying her head deep into the cushions before bringing her arms over her. No light breaks through the tight confines and Kaira likes it that way as she breathes heavily into the darkness. Here, it feels like she can't be touched by everything happening outside of the vehicle.

Until it doesn't.

Mikko—not Forren—was out there alone. Mikko who wasn't the harsh soldier she'd thought he was when he was Forren to her. It shouldn't matter if Kaira's here reeling from the truth; Mikko's just lost his father.

But he'd kept it from her. He hasn't once hinted at who his father is. How is she meant to trust him now? Does it even matter if she did or didn't? Will the Golden Games still go ahead?

Stop it, Kaira berates herself. It doesn't matter what happens with the Golden Games, not when there are other things at hand. She pretty much promised Forren that she'd choose him over winning the Games and that means being with him now before thinking about how losing the King will affect the games. First and foremost, he's lost a father. Even if he didn't get along great with him—which Kaira presumes given the almost stricken look that'd been on his face when Mila had announced the death, the look that hinted that even he feared the fact he was feeling something for his lost father— he's still grieving.

Determined, Kaira unravels her hands and pulls herself up from the seat. Her friend needs her now more than her partner in their agreement and she'd be there for him, no matter how much it conflicts her own feelings.

Reaching for the door handle, Kaira lets out one last sigh, washing the last of her misgivings away.

"Argh!" Kaira scrambles back, feeling her muscles lock up as the door is torn open from the other side.

"Oh!" the intruder gasps, caught as much unaware. "Sorry, I'll go. I didn't mean to... Didn't know you... I, uh, yeah..." Forren stumbles out fast.

He goes to step back from the door and draw it shut, but Kaira reaches out, stalling him.

"No," she says. "It's okay. Sit."

Forren watches her carefully, tears glistening in the backs of his eyes before he casts one last glance at the scene behind him and clambers into the vehicle.

Kaira bothers to look out the window for the first time since entering the vehicle as she gives Forren space to wipe his eyes and get settled. The sandstorm has mostly passed, now just a shadow on the horizon. Back a few vehicles, masses of soldiers still lie on the ground, their faces pressed to the earth, but some are wandering around the wreckage. Mila's at the centre of it all, the eye of the tornado, a spot of composure and poise. Kaira spots Tuomas standing near her, a silent support.

"Mila's trying to find the cause of the explosion," Forren offers, keeping his gaze on the rearview mirror.

Kaira turns towards him. His hands are fisted tight in his lap, his knuckles turning white. His lips are turning the same colour as they press together, keeping something back, imprisoning it.

"I didn't even think about that," Kaira responds. Of course, it isn't enough for Mila to have to pronounce her own father's death; she's going to have to investigate it.

"They think..." Forren stalls, his eyes glancing over her and back to the mirror so fast Kaira might've missed it had she not been paying so much attention to him. "They think it might've been your people."

Kaira presses her own lips together before nodding. She knows what this means: even if there's never any clear proof, they'll still be punished for it. The treatment at the camp will only get worse; her treatment will only get worse. On that train of thought, what will happen to her now the King is dead? He'd been the one to assure she wouldn't be harmed before the end of the Games.

"You'll be okay, Kaira," Forren says, following her thoughts in that way he does. "I promise."

"For once, it's not me that I'm worried about." Kaira shuffles closer to Forren. "How—"

"Don't," Forren cuts in. "Don't ask me how I am. I don't know how I am."

He looks over at her, his lips trembling and his green eyes glassy beneath the golden mask that has slipped out of place.

"I don't know how I am," Forren repeats and, this time, the dam wall in his eyes collapses and tears flood out.

With it comes the release of his anger. At himself, at his father, at the people responsible—Kaira doesn't know.

Manically, Forren tears at his mask, discarding it carelessly on the dirty truck floor. Then, his hands go to his guard's uniform, attempting to pull off the layers suffocating him. The beautiful, golden buttons on the coat pop off, flinging across the space and tumbling into hidden spots, never to be found again. His hands fumble wildly for anything in reach, tearing up papers from the dash and throwing pens and little trinkets.

"Stop, stop, stop." Kaira grabs hold of his hands. At first the words are hurried, urgent, but they soften out, turning into a coaxing murmur that stalls Forren's anger. Her hands wrap around his wrists, pulling them to her body to use her weight to keep them imprisoned.

Kept from the physical outlet of his pain, Forren's tears fall harder, trekking down his face in long, unbroken streams. The ferocity of them reminds Kaira of the waves crashing against the cliff's edge back in the camp.

"Mikko," Kaira whispers.

Forren halts his rampage completely, going limp in her arms as he lets out huge, stuttering breaths. Kaira stays silent as she patiently waits for him to be ready.

Slowly, his breathing evens out and the tears trickle to an end. Despite the desert heat surrounding them, shivers race through Kaira's body as she gazes at the broken boy in her arms.

Forren drops his head onto Kaira's shoulder, letting her wrap her arms around him.

"I don't know whether I just imagined that or if you actually did it," Forren says sorrowfully.

"I did," Kaira responds, her racing heart calming now that Forren's more composed.

"Mhmm, it sounds nice coming from your lips."

Kaira lets the silence consume them, giving Forren the chance to speak when he feels ready to. Kaira expects him to move out of her grasp and right himself, putting back on the mask he wears even when he isn't wearing the physical one— the one that hides his true, ardent self. The self that's caring and feeling, selfless and compassionate.

"I don't know what I feel," Forren once more repeats. His fingers play with Kaira's, using the motion to ground himself.

"That's okay," Kaira responds. Her free hand plays with the curls in his hair, pulling out the knots gently.

Forren's face is red and slightly puffy, yet Kaira is still breathless from the sight of his features. Maybe the Keranian army have to wear masks because otherwise everyone would be distracted by their beauty.

"You know, don't you?" he asks, his body tensing.

"Yes."

Forren swallows, hesitating. "It isn't common knowledge that he is—was—our father. It's common for children to be raised in the barracks; many people don't even know their parents because it's like that." Forren lets out a heavy sigh. "We never had much to do with him."

Forren shifts in his spot, seeming to get more comfortable although Kaira guesses it's also to stall.

"Seeing how he ignored us yet always expected us to make him proud made me realise how twisted our concepts of family were. In contrast, I saw your country's idea of family and community and it made me believe in what your country could be. So, I understand if you cannot believe me given my father is at the top of your enemy list, but him being my father changes nothing about who I am."

"You're you, Mikko. You're not your father. My opinion should not be influenced by something you can't control. Besides, we've come too far to give up when there's a slight bump in the road. Now is the time to push—your country will

214

be in disarray. If that's the conditions under which you took control of my country as we were reeling for a new ruler, then what's to say it'll not work for taking your country?"

Forren sits up, turning to peer out the back window.

"What are you thinking about?" Kaira asks, watching with him. More soldiers have risen from the ground and are being directed by Mila. Some are studying the burned vehicles whilst others set up a safety perimeter.

"What's going to happen," Forren responds. "Mila's likely to take up the temporary ruler position, given she's the only High Guard not participating in the Games. If we can convince her to still hold the Games, then we still have hope. We have to push whilst, as you said, the country is in shock. We cannot give the people the chance to recover."

"And you?" Kaira asks.

"What?" Forren turns to her with furrowed brows.

"You lost your father, Forren, even if you didn't like him. Are you really in the right mindset to fight in the most demanding event of your country?"

Forren moves to the driver's door and opens it. "I'm more ready than ever. I don't have to betray my father now."

CHAPTER THIRTY ONE

The King's Hounds are here. The three of them pace around Mila, their giant paws digging into the sand as they sniff about the ruins of the vehicles, their lips curled in snarls to reveal teeth the size of knives.

Kaira clutches Forren's hand, as if preparing to push him in front of her at a moment's notice when the hounds turn to her. A low growl emanates from them before Mila shoots the animals a sharp look, silencing them and making them sink to the floor in submission.

"Good. You're here," Mila states matter-of-factly, pushing her hair back from her face as she watches Forren and Kaira approach.

Kaira watches her carefully, attempting to peer under the mask—literal and figurative—that's hiding her emotions. How can she be so calm even in the face of her father's death?

"What do you need me to do?" Forren asks, looking at the action around them. His eyes don't stay long on the hounds, as if their presence is completely expected.

Kaira follows his gaze. Most of the soldiers—at least those that have risen from the ground—have established a secure safety perimeter, which looks hilarious to Kaira. Do they really think there's going to be another attack? The King is dead—the mourning tradition of falling to the ground would've told anyone that—so what more is there to accomplish? A few soldiers are moving beyond that perimeter, mostly golden and blue decorated ones.

"Kaira."

Kaira spins back to Mila, raising her brow in answer to her name being called. "Yes?"

"Would you be willing to help?"

Kaira presses her lips together. She's tempted to say no, not wanting to have any part in minimising the impact of what happened, but another part of her knows she'll only delay them if she doesn't help. If she wants the Golden Games to go ahead, that isn't in her best interest.

"Yeah," Kaira responds. "So long as I'm put nowhere near the King; I might succumb to the urge to make sure he's really dead."

Kaira doesn't realise how insensitive that might be until the words fall from her lips. She clamps her hands to her mouth, her eyes going wide as she pleads with Mila—and Forren who's still standing beside her—that she didn't mean it.

Mila bursts out laughing, seeming to shock even herself as she quickly regains her composure. "Well," she says, her voice perfectly even, "there's a reason why I'm not assigning myself the duty of overseeing the procession back to the castle."

Mila's eyes slide to her brother before the corner of her mouth relaxes. The red in his cheeks visible beneath his mask shows his own struggle to maintain his composure.

Despite the seemingly good reaction the siblings had to her comment, Kaira still feels bad. She opens her mouth to apologise, but, as if anticipating what she's going to do, Mila begins speaking again.

"I want you to oversee the search party; we should find whoever is responsible and bring them to justice. Given that you know the desert best, you'd know where a group would go to wait out the sandstorm whilst hiding from us," Mila says. Kaira doesn't experience the sinking feeling in her gut at being the one to locate those responsible—likely her own people—because the tight press of Mila's lips tells Kaira of her intentions; Kaira knows where to lead the guards away from.

Kaira nods once sharply.

Mila in return gestures her head towards the group milling beyond the established perimeter. "If you're unsuccessful by nightfall or the sandstorm is coming back over, head back. You" —she points at Forren sharply— "keep the soldiers under control."

Mila leaves, walking determinedly over to another group of soldiers looking for something to do.

Kaira turns her attention to the sky, reading it to see whether it's going to bring the red cloud back over to them.

"What's your plan?" Forren asks, straightening his uniform.

Kaira shrugs, her eyes moving from the sky when she's sure they have a bit of time. "Given how the sand lays and the way the wind came through before, along with the general location we're travelling towards, the Kolt Canyons are to our left."

"So, we go right," Forren concludes.

"Yep."

They make it to the established perimeter and, with a quick gesture from Forren, they're let through. Kaira's eyes linger on the weapons strapped to the soldiers now that they're in their formal fighting gear, not just their standard decorative uniforms. The sight sends a chill down her spine; she'd almost begun to feel comfortable within their ranks. This reminds her of the real threat they are, the threat her country will be facing if the Golden Games are postponed.

If they cannot get better treatment for her people now, in the confusion of the King's murder, it's certain that the treatment of her people will get worse.

"Listen up!" Forren calls, mustering the attention of the group.

Relief washes over their faces at the sight of Forren and Kaira's washed with the realisation that she's underestimated her enemy again. She's grown so accustomed to Forren that she's forgotten how much respect he commands from his comrades.

"I know that it's unfortunate circumstances today and I applaud you for having the strength to move forwards. The most important thing right now is bringing justice and returning power to our country. Whilst it may feel like we've been bested, we'll not let them gain more in seeing us weak," Forren commands, his voice strong. It's almost possible for Kaira to forget how broken he'd been in the truck with how he is now. "We'll advance and use this situation to better ourselves in the future, make us stronger."

Cheers go up in the group, but Forren continues with his speech. "The best thing we can do is find the assailants so we can assuredly move forwards with the Games. We cannot allow a delay that'll only give time for unrest to fester within our ranks and homes."

Forren clears his throat, gesturing to Kaira. "I know some of you might be hesitant to do this, but Miss Aziz is the best chance we have at prosecuting those responsible. Yes, she's Altairian and, yes, that might make some of you uneasy, but the very fact is that she's Altairian. She knows this land better than anyone, better than I, even, who has spent the last four years in this country. As such, we'll be following what she says. Are there any problems with that?"

A few arms shoot up, the owners of the limbs gazing at Kaira with evident distaste in the curls of their lips.

Forren smiles. "Good. All you with your hands up, leave. You're clearly not willing to do whatever it takes for our country." The tone in his voice leaves no room for dispute and the few soldiers grumbling among themselves slink past Kaira. "I hope any of you that are High Guards are disappointed in yourselves. I'd recommend reconsidering participating in the Games."

Kaira looks at the group remaining, who look too cocky for their own good at having remained, reading into it as an endorsement from Forren. As they snicker at the leaving members, it's clear they're already turning on them. Even if they choose to remain participants in the Games, they'll have no allies.

Forren watches the group, feeling the same underlying prejudice as he hums to himself. "It's good to see you aren't intimidated by a little Altairian girl," Forren says with the lilt of someone accustomed to people cracking up at their jokes. Kaira picks up on the crack in his tone, however, that gives away the way he stumbles over the comment.

"Anyway," Forren says, drawing Kaira's attention back to him and not her thoughts considering why he stumbled, "I'm sure you've heard enough of my voice. I'll hand us over to Miss Aziz."

Kaira nods appreciatively, stepping up beside him. She ignores the gallop in her chest as all eyes land on her with varying emotions. She clears her throat. "Right. Well, if we want any chance of finding the assailants, we must do it before nightfall. That gives us little time—a few hours at max—to search, ruling out sequentially searching all directions."

"Can you count?" a voice calls from the crowd. Forren steps forwards again, ready to berate them. Quickly, the voice continues in a tone clearly meant to appease the guard at Kaira's side, "What I meant is that there are enough of us; we can split into groups."

Forren opens his mouth to say something, but Kaira gets in first. She appreciates him being ready to stand up for her, but she can do it herself. "Only people who have lost their minds would ever split up in the desert," she explains in a belittling tone. "Go ahead if you don't mind being the perfect example of a silly goose."

The group lets out a small chuckle at the expense of their friend, but it's quick to die down as they realise they're laughing at something Kaira said.

Once the silence has been reinstated, Kaira speaks again. "Now, as I was saying, we can only comprehensively search in one direction. There are huge canyons in that direction." Kaira points to one side. "Who thinks we should go that way?"

There are a few muttered "obviously" statements as all hands in the group go up.

"Wrong," Kaira says sharply. "Unlike you might've assumed, we're not within the canyon. We're at the top of it. If you'd blindly went there in this visibility, I wonder how many of you would've met the bottom in a nasty manner. Again, only insane people would choose that direction." But, of course, the people that pull off killing the Kerani King within the midst of every high-ranking soldier are insane. They'd have no issue finding one of the few paths that'd lead them down into the depths.

"So," Kaira says, "we're going in the opposite direction. Now, we've wasted enough time with your foolishness, so I want you to get into pairs and make a line. Hurry up."

Surprisingly, Forren doesn't have to repeat the order. With red cheeks from their reprimanding, the soldiers follow her command.

Forren turns to Kaira, wiping sweat from his brow. "I'm sorry about the comment I made," he says, his green eyes glimmering behind the golden frame of his mask.

"You were keeping their respect." Kaira shrugs. "I mightn't know much about the Games, but I know enough to know that if you go in without any allies, you won't be coming back out."

Forren opens his mouth, likely to say that he's still sorry, even if it was well reasoned, but Kaira silences him with a look before turning back to the guards.

"It's nice to see that you aren't so incompetent as being unable to follow such simple orders," Kaira says, raising her brows. "Now, move out. If you see any signs of people or possible evidence, call out 'halt'."

"Yes, boss," one of the guards calls out, bringing a few laughs from their friends.

Kaira doesn't bother responding as she waves her hand impatiently, getting them to move along.

"How are we planning on doing this?" she mutters as the group moves off. She refers not just to keeping the group away from the canyons, but also winning the Games and re-establishing the way things once were.

"One step at a time, Kaira. One step at a time," Forren responds, exaggeratedly taking steps forwards.

Kaira looks over at him, meeting his gaze and the solid belief that's there. She nods, closing her eyes and breathing in the dry air around her. "One step at a time," she repeats.

CHAPTER THIRTY TWO

———— + ✳ ✳ ✳ + ————

"Over here!" an urgent voice calls out, drawing Kaira's attention.

Her head shoots up, pulling her eyes away from the red sand. Above them, the sun shines brightly, burning their skins.

Kaira pushes into a run as Forren does too. By the time they make it to the Keranian soldier who'd called out, the rest of their group is already there.

"Move out of the way," Forren demands, making the crowd part. Kaira follows him, acutely aware of the tensing of his back as he looks at what's drawn the attention.

A shiver runs down her spine. Had she been wrong about the direction the attackers might go?

"What is it?" she asks as she steps beside Forren and squats, her own eyes taking in the scene. There, stark in the sand, is a printed mark of a foot—or at least what looks like one. A laugh bubbles up her throat before she can stop it and Forren, along with the rest of the soldiers, look at her with concern.

"Well?" Kaira asks. "What are you waiting for? We must be going in the right direction."

The soldiers spring to their feet, separating back into their pairs. Excitement courses through their bones as they murmur in hurried whispers.

"Kaira," Forren asks, turning to her as the soldiers move further away. "We should be coming up with some reason to lead them back. We can't let them have any chance of capturing anyone, even if from the softer edges of the footprint it seems like it was made a little while ago."

Kaira spins away from him, looking back over the direction they came from. The ruins of the procession are completely out of sight, though the imprint of the explosion still lingers in the colours of the sunset beginning to illuminate the desert plains.

"Look at the mark, Forren. As you said, it has soft edges." Kaira feels a smile pulling up the corner of her lip as the concern on his face only grows. "Other than hope and the need to do something in the wake of the King's demise, there's nothing suggesting that's a footprint. Do you see any toe shapes? Shoe marks? Do you know anyone with a foot that big?"

Forren's face relaxes as he begins to catch on to what she's saying. "So, you mean..."

"Yep. That mark's nothing more than where the sand laid funny during the sandstorm, happening by pure chance to take the form of a rough oval."

"You're certain about this?" Forren asks. "If we're wrong..."

"I've lived in the desert my whole life, Forren. I know how to read marks in the sand as well as I know the back of my hand."

"So, we're in the safe, then?" Forren asks, his face finally relaxing.

"Eh, not quite," Kaira says, the skin between her brows scrunching up. "We've got one mega sandstorm rolling our way and I don't know how we're going to pull these soldiers in after dangling success in their faces."

Forren's green eyes follow Kaira's sight as she looks up to the sky. In defeat, he sighs. "How long do we have before we need to be heading back?"

"An hour at absolute max and that'd be travelling the last few kilometres in darkness. It'd be almost impossible to assess then whether the sandstorm might catch us before we reach the vehicles."

"Looks like we better get moving."

Forren leads the way, spinning on the heel of his boot to make his way towards the soldiers under his command.

Kaira draws in a deep breath, praying to her gods that they hold back the storm long enough. With one final look at the darkening sky, she pulls her headscarf further over her face and follows Forren.

The wind howls across the plains, bringing the start of the storm as specks of sand prick their skin. For the last half-hour of walking, Kaira has kept a hand steadily gripping Forren's upper arm out of fear he might accidentally take a few too many steps away from her and get lost. She can't say that concern extends to the other soldiers.

It seems they at least keep some of their senses about them even in the face of their intense desire to bring the perpetrators to justice. Slowly, their ranks have closed in, until now they walk in one steady line, their shoulders brushing together.

Their backs are hunched, the excitement of the earlier find sapped out of them as they too can now read the sky that so clearly displays its anger.

Kaira hopes their dejection is enough to convince them to turn back. How far does their loyalty to the King, even when dead, really run?

"It's time," Kaira says steadily.

Forren gives her a sharp nod before calling out to his men. "Halt!" The ease in which the soldiers do so is admirable. "It's too late to continue and, as you've noticed, the sandstorm is coming back. It's going to be impossible to find anything in these conditions, so we'll be turning back."

Mutters of disapproval go through the crowd, but no one works up enough courage to say anything out loud.

"Let's go," Forren orders. Abruptly, he spins on his heel, beckoning Kaira to follow, which she does easily.

"They aren't following," Kaira says once they're a few paces ahead.

Even in the low lighting she can see Forren shrug before he responds, "So be it. I wouldn't mind some of my competition perishing before the Games."

"You'll just leave your men to fend for themselves?" Kaira asks.

"I'm not the one abandoning them. I gave them an order and they're the ones refusing to follow it. Besides, it won't take them long to realise that they have no chance of surviving these conditions without your expertise."

As if on cue, the soldiers stomp after them. Forren ignores the disgruntled rumblings, keeping his pace with his head held high.

Kaira follows his lead, ignoring the prickles tingling her back. Oh, how much has changed in so little time that she's willingly presenting her back to her enemy and walking side by side with one of them.

She's always dreamed of getting to walk freely over her land once more, but playing a part in chasing the freedom of her people is beyond anything she could've ever imagined. After all, she was just herself. Just little old Kaira who liked reading and teaching children. And she's still that person—she's just become so much more.

"What do you look so happy about?" Forren asks, making sure the soldiers don't overhear.

"Everything," Kaira says with a shrug. "What isn't there to be happy about when there's the possibility of everything gloomy in my life being corrected?"

CHAPTER THIRTY THREE

The cool desert night has effectively swamped them by the time the awaiting vehicles come into sight, their headlights the guiding lights home for the soldiers trudging along behind Kaira and Forren.

A figure stands assuredly in front of one of the lights, a second shadowing them around the edge of the vehicle. Kaira beelines for them, leaving Forren to follow her as the rest of the soldiers break away to find their own vehicles.

"I was beginning to wonder if I'd have to send a search party out." Mila huffs as the pair come to a stop before her. "Anything?"

"The soldiers found a footprint" —Kaira places emphasis on the word to disagree with the fact— "in the sand they believe to belong to the perpetrators. We followed the direction until it was unsafe to do so."

"I see. Do you think it's worthwhile to send out another party in the morning?" Mila asks as another figure, illuminated hauntingly by the headlights that stretch their shadow out into the night, makes their way towards them.

"So long as the storm has passed, I can see no harm in doing so," Kaira answers as the figure parks themself next to Mila.

"What do you want, Charlie?" Mila grumbles, turning to the newcomer.

"We need to be moving out right away, ma'am, if we want to reach Burgeston before the storm hits again," the newcomer offers, wringing their hands together.

"Right, let me finish this conversation and then we'll be moving along," Mila says. "You know what, why don't you meet Kaira—"

Mila breaks off as a steely silence washes over the group. Kaira's whole body locks up as Charlie turns to face them.

No. No, this can't be. This isn't fair. This can't be true.

"Kaira?" Forren asks, his hand landing on her shoulder.

Kaira shakes her head, clearing her mind of thoughts as she stares at the newcomer who has had much the same reaction as her, their body frozen mid-turn towards her.

"No," Kaira mutters, feeling her whole body give out as she hits the sand. Forren only just manages to break the fall.

"Kaira," he says more forcefully. "Kaira, what's wrong?"

"No. No. No," Kaira mutters more urgently, shaking her head harder as if it'll take her back in time.

"Kaira."

That one voice is enough to break through the moment, making Kaira pause before she lifts her head to meet Charlie's gaze. He has dark brown hair that's now greying and wears thick glasses hiding brown eyes so similar to her own.

"Why are you here?" Kaira asks, her disbelief churning in her gut so much it begins to form into something else: anger. Red hot anger that has her steeling her jaw and pushing to her feet, slapping away Forren's hands as he tries to steady her.

"You were dead!" Kaira screams, not caring as Mila jumps back in fright. "They shot you. They shot you and you were dead." The first tear falls, splattering hard onto her cheek.

"I wasn't, Kaira. I was never dead. I..." Charlie stalls, swallowing before he pushes on. "I had to make you believe that so you'd leave. I thought I was dying, Kaira, and I was never going to let you die right by me. If I was dead, you'd keep fighting. That's all I ever needed you to do: keep fighting."

"Then why aren't you dead?"

"They captured me. They knew who I was and" —his eyes dart from Kaira to Forren— "they took me to be healed so they could...use me. Use my knowledge."

"You were alive this whole time," Kaira mutters, her voice no higher than a whisper. Charlie—Carlisle, to Kaira—nods dejectedly, knowing what's coming next. "So, why did you never come after me?"

Is fate so rude as to give Kaira back her father the very day Forren loses his?

Kaira leaves her father standing there, shock still covering his features. Forren guides her to his truck. Kaira opens her mouth a few times to tell him to bugger off, but she can't find the strength to.

She'd always imagined this moment. Always dreamed of reuniting with her father and feeling like everything was complete. So, why doesn't she feel the happiness she'd always dreamed of now? Why does it feel like a betrayal?

Forren opens the truck door, steadying Kaira with a hand on her lower back as she scrambles into it. She collapses over the length of the bench seat, letting her hair cover her face as more tears begin to fall.

The bench seat squishes as Forren hops into the truck behind her, drawing his door shut.

"How long has he been working with Mila for?" Kaira asks, using her sleeve to wipe away the snot falling steadily from her nose. Forren offers forwards a handkerchief. She takes it, sitting up to stare out the front window.

"Since I...I captured him," Forren says, shifting uncomfortably in his spot.

"What has he been doing?"

"I think you should be asking him these questions."

"I asked you, Forren," Kaira states sharply.

Forren sighs. "He's been our main source of knowledge about Altair since he was captured early into the conquest—"

"I know that," Kaira cuts in sharply. "He's my father. You don't have to tell me the moment I thought he died. What did he do under Mila's command?"

"The prisoner-of-war camp was his idea," Forren responds. "We'd initially planned to eliminate all Altairians, but he argued that we could keep you in the camp and use you as forced labour. Once the King had that idea in his head, it was full steam ahead. Within two months the camp had been established and, by the end of the year, everyone was in there."

"He did that to us," Kaira mutters. "He took away this freedom I've been fighting. It was never you that did anything; it was him." Kaira pushes her lips together as if to hold back the flood of words she wants to let out.

Hesitantly, Forren asks, "Does this change anything?"

Is this the thing that'll break their plans of winning the Golden Games?

"No. I'm going to show him all that he's taken from us."

231

CHAPTER THIRTY FOUR

———— ···· + ✳ ✺ ✳ + ···· ————

Kaira sleeps through the night, her mind running circles planning everything she'd say to her father. It'll all wait until the Golden Games are won, though. For when the freedom of her people is assured and the truth of everything he took from them is stark.

Turns out, she also sleeps the whole day. And the night after that as well. By the time Forren shakes her awake, the scenery around them has completely changed.

Instead of flat desert plains, they're within the ruins of a large city that spans as far as the eye can see. Before them is a towering sandstone building, the only thing remaining upright and mostly untouched from the conquest. The building is shaped as a circle, with the first two floors decorated with open archways. Sitting above this are three domes whilst four decorative columns mark the perimeter of the land upon which the palace sits. Because that's what the structure was: the Royal Fortress of Erasme. Despite it being monotone in its shades of yellow, its beauty is undeniable and Kaira gawks at it regardless of having seen it multiple times in the past.

There's an unshakeable energy in the air as soldiers emerge from the vehicles surrounding them. Kaira's surprised that none of them head straight for the structure, instead wandering around the perimeter of the building.

"Where are they going?" Kaira asks, turning to face Forren who'd silently been letting her take in the sight.

"Buckle up, little birdie," he replies. "The first event of the Golden Games is about to begin."

After following the bustling crowd, Kaira's allowed her first sight of the arena within which the Games will take place.

It's a large circle complex made of sandstone blending into the surroundings. They pass under the arch entryway, beneath the sharp teeth of the gate that's currently lifted, coming out into the centre of a field. Packed dirt and sand makes up the ground and lifting into the sky are rows upon rows of elevated steps. Already hundreds of soldiers are crowded into the seats, jostling with excitement as the colours of their uniforms glint in the sunlight falling over the scene.

Directly across from the entryway is a tall boxy building. At its peak, at the height of the rest of the seating, is a glass windowed room protected from the elements. Behind the glass, it's just possible to see lounges and extravagant decorations; it's where the King was meant to observe the event.

Kaira turns back to Forren, drawing his eyes back to her and away from the jail-like cells that Kaira hasn't noticed sit under the end building. "What happened with the King's body?" she asks.

"Mila arranged to transport him back to Kerani lands." Forren shrugs, as if he's given little thought to it. He jolts suddenly, startling Kaira as he digs into his pockets. "I brought this in case you wanted to put it back on." He offers forwards a piece of chain jewellery—the forehead piece Kaira's been wearing.

"Just so you know, it won't hurt my feelings if you decide not to wear it," Forren laughs as Kaira doesn't make a move to grab it, still startled from the sudden change in topic. "I mean, really there's no point as it offers you little protection. I doubt my sister will be ordering your murder before the conclusion of the Games. After that, you'll either be protected for life or...it'll do little."

Just as Forren pulls it back, accepting her not taking it, Kaira reaches for it. "Help me put it on?" she asks.

Forren smiles, his green eyes dancing behind his recently polished mask.

Is it so easy for him to be carefree after everything that's happened? Kaira wonders as she tilts her head down to let him place the jewellery on her.

As soon as the main jewel slips between her brows, Forren steps away, taking a deep bow that has Kaira giggling. "Well, my lady, this is where we part ways, for I must go win us a country."

With one last smile, he slips into the crowd, heading towards the central building that towers over the scene. Kaira spins around, almost running face first into Tuomas.

"Oh gosh, how long have you been standing there?" Kaira gasps, holding a hand to her chest.

"Don't worry, not long. Whatever secrets you were sharing with your lover are very much safe with me." Tuomas smiles teasingly before gesturing with a tilt of their head to the stadium seating. "Let's go find a spot, hey?"

"What's the first event?" Kaira asks as she follows, a pep in her step. Surely on a day like today nothing can go wrong. The sun's shining. Her country's welcoming her. Her heart is...still reeling over the fact her father is alive.

Kaira sighs. Everything's going to be fine. She must focus on the Games before she can think about her father.

"You should know Mila would never give away such information so freely. She's going to make it into the spectacle it deserves to be," Tuomas answers. "It begins in an hour. The participants won't find out until they get on the field."

"But she didn't even tell..."

"Nope. Mila plays fair and square. Everyone knows that and, even if they didn't, they have enough trust that she hasn't had the opportunity to tell Mikko considering they've not seen each other for reasons other than dealing with the King's death since she took over as regent."

Tuomas squeezes past the crowd and the second they find a gap just big enough for them both to sit on the stone steps, they slip in, patting the seat next to them for Kaira to sit.

Kaira does so and, looking out over the arena, she takes a deep breath. This is it.

"Popcorn?"

Kaira looks over at Tuomas, who offers out a box of the white pieces coated in what looks to be double the amount of salt. She digs her hand into the box. "Thanks."

There's silence all around. Encasing. Consuming. Compelling.

Suddenly, it's broken by the toot of a trumpet and the echoing beat of a drum. Instantly, the atmosphere is electric. The crowd, which has settled down and found their seats, rise to their feet, shouts of support being called out as one by one the competing High Guards march out onto the field, their golden decorations glinting.

Forren is the last to be called and Kaira cannot claim it's only the addition of hers and Tuomas' voices that have the noise increasing as much as it does.

Kaira watches as Forren's eyes scan the crowd, landing almost instantly on her as if he knows how to seek her out no matter the barriers between them. His next wave is for her.

As the competing soldiers—less than thirty of them—line up in the centre of the field, the crowd again goes silent, awaiting what comes next.

"Kaira," Tuomas says with a sharp nudge of their elbow.

Kaira follows the gesture of their head, turning to stare at the tall building's opening. Her gaze manages to focus in time for her to catch as two brilliant red and golden feathered birds take flight from the rooftop.

The majestic animals soar out over the crowd before entwining with the golden soldiers, twisting through their ranks. Then, with the attention of the whole arena on them, they fly to the top of the prominent sandstone structure.

Now, within the window, is a sight just as stunning. In a tight fitting red sequined dress, Mila stands. Kaira peeks at Tuomas, watching drool fall from their lip.

"Fellow citizens of Kerani," Mila's voice rings out, projected by some hidden system, "and, of course, our esteemed guests. Welcome to the Golden Games! In the wake of recent events, it's pertinent that the next ruler of our country is declared. In addition, let it not be forgotten that that's not the only prize this year."

The crowd is enthralled, waiting on the edge of their seats. The same energy buzzes through Kaira's system, even though she should be nervous. This is the fate of her country, after all.

"The conclusion of these Games will also crown the next ruler of Altair. The opportunities with this are endless as it'll be their choice whether Altair remains an independent country or whether they join our empire." Mila leaves a moment of pause; the only sound heard is the ruffling of the two birds' wings. "There will be three rounds for these Games. Without further ado, you have one hour; don't lose your blood."

And with so simple instructions, the Golden Games begin.

Forren's the fastest to move, taking out the soldier on his right side with one of his swords before moving out of reach. He takes a position outside of the immediate fighting ring, content with watching his opponents as they eliminate each other. By the time Kaira draws her eyes away from him to watch the other competitors, another five have already been eliminated, clutching bloodied wounds. They make their way to the jail-like cells in defeat.

In the crowd, murmurs and jeers flood the air, as buddies whisper, 'told you so', and others mourn the loss of the fighter they're backing. The mix of weapons is expansive: swords, axes, spears. One of the eliminated soldiers even had a bow and arrow, though they'd quickly gone down before getting far enough away to use their weapon.

A cheer goes up through the arena, cutting over the sound of weapons clashing. With the dust of the movements clouding the air, it takes Kaira a while to see the source of the cheer. The sight of it rolls Kaira's stomach.

A Keranian guard had fallen dead.

And the soldiers in the crowd once standing by their side, fighting with them, had cheered at their demise.

Kaira's eyes glance up to the on-looking glass room, searching for Mila's reaction. She makes no move and it tells Kaira everything she needs to know. This is just the way of the Games.

You win or you lose.

Kaira's eyes fall back to the dusty grounds. The soldiers are moving carelessly around their fallen comrade, who's been joined by more. Her fingers twiddling nervously in her lap, Kaira continues to search the field. *Where is he? Where is he?*

There. Forren stands in the shadows of the building. He's taken on a different approach to the other competitors, who were out to get as much blood as possible, as if that's the decider of the winners and not who's left standing at the end of the time.

Kaira takes a deep breath. At least Forren's pretty much guaranteed to survive this round. So long as nobody particularly seeks to find him, he's hidden in the shadows; out of view, out of mind.

But what about the following rounds?

CHAPTER THIRTY FIVE

The hour passes quickly. Once half of the contestants have been eliminated, either making their way to the cells or meeting the after-life gods, the fighting slows. It's by no means any less deadly—anyone who'd not trained under the Kerani's strict program would've easily succumbed—but the fighters become more evenly paired.

For the final ten minutes, Tuomas' hand has been tightly clenching Kaira's, their popcorn long forgotten. The crowd had gone quiet but is once again picking up in tension as it's debated what the next round will be and when. Most are betting on it coming straight after, whilst the fighters are exhausted.

Kaira flinches before relief floods her as the two fire birds dive bomb towards the arena, signalling the end of the round.

The remaining soldiers back away from their competitors, some hand shaking each other in a dramatic change of tone.

"And with that, eight soldiers remain standing." Mila's confident voice echoes around the stadium in the falling silence.

Kaira's eyes jump back from the girl to the scene before her. Her eyes seek Forren, who's making his way confidently from the shadows, as other soldiers dressed in mostly blues enter the arena. In groups they carry large wooden structures that have one central wall with a rectangle window cut out of the middle. There are supporting structures on the four edges to keep it upright when it's set into the dirt. There are seven in total.

Each remaining competitor is directed to stand on one side of the wall in their designated structure.

"...and with all that said, it's my joy to announce the second round of the Golden Games."

Kaira shoots her head up, realising that Mila has been droning on about the traditions of the Games.

"This round will test integrity, moral and honour as presented before you will be three prisoners. You'll have as much time as needed to interview each and decide on their fate. At the end of the challenge, it'll be revealed what sentence each has been formally charged with. If you've picked the same, you'll remain in the Games." There's a suspenseful pause as Mila lets the rules sink in. "Let the Games proceed."

The jail-cell like enclosures on the floor-level of the arena open and an array of guards in their neatly pressed uniforms are juxtaposed to the ragged prisoners being led across the field.

Kaira watches, her body almost numb as she takes in the torn and bloody clothing of the prisoners. They aren't just any prisoners tied up and dragged along, fighting the whole way. No, they're from Akuma.

A hand pulls Kaira's into their grasp and she lets out a breath at the calming touch.

"This round is basically set up for failure," Tuomas says.

"Why?" Kaira asks, letting them take her mind off the sight of the prisoners as they're separated in groups of three before each stall.

"Our legal system is about as consistent as the Altairian weather," Tuomas says with a huff of disapproval. "There's no way you could ever figure out what their sentences are as it depends on what mood the judge was in at the time."

"So, how's Forren meant to win?"

"Well, you mightn't be able to figure out what the prisoner's sentence is by interviewing them here, but if you'd taken the time to get to know the prisoners under your care..." Tuomas trails off.

"Then you'd already know what their sentence is. This isn't about seeing how fair you are and how much you know the Kerani laws; this is about how much attention to detail you pay in completing your job," Kaira finishes.

Tuomas' nod confirms she's right.

Kaira's brows furrow. How much attention could Forren have paid given he gave up serving in Akuma prison to oversee the camp? She doesn't get the time to ask Tuomas before the prisoners are deposited before Forren and her mind goes to other things.

She watches him nod once at the prisoners before he picks up his piece of paper and scribbles down a few sentences. Then, before the rest of the guards have even begun questioning their inmates, his hand goes up in the air.

With a loud squawk, one red bird soars up into the sky. Kaira gasps as it looks like it's going to fly right into the burning sun before it seamlessly changes directions and dive bombs for Forren's answer sheet.

The bird grasps the paper in its outstretched claws and flies back to the main structure, where it disappears around the edge and out of sight. Its friend has also disappeared.

Kaira turns her attention away. Her eyes glance over Forren, who's proudly leaning against his stall as his prisoners are led away, before studying the remaining golden guards.

It seems they all have the interrogation training that Forren does—not that he'd needed to use it. The guards bark out quick questions, leaning through the little windows to get in the faces of the prisoners, who are unable to move away given they're chained to the walls. But even with the intimidation tactics, the prisoners don't cower. They stand stoic and indomitable, giving little answers. As much training as the guards have received in interrogating, the prisoners have learned in avoiding the questioning.

Kaira presses her hands into tight fists as the questioning goes on. The heat is beginning to weigh down on them now, pooling sweat and searing their skin.

As if reading her mind, Tuomas stands and gestures for her to follow. "Let's get water."

Kaira pushes to her feet and accompanies them as they slip between the rest of their row. The crowd looks in even worse shape than Kaira: their hair sticking to their heads with sweat, sand clinging to their pink-tinged skin. Still, it doesn't seem to be hampering their excitement.

Making her way through the hundreds of people, it's impossible to forget what this is. This isn't just entertainment. This isn't just guards training. This is the naming of a ruler.

Kaira shakes away the thoughts as she focuses on keeping up with Tuomas, who's found a gap in the crowd and is slipping away from view. She can just see their fluffy blonde hair over the other guards.

By the time Kaira catches up, they're standing in line at one of the food and drink stalls that Kaira's failed to notice. They're only a metre away from the wooden fence that holds the masses from tumbling into the arena.

Kaira peers over the edge, her eyes trying to calculate the new position they're in to find Forren. All there is in the place he was before, though, is the empty wooden stall. *Where did he go?*

A large shoulder bumps into Kaira, knocking her into the rough sandstone wall at her side.

"Sorry—" the voice goes to say, before they abruptly cut off. The large, burly, green-decorated guard lets out a huff of breath before turning his attention from her.

Suddenly, a hand reaches out and clasps the soldier by the fabric at their neck. Kaira turns her attention to Tuomas, who even though they're much smaller than the other guard, is almost lifting him from the ground. They put enough pressure on his neck to make the green guard turn red in the face.

"Apologise to her," Tuomas orders sharply, tightening their fist.

The other guard looks for a second like he's going to argue but the serious look in Tuomas' stormy blue eyes has him lowering his head and muttering an apology.

Tuomas lets him go with a sharp thrust that has the guard stumbling a few feet into the fence.

"Don't speak like that again or I'll be reporting you. Got it, Guard Redfern?" Tuomas questions.

The green guard, Guard Redfern, looks slightly surprised for a second that Tuomas knows his name, but he simply nods and mumbles under his breath, "Yes, sir."

Tuomas nods sharply before Kaira feels their eyes fall on her. "Are you okay?" they ask.

"Nothing I'm not used to," Kaira responds with a shrug.

"Well, not for much longer, right?" Tuomas says.

As if agreeing with their words, a loud screech comes from the sky. Kaira looks up, using a hand to block the sun, as both fire-red birds alight from their perches right above them, as it turns out the wall Kaira had been pushed into is the main building from which Mila has been publicising.

Kaira's head follows the path of the birds, like their gleaming colours are a magnet her eyes are drawn to. They sweep in and collect the rest of the papers.

The crowd goes silent, feeling like a shaken soda can about to explode. Everything's moving too fast. How can they already be so close to the final round? At this rate, the trip to Erasme took longer than the Games themselves.

"Tuomas," Kaira asks, turning to them urgently. "How bad is the final round going to be?"

Tuomas grimaces, having the same realisation as her. Surely, even if this round was meant for failure, a decent portion of the guards will be left. What will be expected of those left to fight for that final spot? Where is the bloodshed, the stress, the high tension that Forren has been preparing her for? This has all been too easy.

"Alright, Kerani!" Mila's voice breaks through the silence like a knife. "Let's see what the results of this round are."

The hush seems to intensify as the sound of paper being sorted through echoes around the arena. It's a soft sound but holds all the power of the roar of waterfalls. Then, it's broken by a soft release of air and an indiscernible whisper from Mila.

"It's my pleasure to announce that two candidates will be progressing to the final round!"

Kaira's breath catches in her throat. She grips onto the nearest thing to her—the railing of the fence—as it feels like her legs give out. A final, deadly fight between a group seemed formidable, but, somehow, this is worse. This will be one against one. This will be the determination of each butting against the other, fighting with their last wish to the end.

"Now, where would the fun be without a grand final reveal?" Mila says. Kaira forces herself to let out a breath. Surely Mila wouldn't be so carefree if Forren hadn't made it to the next round. Or could her breath of relief be because he hadn't and is safe from what's to come? "Contestants, you may make your way back to your allocated residences. If you're progressing, you'll find everything you need for the final round there. We'll see you back here at sunset."

There's a short tick of silence before the arena breaks out. As one, the crowd surges up, falling out of the stands and flooding the main gates to disperse into the ruins of the city.

Kaira stays in place, watching as the competitors exit the arena and go into their little cells, which must lead back to their residences.

A hand lands on her shoulder and she plummets back to reality. Kaira spins and faces Tuomas, who offers forwards an icy drink.

"If you don't tell anyone," they begin, switching to her language, "I might be able to sneak you back to find Forren."

"Is that a good idea?" Kaira asks, though already she's wringing her hands in anticipation.

"When have you ever shied away from a bad one?" Tuomas smirks. "Surely it hasn't been all good ideas that have led to you standing here in the middle of the Kerani army about to see the next ruler crowned."

"You've got me there," Kaira replies, smiling back at them and, finally, taking the proffered drink. "So, how are we going to achieve infiltrating the future ruler's accommodations?"

"Watch and learn."

CHAPTER THIRTY SIX

Turns out, there isn't much sneaking needed. Tuomas leads Kaira from the arena before following the outside of the circular structure. Just before they make it to the opposite side, marked by the tall building, they pull to a stop.

Kaira looks around. Other than the sandstone wall of the arena, there isn't much: a few ruined buildings, piles of sand that have built up over time and a few twiggy bushes adding to the abandoned feel.

Then, Tuomas pushes against the wall and the bricks slide inward, opening to a hallway built beneath the stands of the arena. Kaira lets out a hum of appreciation and follows them in, ducking her head to pass through before pushing the bricks back into place.

The air tastes of sand, thick and gritty in their throats. It's also stiflingly hot, even more so than outside. As they make their way down the shadowed corridors, torches light the way. Their footsteps echo through the space, sounding like drums being beaten before war. Those drums were one of the last sounds Kaira heard before everything in her life turned into a nightmare. By the time her village was reached, it'd already been said that the Capital had fallen.

It doesn't take long before Tuomas is again pushing against the wall at a seemingly random spot before it opens into another room. Within, it appears to be a spacious living room, furnished with a lounge and, in the corner, a wardrobe and a bed that can be folded down from the wall.

"Mila, I told you it wouldn't be a good idea to come—" The voice suddenly cuts off as the person emerging from the room to their left—a bathroom—sees them. "Oh."

Forren finishes pulling on a fresh shirt, ruffling his wet hair, before he walks over to the lounge and sinks down onto it. Even with how familiar the sight is to her now, Kaira still startles at seeing him without his golden mask on.

"I didn't expect you to come by," Forren says casually, as if he isn't one round away from being crowned the ruler of two countries.

Kaira's eyes glance around the room, attempting to look for some object that'd tell her Forren has made it through, but nothing looks out of place.

"It's a uniform," Forren states.

Kaira looks over at him as Tuomas asks, "What?"

"It's a uniform," Forren says again. Kaira knows he's answering what she's thinking. "It's the thing we'll need for the next round."

"Holy crap, you actually made it?" Tuomas exclaims, practically launching over the lounge to tackle Forren into a hug.

Forren laughs, fluffing up Tuomas' already unruly hair. "You should have a little more faith in me, man."

"Congrats, I suppose?" Kaira says as he looks up at her over the lounge. She doesn't really know what else to say. It feels bizarre to be here, to be this close to their dreams. It's like she never fully expected that they'd make it here.

"I know how you feel," Forren says, straightening up as he pushes Tuomas off him. "I...I don't know how I expected it to be, but this feels...too calm. I expected more: more pressure, more energy, more anticipation. But, instead, it feels like...whatever happens is what's meant to happen, like what I do doesn't even matter. Which is ridiculous because I'm literally one of the final two standing and everything comes down to this."

Despite Forren's outwardly composed appearance, his tirade reveals his anxiety.

"Have you eaten enough?" Tuomas asks, also sensing Forren's overthinking. "You're going to need your energy."

Forren gestures over to a desk in the corner that's laden with food. "I've already consumed half of that. You guys can have some if you like."

Kaira wants to—her aching stomach begs her to—but she fears whatever the next round is will see all of it making a reappearance.

"Do you know what the next round is? What does the uniform look like?" Kaira asks, ignoring the irritated look Tuomas shoots her at having drawn Forren's attention back to what's possibly his impending doom.

The door slams open before Forren can respond. Mila stands in its midst looking frazzled.

"Get out," she barks at Kaira and Tuomas.

There's no refusing her as she stares them down, her eyes holding an anger reflected in the red gown she wears. Forren stands to meet his sister. Tuomas copies his action, walking to the door as Mila strides into the room.

Kaira hesitates, but before she can second guess herself, she launches at Forren. She pulls him into a hug, burying her head into his shoulder as his strong arms come around her.

"Stay alive for me," Kaira says before forcing herself to pull away from him.

Before he has a moment to say anything, she leaves, letting the heavy bricks fall back into place behind her as she begins up the corridor with Tuomas keeping pace at her side.

"That can't be good, can it?" Kaira asks, her voice a whisper in the shadows.

Tuomas' silence is her answer.

CHAPTER THIRTY SEVEN

—— ······ + ✳ ✳ ✳ + ······ ——

The pair end up distracting themselves—well, attempt to—by wandering the ruined city. Kaira spurts out random facts about the place, her culture and her people at Tuomas' prompting, but she's embarrassed by how little she really knows. She'd only come to the Capital for cultural events or similar.

Looking at the ruins only makes the impending moment more heightened. The few parts of structures that remain upright, which are mostly the decorated arch doorways that once led to welcoming shops and warm homes, evoke memories of what life was like before the conquest. The juxtaposition of that to the army that crawls around the structures, lazing on the remains with drinks in hand, sticks out sharp in Kaira's mind.

Even if Forren wins, how long will it take to rebuild all that has been lost? And that isn't just talking about the physical structures. There are years of cultural, emotional and social damage that can't be repaired with the naming of a better ruler.

"Come on, we should be heading back," Tuomas says gently, breaking into her thoughts.

Reluctantly, Kaira draws her eyes away from a building she can only tell once stood there by the purple pole with a blue star atop it that stands in the space, having refused to topple and succumb. It's one of the most recognisable symbols for her people. It signifies a House of Worship for the Goddess of Kinship and Community.

With her heart feeling like it's drowning in her chest, Kaira follows Tuomas towards the towering arena, that even in its sandstorm form stands out like a sore thumb. It doesn't belong here amongst the ruins of her country.

When they make it back, it's already filling up, but Tuomas is quick to spy a free length of step in the front row. Here, they have a clear view beyond the fence to the arena.

The crowd is alive with excitement and elation. Last minute bets are being placed and murmurs about what the last task might involve are being discussed. Nobody expects anything less than a fight to the death. They just like fantasising about what else might be added: different beasts, weapon restrictions, the taking away of senses by blindfolds or other means.

"It's time," Tuomas murmurs from her side.

Kaira raises her gaze to the glass lookout on the towering building, but she can't see Mila within it.

The arena suddenly goes quiet as if in response to some unknown signal and the girl in question strides out into the field. Now, she's dressed in a different golden and red gown that's somehow even more breathtaking than the last. It's designed as an ode to her country's flag, with a dragon wrapping its way down her body.

"Now, you all know what comes next in the Golden Games," Mila announces, her voice clearer and more powerful than it'd been when she was standing in the glass room. "From a young age, you train to become a High Guard to have the honour of participating in the Golden Games, even whilst knowing it might end in you giving your life. A fight to the death has traditionally been the final round to the Games, but being able to beat the person at your side is not the only skill you need in a war. As such, this round has been designed to test this, as

251

more important than being able to best the finest soldiers Kerani offers is being able to work with them."

Mila pauses to let a silence settle over the arena. Kaira clenches her fists at her side. She just needs to know who Forren will be battling, though she doesn't know what difference that'll really make considering she doesn't know the other soldiers well enough to judge their ability. She should've studied them in her spare time during their travels.

"So," Mila continues, "this final round will have two parts; the two contestants will pair up to take down a common enemy before they're allowed to turn on each other and crown the winner."

Murmurings begin to rise in the crowd.

"What's the matter?" Kaira asks Tuomas. Weren't conditions like these common?

"They've never had to specifically work together to defeat the enemy. Even with other distractions added to the field, it's always just been fighting to save your own life," Tuomas answers before looking over at her. "Even though we're a coherent unit as an army, the number one thing we're taught is to save yourself. If you find yourself in a situation where you might die, you're the weaker link and it isn't worth risking the better soldiers that have avoided that situation to try and save you."

The way Tuomas says it so factually, like it's something so ingrained in them, has shivers running down Kaira's spine. How can any army function like that?

"As well," Mila says, breaking through the doubtful mutterings, "in a war, you'll find yourself often overcome by unidentified enemies. As such, our contestants will be announced first, only allowed to bring one weapon into the field with them. After that, we'll reveal what they face."

Tuomas' hand finds Kaira's again and she squeezes it tightly.

"Without further ado, please welcome High Guard Arias!" Mila cheers.

Her sentiment is echoed as the crowd rises to their feet. Kaira follows, standing before she's crushed. Her eyes trace over Forren and her breath catches in her throat at the sight of him. Well, his attire, because it's the colours of her country, the purple and royal blue stark against the pale sand around him. There's no way this isn't intentional.

Then, her breath catches again. "Tuomas," she mutters sharply, clinging onto their upper arm.

They don't need her to continue to know what's taken her breath this time. It only takes a quick assessment to notice that Forren's standard double swords are missing.

Kaira's eyes hurriedly take in the rest of him. Surely, he has something hidden somewhere: a smaller sword, a dagger, even throwing stars. Anything. The thick, pressed fabric of his uniform reveals nothing, however.

"Unveil the foe!" Mila's voice is final, breaking through the air markedly as the crowd roars.

Kaira's hand digs tighter into Tuomas' side as her eyes scan the field. How has she missed the announcement of the second competitor? Where are they? But there isn't anyone else or at least nobody Kaira can spy before the jail-like gates are rolling open and the common enemy is revealed, flooding the scene. It's the prisoners.

As her gaze lands back on the centre of the field, where Forren now stands facing his sister, it all makes petrifying sense. Mila's announcement at the end of the first round that eight contestants were through but then only seven stalls being brought out. The second fire bird shortly disappearing after the first collected Forren's piece of paper. Mila's visit to Forren's accommodations with such a hustle before.

Because Mila's the other competitor.

And the siblings are about to murder Kaira's people before fighting each other to the death.

The Keranians are all but frothing at the mouth, their desire for bloodshed heightened by the possibility of it being sibling against sibling.

Kaira launches over the fence in front of her before she spends a second thinking about her action. She has to stop them. She can't let them do this, no matter what the results might mean for her people.

She ignores the voice calling out for her as she lowers herself on the other side of the railing and, with a practised ease, drops down to land in the sand.

Shaking her head from the thoughts, Kaira scans the scene before her, trying to plan whatever she's expecting to accomplish.

Step one: get to Mila and Forren.

Step two: figure out how to convince them not to kill the prisoners.

Step three: convince the prisoners not to kill them.

Step four: solve how to stop the rest of the Kerani army from revolting at the cancellation of their Games.

Simple, right? Well, there's no time for something more comprehensive as Kaira launches into movement. As her feet push into the sand, however, something brings her up short. It has nothing to do with the scene in front of her that feels like it's moving in slow motion.

Kaira turns her head, sand grits slapping her from the dust the movement in the arena is kicking up. Her stomach drops as the situation gets tenfold worse.

Without allowing a second to doubt herself, Kaira pivots, heading for the jail cells the prisoners have come from. She hears Tuomas shout for her again but doesn't look back to see if they're following. There's no time to waste as she sends a prayer to her Gods that she can trust Mila and Forren to stick to what they've been telling her.

She comes around the corner and darts into the cell with a speed that startles the figure hiding within the shadows. They lower their bow from where it's aimed at the siblings.

"What are you doing?" Kaira screeches, launching forwards to take the bow.

"What are you doing?" the potential assailant responds. They recover themself enough to jump back from Kaira, hugging the bow to their chest.

Kaira looks up, pushing her hair out of her eyes as she meets the gaze of her father. "Don't you dare do anything to either of them," she threatens.

Her father looks down at her with an emotion Kaira can't quite pick. "They're killing our people, Kaira. How can you hinder me from stopping them?"

"They wouldn't—" The words die from Kaira's lips as the crowd goes wild from behind them. No. No, they can't have made a move...

Kaira spins, pleading as she looks back over at the scene, not wanting to but having to look to see if her people have fallen.

A shadow moves in her periphery. Kaira pivots and throws her weight into her father's side. The bow that'd again been raised and ready to fire clatters to the ground as Kaira's father is pressed against the wall.

Kaira's heartbeat roars as she keeps him pinned, watching the blood that trickles down his brow from where he's hit the sandstone. *She did that.* Her stomach drops, her hands beginning to shake.

"Kaira."

The voice brings her back to the present, but it hasn't come from her father. Taking a deep breath, Kaira swivels her head to the bright opening, blinking a few times to see who's standing in the light.

Tuomas.

Kaira turns back to her father, feeling his heavy breaths under her hands. His eyes are turned to Tuomas, familiar with the sight of them, too.

Steadily, Tuomas approaches and, with one sure movement, stomps on the bow. The snap of the wood punctures the air and Kaira backs away from her father, letting him slump from the wall.

"What are you doing, Kaira? We need to stop them from—" Her father's voice is weak, hopeless.

"They're my friends, Father. They wouldn't do something like that."

"What do you think is going to happen? How do you think they'll get out of that?"

"They'll find a way. They must," Kaira states, ignoring her thoughts that roar with the same questions. "Forren promised me that he'd help me see a better future for Altair."

"A promise? What does a promise mean to a Keranian?" Her father all but spits out the words.

"I trust them," Kaira says with finality in her tone.

As if agreeing with her, a change in the air sweeps over them. Cries of confusion ring out and, as one, the three of them twirl to see what's happening in the arena.

It goes silent for a few tense beats as everyone tries to work out what's happening as the siblings reach out and shake hands while the prisoners begin falling away, slinking back towards the jail cells.

"Kaira, let's go," Tuomas says, grabbing her hand and moving them towards the light. His eyes show a mixture of worry and relief, reflecting what Kaira feels inside.

She turns to her father, but no words come to her mind that she wants to say. What could be fitting in a moment like this? Instead, she lowers her head a fraction, a sign of respect to Elders in her culture. "The Gods will have us meeting again."

Then, she adjusts her hand in Tuomas' grip and follows them out over the now deserted sand apart from the two golden guards standing in the centre. The crowd has gone quiet, as if waiting for something else to come.

Kaira's heart erratically beats in her chest as she too awaits.

When Tuomas and herself are halfway across the sand, the next move plays out. Slowly, Forren lowers himself to his knees, bowing before his sister. The silence is like someone has walked into the middle of a worship service.

Kaira's breath catches. What is he doing? He can't be giving up his spot. Sure, Mila might be better than the other contestants, but will she be on board with the plans they've made?

Mila lowers her head in acknowledgement to her brother before holding out her hand to help him up. With confidence, she turns to the awaiting arena, her eyes only hesitating a second on Kaira and Tuomas' approaching forms.

"Citizens of Kerani!" Mila says, her voice amplified by whatever system she'd been using earlier. "I know this mightn't be the ending you're hoping for, but I hope you understand the decision that's been made."

A few murmurings arise in the crowd but, overall, it's quiet.

"Lucky for us, this year has uniquely offered the possibility of crowning two rulers," Mila resumes. "As such, High Guard Arias and I have come to an agreement. I'll be taking Kerani's crown whilst he'll accept the position of Altair's new ruler."

A trickle of sweat releases its hold on Kaira's brow, falling down her face as her body relaxes. She lets out a deep breath as everything falls into place.

The whole stadium seems to let out a collective sigh as their doubts receive answers.

It doesn't take long, however, for the moment of peace to shatter. Doubts come rushing back to the surface, as for the hundredth time today Kaira feels herself freezing over.

"But what about the people?" Kaira asks Tuomas, turning her eyes to the crowd. "What if they revolt? We're four people; how do we ward off a whole army and convince them to accept this?"

"Mila is—was—the regent, Kaira," Tuomas says as if it's common sense. They add, as her brows draw closer together, "She's technically in charge until the coronations. Nobody can go against what she says unless she's committed a crime that voids her ruling."

"And this isn't a crime?" Kaira asks. "Calling off the Games?"

"The Games are essentially lawless. Nothing says all contestants can't back out and leave one person standing."

"So..."

"So, they're officially the new rulers of the two countries. Forren is Altair's new ruler."

Then, Kaira's running for Forren.

He's prepared as she lands in his arms, wrapping herself tightly around him. Amidst the chaos, she hasn't realised the rest of the tension leaving her muscles knowing that Forren's safe. That he won't die fighting a contestant or kill a part of himself slaughtering his sister.

As she finally works up the courage to pull away from him, convincing herself that doing so won't pull her out of the dream, he's looking down at her with a smile lighting his entire face. His golden mask has never looked more beautiful as it glistens beneath the Altairian sun.

"Will you marry me?" Forren asks.

Kaira blinks. Then blinks again. Is he suffering from heat stroke? "What?" she asks him, stunned.

"Will you marry me?" he repeats. "Trading one Keranian ruler for another isn't enough; I want Altair to have its own people back on the throne. Marry me and become the Queen of Altair."

Kaira should visit a healer with all this heart stuttering. Her throat feels thick as she wades through her thoughts and comes out with a coherent answer.

"Mikko," she breathes, ignoring the jittery feeling in her stomach as his smile grows at hearing his name upon her lips. "Yes, yes, yes!"

This time, it's Forren—Mikko—pulling her into a hug and crushing her tight against his chest. Kaira laughs giddily, feeling like she's in a dream. Is she going to wake up and find she's still in the camp?

"Ahem," someone coughs from nearby.

Hesitantly, Kaira pulls away from Mikko, though her fingers curl into his jacket which proudly displays the colours of her country.

"Are you two done with your little moment?" Mila asks with a smile spreading across her face. "Because this fight's a long way from over."

And even though her dream is shattered a little at that, Kaira isn't sad as, in its place, a hundred more wonderful ones grow.

EPILOGUE

Kaira's pulse pounds as she watches the pen slide across the paper, marking Mila's signature. Her chest constricts as it feels like she hasn't taken a single breath the whole time the paper has been under scrutiny.

Calmly, Mila lifts the ink pen from the paper, puts the cap back on and lays it down on the table neatly. She lifts the documents and hands them over to Kaira.

The tears start falling.

Strong, familiar arms wrap around her shoulders as she clutches the agreement to her chest. It's really, finally happening.

As per Keranian law, the newly reinstated Altair had to pay for the release of its citizens from the prisoner-of-war camp, but it never specified how much had to be paid. Two hundred dollars and a donkey—Kaira still doesn't understand why Mila requested that—as well as a few signatures on the piece of paper Kaira clasps and Kaira's people are free.

Kaira isn't deluded that this is the end of the road. No, this is just the beginning as they set about returning the country to its original glory. But this is one colossal leap in the right direction.

Besides, with Mikko at her side and the continued support from Mila and her newly appointed viceroy, Tuomas, Kaira's more than confident that they'll continue to see her dreams coming true.

Taking a deep breath to ingrain in her mind that it's real, Kaira hands over the documents to Mikko and twirls out of his comforting hug. With only slightly shaking hands, she strides across the room and pulls open the solid doors.

She steps out onto the balcony of the Palace of Golden Kings and eager eyes land on her.

"It's done," she announces to her family and friends: her mother, her father, Nora, Benji, even some of the Elders.

Benji runs over to her, pulling her into a tight embrace.

"You did it, Miss Kaira. You've freed us," Benji says, tears staining his cheeks.

"*We* did it," Kaira responds, knowing how important the motivation of freeing her loved ones has been to her success. She couldn't have done it without them.

Soon, everyone joins in on the hug until only one figure stands off to the side. Carlisle keeps his distance, but pride shines in his eyes. They still have a long way to go in repairing their relationship, but Kaira knows it'll happen because, beneath the burning sun, the future has never been brighter.

Acknowledgements:

This book would not exist without Abby and Ellie, my two youngest sisters. Little girls, I hope you enjoy reading this book (even if it takes you months or years to finish it as you don't share the same obsession with reading as me).

Additionally, an enormous thank you goes to Bex from Serpents and Doves Publishing. You brought this story to life in the cover design even if you didn't know what the story was about when you made it. I could not imagine a more perfect first-impression for my book.

Also, as always, thanks go to my alpha and beta readers. Whilst it was at times hard to take your feedback, I am immensely grateful for how it has shaped this book.

I would also like to specially recognise my Nan in QLD. You passed away the day before I wrote these acknowledgements, but I hope wherever you are now peacefully resting that you can continue to read my books. Nothing made me feel your love more than meeting your friends at your memorial and hearing how proudly you had told them I am an author.

Hello! I'm Anna, a young Australian author. *Beneath the Burning Sun* is my first young adult novel. It presented a challenge for me to write and I went through many stages of furiously hating, loving or being indifferent to this story. However, as I persevered through the challenges it presented, it showed me the importance of the themes in the story, including pursuing what you want and never giving up.

If you enjoyed this book, I'd love for you to leave a review where reviews are accepted!